F I V E

Jeffrey Kelley

Experiment Five Media

Published by:
Experiment Five Media
Saint John, New Brunswick, Canada

First published in Canada
Archived with the Library and Archives of Canada

Catalogued Editions
Hardcover: ISBN: 978-0-9951907-1-9
Paperback: ISBN: 978-0-9951907-0-2
Electronic Book ISBN: 978-0-9951907-2-6

For my father, Peter.

FIVE

Five men.

Four Bullets.

One gun.

No clues.

"In the face of pain, there are no heroes."

(George Orwell, *1984*)

PROLOGUE: COLOMBIA

It was deep in the jungle, and it was very humid. The vegetation was thick and dense, and led to a sharp, steep cliff that gave way to a long drop into an even denser area of jungle.

It was growing late in the afternoon and the sun was making its way west, leaving a darker hue of blue sky as it moved closer to the Pacific. It was then that, just inches beyond the edge of the cliff, the blade of a machete rose up straight and erect, with the sun glinting on its steel. At first just the tip of the blade was visible, but it continued moving upward, slowly, revealing as it did the full length of the blade, and the handle, gripped tightly by a hand. The blade and the hand that held it were stained with blood. As the hand rose, a portion of an arm, also covered in blood, became visible, and then the machete was turned one hundred and eighty degrees, pointing the tip towards the ground.

The machete stayed suspended above the earth for a moment, with the blade pointing down, and blood dripping from the tip onto the soft ground. Suddenly, the hand gripping the handle of the machete drove the steel deep into the dirt. A moment later, a duffel bag flew up and landed on the ground; levitating just inches beyond the cliff was a second, bloody hand. The hand drove itself downward, putting itself palm down in the ground. The hand gripping the machete pulled hard, and the hand that was palm down on the ground pushed hard, and united in a great strain, the weary body of a soldier was pulled up and over the cliff by the two bloody hands, and dumped to the ground.

The soldier was covered in blood, some of it his own, but most from others. The soldier lay still a moment to catch his breath. Once he had taken a few deep breaths, the soldier rolled over to his back, and then sat up. He slid himself back a number of inches and rested against a tree as though it were the back of a chair, and dangled his feet over the cliff.

The soldier reached into the pocket of his fatigues and hauled out a solid plastic tube; he opened the tube and dumped out a cigar. Next, the soldier bit the end off his cigar and then put it between his teeth as he fished out a lighter. He opened the lid of the lighter and clicked the flame on, raised the lighter to his face and sparked the end of his cigar. The soldier clicked the lid of his lighter shut, smothering the flame and then put his lighter back into his pocket.

In the humid jungle now sat a soldier against a tree, looking out past a steep, sharp cliff, covered in blood, smoking a cigar.

CHAPTER ONE

Charles Washington was nearing the end of his life, and consequently, the end of his career. Washington had terminal pancreatic cancer and quite likely only a few months left to live, and he was well over a year away from reaching a pensionable age. Charles Washington would never know retirement, though truthfully, even if Charles Washington were healthy he would not retire. Washington was the sort of man that lived to work; for Washington, work was an escape from the hardships of his life and the demons that haunted his memories. Ironically, the demons that haunted him came to find him by way of his career, and over the many years he was consumed, possessed, by these demons; Washington could not exorcise them. There was only one sure way for him to ever find a release from the clutches of his demons, but it was his fear of this recourse that had always left Charles Washington gun-shy. This was the price, the curse, and the penance that Charles Washington carried with him for knowing what he knew, and he only knew it because he innocently chose a career with altruistic motives and a dream of contributing to society in a meaningful way.

As an investigative reporter with a thirst for adventure, Charles Washington had spent his entire life chasing stories, and as a consequence he had let his life pass him by. Washington never put down roots, he had never married, and never sired any children; Charles Washington had never so much as owned a dog, or a cat, or a fish. For him, anything, no matter how large or small, that could impact his ability to pick up and chase a story halfway around the world was a burden. Charles Washington was decorated, trusted, and world renowned, and Charles Washington was all alone at the end of his life, with a painful disease that had no cure and limited treatment.

Charles Washington lived in a modest home in a modest subdivision surrounded by other modest homes and modest neighbors he had never taken the time to know. Washington's house itself was a small war-widow home, and it was sparsely furnished, as he had no need of much furniture, or nice furniture. Washington had lived in the same home for over thirty years, and he still had the appliances that had come with the house when he purchased the property. Other than the appliances, there was not much to speak of for furniture in the bulk of the home, and even the bedroom was outdated with a bedroom set that was nearly as old as he.

As his cancer progressed, and Washington went through the feelings of grief and anxiety that one experiences with a terminal diagnosis, he had decided to remain in his home. He wanted to die on his own terms doing what he loved: reporting on the stories no one else could, or would, report. It was one night, late, when Washington was reflecting on the leeway he would have being so well-established as a top globe-trotting reporter for over forty years, and the advances in technology that were about to make his job easier, and doable from home. Washington had realized that dying at home was not, in and of itself, dying on his own terms. If he wanted to balance the scales before he met his maker, he had one more scoop to report, a story that Washington had buried over thirty-six years earlier: a dark story that had been eating his soul and haunting his memory right through from the time he was an eager young man to the present, when he was enfeebled, old, and dying.

Washington made his way through his modest home to his kitchen, and over to his small refrigerator, where he opened the door, took out a bottle of beer, opened it, and drank the whole bottle in one shot. Washington reached back into the fridge and picked up the six-pack that now contained only five beers, then closed the refrigerator. He made his way through his house to the basement stair and proceeded downward.

In the basement of his home, a basement that was blocked in by the grey walls of the foundation and never finished, with cement floors and a cold feel, Charles Washington had all the equipment he would need. Washington hung a black bed-sheet against one of the walls and shined a light at it. Washington put a stool in the center, and he moved a microphone stand with a cold, grey, microphone in front of the stool. Washington set up some cameras, and framed the stool dead center, and fed the signal back into a monitor that he turned so he would be able to see it from the stool. He put a table beside the stool and then put his beers on the table; beside them he placed a remote.

Next, Charles Washington looked himself over as best he could without a mirror, using the monitor for an inspection. Washington buttoned his dark blue suit and straightened his tie. He made sure his hair was neat and combed, and he had trimmed his beard adequately earlier in the day. Washington knew this would be his last report, and when he filed it, he was filing it with every major news network in the country, and a few abroad, because this was the privilege, the power, of his name in his field. Charles Washington was a legend, and for the first time, he was going to trade off that to scoop the world with a story that needed to be exposed. Washington was ready, and for the first time in nearly forty years, Washington was nervous about the camera. Washington climbed on the stool, opened a bottle of beer, took a long sip, and then he picked up the remote from the table and after taking a deep breath, Charles Washington pressed *Record*.

Washington looked off and to his left, or slightly to the right of the camera; he was a pro, and this filing was to be his legacy to the world. Washington took a deep breath, exhaled, and then he spoke:

Hello. My name is Charles Washington, and I have been a trusted reporter, broadcast throughout the world, for forty-seven years, and I am dying. I have pancreatic cancer, and I am nearing my end. This recording is the last story I will ever file with you, and I have arranged for it to be broadcast by my colleagues at various networks simultaneously. This recording will serve as my confession, my penance, my last will and testament, and my legacy; a legacy that will be tarnished, and perhaps viewed harshly, because I should have filed this report decades ago.

In my time as a reporter I have covered every manner of story from crop reports to foreign wars. I have stood out in hurricanes, delivered news about economic downturns. I have spoke to you about miraculous events that showcase the best of what people are capable of doing, and I have shown you the evil side of society with horrific detail, but only one story ever chilled me to the bone. Only one story ever made my skin crawl as if the devil himself were walking over my grave, whistling, and it is this one. I have kept it secret for 36 years because I have lived in fear my entire life of what might happen to me if I broke this story to the public. This story, a story so sinister it belongs in the dark, is a story about the dark side of democracy, a story that changed my view of our world and its leaders.

It was 36 years ago, and I was still a young and hungry reporter looking to break through to larger markets, naïvely believing myself to be seasoned and hardened by what I had seen in my idealistic early days of reporting. I received word from a man, a man who said he could make my career with a story that would change the world. He instructed me to come to his home that night for an interview – it was a one-time offer and he told me it would be a story that would take all night to tell. He gave me his address and told me no earlier than nine o'clock.

It was a dark, stormy, November night, the dead of the year, and at the time the omen was lost on me; now the irony re-introduces itself

9

whenever I try to rest. The very night had a unique, foreboding feeling, as if the world had died and I was the pallbearer, and in a sense, that is very much what happened to my world that night.

The old man had given me directions to his home. It was a large Victorian manor beyond the outskirts of town, and the driveway itself was long enough to be a road. That is what I would have thought it to be if it were not for the large metal gate at the foot of it, a gate that I suspect was closed most nights but was left open for me on that occasion.

The rain, a cold, dead rain, was bouncing off the roof of my old sedan as I pulled along the drive and approached the house. I pulled my car up alongside the front of the house as best I could, and I glanced right, past the passenger's seat and out the side window at the house. I was amazed by the over-sized gothic doors; in hindsight I should have been less amazed and more afraid. I grabbed my notebook and pencils, and I opened the door, placing the notebook above my head, foolishly thinking it would protect me somewhat from the rain. I climbed up out of my car and slammed the door quickly, and half ran around the sedan towards the house. As I clambered up onto the small porch to get under the overhang and out of the weather, the door opened wide before I ever had a chance to knock.

When the door opened it revealed a man, an old man. I recall thinking to myself, through the eyes of my youth, that he was well over one hundred, but by the morning I would come to realize that living with this story had likely aged his body far beyond his years. The old man stood aside, and without a word, motioned me into the house. As I stepped in, the old man pulled the over-sized door closed with an over-sized slam.

Next, the old man motioned me towards the interior, and I took his

10

silent invitation to head deeper into the parlor. The house itself was cold, both in spirit and in temperature, except for the parlor, which had a large fireplace and a roaring fire that gave it warmth by comparison, yet I still had no desire to remove my overcoat.

In the parlor the man had set two over-sized chairs in front of the fireplace with a small table between them, and a decanter of brandy upon it along with two glasses. The old man motioned to one chair, and I took it as he stepped to the fire and used the poker to stoke it somewhat. After completing his task, the old man set the poker down and then poured two glasses of brandy, placing one in front of me and holding tight to the other as he sat down into his chair in a drawn-out fashion that allowed me to see how feeble his body truly was in his old age. As he finally settled into his position in his chair, I told him I was not a drinking man, and in a raspy, near-whisper voice, he told me that by dawn I would be.

CHAPTER TWO

The old man's story began in a small, dark room. It was less of a room and more of a space. The space was four feet by eight feet, enclosed by long black sheets that served as partitions, similar to what you would expect to find wrapped about the beds in a hospital or an asylum. In this space there was a small, uncomfortable cot and a man on it; the man was Special Agent Hal Northrop, a devious man from a dark, shadowy corner of the government that few know exist. All those that are aware of this corner fear it, using only the uneasy whispered tones of conspirators when they discuss its existence.

Hal Northrop woke, entering the world of consciousness and leaving behind the sedated world of unconsciousness. He did not rise easily, and he was groggy. Northrop's vision was dark, at first, but as moments passed it gave way to blurry, before finally settling on tired.

It was an arduous task for Northrop to rise from a laying position on his cot to a seated one, and the process took nearly twenty minutes of effort before Northrop's legs were slung over the side of his cot and his feet were on the floor.

The floor beneath Northrop's feet was cold, grey concrete. Northrop's shoes were black and shiny, meticulous. Northrop was all about appearance. He believed in looking the part, and that by looking the part you were the part. Northrop's biggest asset was his ability to feign sincerity, and his greatest liability was his hubris; he was the archetype for the non-military government operative. Northrop was a man of secret sins and no regrets.

As Northrop became more aware of his surroundings, he slowly, gingerly made his way to his feet and scanned his small space. Northrop identified the curtains on either side and at the floor of his cot as what they were, and he noted that the head of his cot was pressed against a concrete wall. There was minimal light in Northrop's area; the only light source came from beyond the curtains, bleeding in, and even then it seemed as if the wattage of the bulbs was not adequate.

Northrop eventually walked to the foot of his bed and pushed the curtain back, and then stepped out into a larger, poorly lit room. The room was a large heptagon, a seven-sided room, perfectly symmetrical. In five of the corners there were long black curtains that each concealed a space with a cot identical in every way to the space where Northrop had awoken. In the corner on either side of Northrop's sleeping area, there was a sleeping area; the remaining two were on the opposite side of the heptagon, side by side.

In one of the remaining corners there was a large and ominous door, it was solid steel with no windows, and there appeared to be no hinges, but it was still obviously a door. The door was inanimate, yet intimidating. The door inspired apprehension and triggered anxiety while bearing no unique markings whatsoever. It was cold, grey, and unforgiving.

In the last corner there was a very large wall clock. The diameter of the clock itself was three feet, and instead of numbers, the clock had abstract faces, each one different, each one clearly the face of a man gone mad. There were two minute hands and one second hand. The clock was both operational and frightening.

In the centre of the heptagon there was a table. The table was round and wooden, and surrounding it were five wooden chairs, the sort of chairs that one might have found in an office circa 1920, with rounded arms and vertical spokes framed into their backs. In three of these chairs there were men.

The first man was Lieutenant Kelley Pike. Pike was a hard man, and a bad man. Pike was the sort of man that could not receive absolution even from the Pope; there was absolutely no doubt where Pike's soul was heading. Pike wore army boots and camouflaged trousers. Pike wore his dog tags around his neck and his shirt was a dirty, white, wife beater style undershirt. Pike was smoking, inhaling his cigarette with the cold calm of a man awaiting an overdue death. The chair immediately to Pike's left was empty, as was the chair immediately to his right. Pike was a difficult man to get close to, in every sense of the word; he was a loner and a loose cannon. Pike's epitaph would be *Effective but Expendable*; he was the ultimate cleaner, the best choice for the most dangerous missions that require success and would ideally not allow for the soldier to return; yet Pike somehow always made it back.

Beyond the empty chair to Pike's left sat Sergeant Michael Paxton. Paxton was dressed in beach sandals, cargo shorts, a cabana shirt, and a wide brimmed camouflaged hat. Paxton was a real soldier's soldier; he had been dropped in the shit many times and he had walked back out of unscathed. Paxton's missions were so classified and top secret, he rarely knew any more than the components that required his personal attention. Paxton had seen more, done more, and lived through more than most soldiers would ever care to experience, but despite it all, Paxton was far from jaded. In fact, Paxton was an optimist, always believing there was a way to achieve mission success, and so far in his career, Paxton had never been wrong. Paxton was strong, resourceful, highly intelligent, and innovative. In fact, Paxton's only sin was that he was a soldier who had always followed orders, an excuse history has always rejected. Much like Pike, Paxton was smoking, but whereas watching Pike smoke summoned a sense of dystopia, Paxton simply appeared to be a man smoking to passed the time of day, if in fact it was day.

In the chair immediately to Paxton's left was Captain Bradley Pell. Pell had never had a cigarette in his life, and despite the fact he was now trapped in a concrete heptagon where smoking was the only entertainment available, Captain

Pell was not about to take up the filthy habit. Pell was a highly decorated air force pilot who had flown all manner of planes, jets, and helicopters. Pell was regarded as one of the best flyboys in the world, and he was wearing his military issue flight suit, with the front zipper down somewhat for his own climate control revealing a white crew-cut t-shirt. Bradley Pell was one of the most outwardly affable men to ever walk the earth, but that was the part visible, above water; below the surface, like an iceberg at sea, there was a larger story. Bradley Pell was the product of some hard demons that he would prefer stayed buried. To Pell's left, there was an empty chair, and beyond that the table came full circle to Pike.

Northrop took in the room -- not at a glance, he was far too groggy to do that – instead, he took it in with a laboriously slow effort, circling it many times, and by default resting his gaze at the table many time, eyeing the men, and in particular Pike. As soon as Northrop recognized Pike, he realized with horror where he was and he began to feel his anxiety rise. Internally, Northrop prayed that Pike did not know who he was, that no one had told him, and that Pike had arrived here only to awake in his surroundings just as protocol had always dictated. Northrop did not know the other men at the table.

As Northrop composed himself, he looked to his left. In the corner beside him sat a sleeping area, and the corner beyond that was the larger door. To Northrop's right there was a sleeping area, and beyond that the large wall clock. Northrop began to walk towards the clock, and it was then that he noticed that a man, crouched down on his haunches, half hidden by a curtain, squatted in the sleeping area between him and the clock. This man was Sergeant J.P. Kaye, a sniper.

Sergeant Kaye was small in physical stature, and wiry. Kaye was also neurotic, but the most noteworthy trait of Kaye were his eyes. Kaye's eyes were always scanning, always moving, and instantly focusing, faster than the normal eye. Kaye never blinked, ever, and there was something inherently creepy about his gaze. Northrop felt Kaye's gaze on him as he passed Kaye and walked close to the clock.

Kaye's eyes were not the only ones that followed Northrop. Paxton and Pell had noticed Northrop's movements, and they were watching him as he crossed the room to the clock. Once in front of the clock, Northrop began to watch the second hand as he took his pulse. Pike never looked towards Northrop; instead, Pike kept his head tilted back and one leg up on the table. Pike was staring at the ceiling, watching the smoke from his cigarette rise and blend into the concrete above. Paxton, Pell, and Kaye studied Northrop quite carefully.

As the others watched Northrop, Pike put his cigarette out on the back of his hand, and the smell of his flesh burning caught Paxton's attention. Paxton began smoking faster so that the two men could move on to their next cigarette. Northrop made his way to the table, and walked around it, selecting the empty chair between Pike and Paxton; from here Northrop could see the clock and continue to check his pulse against the movements of the second hand.

"And then there were five." Paxton was the first to speak, and he spoke in a flat tone, unimpressed with the new arrival.

"Well," Pell chimed in with an optimistic tone, "we finally have enough for a good game of poker."

"I hope you brought cards, Company," Pike said with hostility and without ever looking towards Northrop. Only a fool sits with his back to a door. Paxton took out a pack of cigarettes and handed one to Pike and put one between his own lips. Northrop motioned for a cigarette and Paxton, somewhat reluctantly, handed him one. Pike then produced an old lighter, a flip top device, took his leg off the table and leaned in to the centre of the table; Paxton likewise leaned in to the center of the table where Pike sparked the flame and they lit their smokes. As Northrop leaned in, Pike snapped the lighter off. Paxton grabbed Northrop's cigarette and lit it from his own, and then passed it back to the company man.

As the tip of Northrop's cigarette turned to ash, he snapped his eyes, his whole head around, looking for a tray for the butts. "There's no ash tray?" Northrop asked.

"Look around you, Company," Pike snapped. "This whole place is an ash tray."

"Point," Northrop replied, defeated but unwilling not to have the last word, despite the futility. Northrop went back to looking at Kaye, still on his haunches and scanning from one man to the next, going around the table and back time and time again. "What's with the anti-social guy over there?"

Northrop asked, referring to Kaye.

"Sniper," Paxton replied with indifference.

"Ah, gotcha," Northrop replied, pretending to fully understand, but in actual fact he was faking it. Northrop had never been in the shit, and although he knew soldiers like Paxton had their own social structure, ways of speaking, and interaction, Northrop did not know what they were. He was a boardroom guy first and foremost, but he was electing to try and fake his way through, hoping to plot an exit strategy. That was, after all, his training.

As they smoked, Northrop kept scanning the others. Northrop was still coming around, and the stimulation from the cigarette was helping him to an extent. "Are you guys groggy at all?" he finally asked.

"No." It was Pell who spoke up. "We have all been here a while now. Days, or weeks, or months…who knows? The effects have long since worn off."

"Weeks or months?" Northrop asked. "How do you know how long you have been here?"

It was Paxton who engaged Northrop's question. "Well, we have all been here a while, all of us longer than Pell except you…" Paxton stopped for a minute and took the cigarette from his mouth and looked at it, then pinched between his thumb and forefinger before continuing "…and I am getting low on cigarettes now. Funny thing, they let me keep my cigarettes… actually they gave me more, but they took my matches. Imagine that, they stole my matches but left me with more nails. Sick sense of humor."

"They?" Northrop asked, trying to conceal the nature of his question, an exploration to see if anyone in the room knew what he knew, or what he really was. "Why do you say 'they'?"

"Well, Company," Pike said gruffly before turning his head and looking right into Northrop's eyes, "it just don't feel like a one-man outfit, now, does it?" The question was clearly rhetorical.

"Point." Northrop replied, still unsure of how to read Pike.

It was Pell's turn to speak again. "Don't mind Pike. He is an acquired taste for a roommate. We all had roommates like him in basic." Pell was not fond of tension, and he was in a constant quest for tranquility in his environment.

"You mean," Northrop chimed up, feeling braver knowing that Pike was not pulling the strings of the others, "he's a jackass."

"Sure, Company," Pike shot back, putting animosity into the word "Company," "you may not like me, and Pell, the others, maybe they don't want me here, but I am just glad to have a more cheerful...entourage...this time." Pike leaned back and took a long drag off his cigarette, and tossed his leg back onto the table.

"This time?" Northrop asked, with some shock in his voice.

"Not my first incarceration." Pike, staying awake, closed his eyes and leaned his head back to rest on the top of his chair. He swung one leg up onto the table, and then he took a long pull out off his cigarette, and calmly allowed the smoke he exhaled to rise upward before he snapped out in a large voice, "Quit staring at us like we're targets, Blinkey! Christ!" Pike made the briefest of pauses as he softened his voice to his usual low, gravelly growl. "You're making poor Paxton nervous."

"That's right," Paxton spoke up. "And when I get nervous, eyes get blackened."

Northrop had jolted when Pike first let his voice boom, and then as he was staring at Pike, he heard Paxton's threat, and his head snapped over to look at Paxton. Northrop was trying his best not to show his fear, but he knew he was in way over his head. Northrop knew better than most what happened when hard men like these were placed in situations like this; he had observed it many times, but he had never counted on being on the inside, and he did not like it one bit. Northrop knew he had to establish control and manipulate the group into seeing him as a leader, not a target for aggression. Meanwhile, Kaye had slinked slightly further behind his curtain, but he remained visible, his eyes hard on Paxton, and then hard on the back of Pike's head; none of this escaped Northrop's notice. Kaye hated Pike, but he knew it was best to keep that information private for now. Kaye was a survivor, and instinctively he knew not to provoke Pike.

Northrop was thinking fast, looking for an opportunity to manipulate his surroundings. Soldiers like Paxton and Pike excelled in the field because they were adaptable – they would adapt to a situation or environment even if it meant sacrificing a part of themselves, but Northrop was different. Northrop manipulated environments to his own purposes, which he knew was happening here on a somewhat larger scale. He had to micro-manage, manipulate the immediate environment, but he needed an opportunity. It was Pell's voice that broke Northrop's concentration and brought him back to the moment.

"Relax, Paxton." Pell said. "Kaye is just trying to calm his nerves. He is just doing what snipers do to keep calm. Don't worry about it."

"And that is exactly why he makes me nervous." Paxton spoke with the firm authority of a seasoned tactical leader. "Snipers sit off in the distance, staring at you through a scope, and planning the moment you die. You never see it coming, you never know they are there. They just target you with their soulless eyes and BAM! They drop you from afar, like a coward."

"Easy, Paxton," Pell countered. "He is just trying to keep calm, and get his mind active, so he's falling back on his training to ease his nerves. It's no big deal. It is instinct. Besides, in close quarters like this there are no long distances to scope out and no hiding places, and no rifles. A big guy like you is the real threat, not Kaye."

It was Pell's position and affable nature that gave Northrop his opening, and he pounced, hiding his intentions in what appeared a very logical question: "Are you guys not getting along?" It seemed innocent, but Northrop knew caging men like these together meant they clearly were not getting along, not expertly. It would take a mutual cause, or enemy, to grow these men close.

It was Pike who answered Northrop's question. "Paxton is just getting stir crazy. Can't say I blame him with Blinkey eyeballing him all the time. Christ." Northrop relaxed and focused on the fact that his instincts were telling him that Pike had no idea who he was. Northrop and Kaye were falling back on training, and in some ways, they had very similar minds.

Kaye, perhaps sensing a comrade in Northrop, or perhaps looking for the same opportunity to take the lead, finally stood up and walked, somewhat stiffly, to the open chair to Pike's right. Sensing what he was doing, and growing curious at the new brazen level of Kaye, Pike opened his eyes and sat up to see what would unfold. Looking at Kaye, he waited, until the sniper had settled in to his chair, and then Kaye spoke: "Why are you always such a bully to me?"

Pike grinned, and then he took a long, slow, drag off his cigarette and blew the smoke right into Kaye's face before grinning again, and whispering, raspy in the silent tomb, "Because I can be, Blinkey, because I can be." Pike flicked his cigarette at Kaye's face, and it bounced off his forehead, causing him to blink. As Kaye opened his eyes, Pike then flicked his finger off Kaye's forehead right in the same spot the cigarette had landed. Pike may well have been a bully and an asshole, but he was also one hundred percent alpha male, and maybe if Northrop had been on the outside looking in, as he generally was, he would have realized this, but it escaped him at this time. Pike threw his leg back up on to the table and leaned back into his chair and closed his eyes, but remained vigilant, alpha.

After Pike seemed settled, and Northrop had finished observing the way Kaye was reacting to him, identifying Kaye as an easy mark to control, Northrop cleared his throat and addressed Paxton. "So, Paxton, was it?"

"Sergeant Michael Paxton, United States Army, Special Forces, sir." Paxton answered as a soldier that respected his institution, and Northrop may have misread this as a sign of contrition...or maybe not.

"So I'll take that as a yes." It was Northrop's attempt to establish control over Paxton.

"Yes sir." Paxton was very ingrained in the chain of command, and even now, here, in this place, Paxton respected the chain.

"Don't you think its funny, soldier, that they took your matches but left you the nails, and that they left...Pike?... that lighter?" Northrop's plan was to trade on his knowledge by presenting it as a deduction, and showing himself to have the higher reasoning skills that people look for in leadership. "It is Pike, right?"

"Who the hell are you, Company?" Pike snarled, but never opened his eyes.

"And I will take that as a yes." Northrop was image-building; he was a natural salesman. The hurdle for Northrop was that he had nothing to sell, but he was not going to let that stop him. "So, Paxton, don't you find that to be funny?"

"Funnier than that, sir," Paxton replied. "Pike said they took his cigarettes."

"Cigars," Pike corrected Paxton. "Men smoke cigars."

"Screw off, Pike," Paxton laughed.

"Not tonight, honey, I have a headache," Pike replied.

"Herm." Northrop made a noise; now he just needed someone to bite, and Pell did.

"Is something on your mind?" Pell asked the company man.

"Just that I know this trick," Northrop responded.

"Well, I don't." Pell was curious, and that was exactly what Northrop wanted. *If I keep them curious and engaged*, Northrop thought, *I will keep them dependent on me*.

"They left the first man with a lighter, but no smokes. Something he needed but nothing he wanted. They then gave the second man smokes, but no lighter, something he wanted but nothing he needed. The goal is manipulation of emotional responses. It's a stress test,"

"Okay…" Pell encouraged Northrop to tell them more. "And so they are looking to learn what exactly?"

"They want to see how the subjects react, how they handle resources and if they can work together. The expectation is they will not, and that the first man will have either played with the flame while he was alone to pass the time and then have no lighter fluid by the time the second man and the cigarettes arrived, or that the second man will not share the cigarettes and waste his commodity on the resource."

"Waste not want not, Company. That's my motto," Pike snarled, his eyes still closed and leg up on the table.

"Well, bully for you." Northrop was feeling challenged and anxious because, though he tried not to let it show, he had again started to wonder if Pike knew.

"Then I would say that Pike got the better of them, by saving lighter fluid and playing nice with Paxton," Pell interjected, once again sensing that tensions were rising and attempting to return the room to a social equilibrium.

"Or he knew what was coming." It was Kaye's voice, and it was the most brazen he had yet been in this holding room, perhaps drawing strength from Northrop's lead and choosing a side. The implication was clear: Kaye was suggesting Pike might not be a prisoner in the way the same rest of them were. And this was exactly the manipulation, dissent, that Northrop needed, and like a politician, he made a strategically timed exit from the event.

"Well, gentlemen," Northrop began by way of excusing himself," the Rohyphenol is still doing a number on me. I think I will rack out for a bit. Thanks for the nail, Paxton." Northrop stood from the chair and steadied himself a moment to overcome the head rush. He exaggerated it to play up a role he was creating for himself, and then he began to walk away.

"You're welcome," Pike snarled, "for the flame...Company." Pike's eyes were still closed.

Caught slightly off guard, Northrop tried to hide the fact he was flustered and replied, "Thanks, Pike." But this pause was a wild card and it gave way to another question from Pell.

"So who are you anyway?"

"Special Agent Hal Northrop," Northrop replied with confidence.

"Special Agent where?" Paxton asked. "CIA, Bureau, ATF?"

"Special Agent Hal Northrop," Northrop repeated. Northrop tried again to leave, but Pell had one more question.

"How do you know it was Rohyphenol? The sedative they gave us?"

"It was likely something stronger," Northrop admitted, "but I am definitely feeling the effects of the sedative." This time Northrop was able to make his exit and retreat back into his sleeping area and strategize.

After Northrop left the table area, the table settled back to its general rhythm. "I like him," Pell said with an upward inflection.

"I don't," Pike contributed.

"You don't like anyone," Paxton added.

"I like you." Pike swung his leg down off the table, opened his eyes, and sat up.

"That's because I have the cigarettes." Paxton smiled, almost audibly, as he reached into his pocket and retrieved his cigarettes. As he did so, Pike snapped his fingers and motioned for a cigarette as he produced his lighter, and then Pike and Paxton did what incarcerated men do: they smoked.

CHAPTER THREE

At night, or what the men perceived to be night, the large heptagon-shaped room became quite dark. It was not dark as pitch, but it was darker beyond the blue hue of dusk. It was darkness akin to the glow of midnight. The five men had no control over the lights, so during these darker cycles, most of the men generally accepted it to be night. When the lights were brighter, but by no means actually bright, more the brightness of a damp English fog, the five men, or most of them anyway, considered it to be daytime.

It was in the darkness of the perceived night that Sergeant Kaye pulled the curtain back from inside his sleeping area and shuffled out. Kaye hugged the wall and moved to his right, shuffling along the wall, under the wall clock and slowly creeping towards Pike's sleeping area. Beyond Pike's sleeping area was Paxton's, then the door, then Pell's, then Northrop's, and finally back to Kaye's, but Kaye did not make a full lap. He stopped at Pike's curtain, looked about the room, and then slipped past Pike's curtain and into his sleeping area.

Pike was on his cot, perhaps asleep, perhaps awake, but completely indifferent to the arrival of Kaye. Kaye shuffled up to the foot of Pike's cot, and he waited, and he waited, and eventually he grew tired of waiting for Pike to speak to him, so instead Kaye spoke.

"Pike. Hey Pike?" Kaye's tone was a hurried whisper. "Pike."

"Yeah?" Pike answered with a snarl.

"Why do you keep calling Northrop 'Company?'"

"He's a big feeling guy in a cheap suit. What else would he be?" Pike was dry, rhetorical, and annoyed. Kaye spent several moments absorbing Pike's words before he responded.

"How do you know his suit is cheap?"

"Go away." For the first time Pike moved. He still had not opened his eyes as near as Kaye could tell, but he did roll over on to his side as if to turn his back on Kaye. Kaye did not like that.

"Okay," Kaye said, and then as he pulled the curtain back enough to slip through he spoke to Pike again. "Pike."

"What?"

"Do you trust him?"

"No."

"Yeah...me neither." Kaye slipped out through the curtain, exiting Pike's sleeping area and re-entering the larger, heptagon-shaped room. Kaye crept to the center of the room, and then he crawled onto the table and faced the corner where the wall clock hung. Kaye's night vision was exceptional, and he could still see the clock. Kaye put his fingers to his neck, as if he were checking his pulse, and he stared at the clock, mimicking what he had seen Northrop do, but not sure what it was this was meant to accomplish. Kaye grew frustrated.

Kaye continued to try and reason out what Northrop had been doing, but he grew more and more tired as he tried to think, and eventually Kaye was overcome with drowsiness and he fell asleep on the table.

CHAPTER FOUR

The lights had brightened in the cell, as if to suggest that night had turned to day, and Captain Bradley Pell was the first to rise from his cot and the first to emerge from his sleeping area and enter the large heptagon cell.

When Pell stepped into the main cell area, he looked to the center of the room and discovered J.P. Kaye asleep on the table. Pell also looked to his left and discovered a tray was sitting on the floor just inside the door, with five bowls of gruel and five glasses of water. Pell sighed and first went to the table.

"Kaye," Pell said to the Sergeant as he nudged his shoulder, waking the sniper gently so as not to disturb the others. "Wake up, Kaye."

Kaye began to stir, and as his eyes opened he slowly came to realize where he had fallen asleep. Kaye looked up at Pell. "Why am I on the table?"

"You were sleeping there," Pell answered.

Kaye sat up, with his legs now dangling off the table, and rubbed his eyes. "Oh, yeah. I was watching the clock, and I fell asleep."

"You were watching the clock and you fell asleep?" Pell repeated.

"Yes," Kaye responded.

"Were you having trouble sleeping?" Pell asked.

"No," Kaye said. "I was trying to figure out what Northrop was doing it for."

"Ah," Pell said. "Did you?"

"No," Kaye admitted.

"Well, Kaye," Pell changed the subject, "you don't want to be asleep on the table when Pike gets up. He'll just shove you right off it." Pell turned from Kaye and went to the door. He kneeled down in front of the tray of gruel and proceeded to say a prayer over top of the food. Kaye watched Pell, and as Pell started to pray, Kaye shook his head, shoved himself up, off the table, and retreated into his sleeping area.

After Pell had said his prayer, he picked up the tray and carried it to the table. Pell sat the tray down and began to distribute the food to each of the five places marked with a chair along the table.

As Pell was distributing the food, Paxton emerged from his sleeping area and looked towards the table. Seeing that Pell was putting the food out, Paxton strolled to the table briskly and spoke. "Mmm, gruel, my favorite," Paxton said in a sincere tone.

"See, Paxton," Pell responded, "it's not all bad in here. The chef serves your favorite every morning."

CHAPTER FIVE

Several days passed before Northrop had fully overcome the effects of the sedative. With his head clearing, Northrop began to focus his thoughts towards his predicament. Northrop knew where he was in the sense that he knew the purpose behind the sinister abductions of the five, but he could not entirely be sure of the physical location as there were five possibilities. He did have one particular location in mind.

Northrop's primary concern now was to read the other men and develop strategies tailored to each one. Northrop needed to make the men believe they needed him; it was a matter of his survival, and reduced to his base needs, his own survival was all that mattered to him.

As Northrop began planning his strategies, he was again standing in the same corner as the clock, watching the second hand tick, his fingers on his neck, taking his pulse. Northrop wanted to be sure that the men saw what he was doing and that they in turn would rely upon him and his intelligence gathering. Northrop needed the other four to believe they needed him, that he knew more than they did, and in turn Northrop wanted to use that to make the other men dependent upon him and become his to command. It was about manipulation.

Paxton was standing outside his sleeping area, watching Northrop, and after a few moments, Paxton wandered over and stood slightly behind Northrop's shoulder and stared at the clock. Paxton took out two cigarettes and began to pass one towards Northrop. "Those nails are no good without Pike's lighter," Northrop said, refusing the smoke.

"Force of habit." It was the explanation Paxton half-heartedly offered.

"So what do you want, Paxton?"

"Want?" Paxton responded.

"Yes, want. The gesture with the cigarette, it was a conversation starter. I know all the tricks." Northrop bragged his point as if it were impressive. "So what's on your mind, soldier?" Northrop believed that Paxton was already beginning to view him as their leader, and that was why Paxton had approached him with the overture of the cigarette. Northrop was wrong.

"You spend a lot of time looking at that clock," Paxton said as he put the cigarettes back into his case.

"Four times as much as you might think, soldier." Northrop was trying to leverage his knowledge, but he was not about to reveal it to the others. His plan was to be cryptic.

"What do you mean by that, sir?" Paxton was professional by design, but he was never one for cloak and dagger games.

"I'll tell you soon enough, Paxton. When the time is right." Northrop grinned and slapped Paxton on his back and then walked away.

Paxton was an intelligent man, perhaps the most intelligent soldier in the room. As Northrop walked away, clearly having designed some sort of window dressing around his revelation of the clock, Paxton reflected on the conversation he, Pike, and Pell had about Northrop during the Special Agent's first day in the cell:

"I like him," Pell had said.

"I don't," Pike had said.

"You don't like anyone," Paxton had said.

"I like you," Pike had said.

"I have the cigarettes," Paxton had said.

Paxton was finding greater sincerity in Pike's words. Pike was a bad man, and his personality was kerosene, but he was not the least bit cryptic. With Pike, you always knew where you stood, and Paxton liked that trait in men. Paxton disliked cryptic people like Northrop, who were always trying to manipulate others and were so much in the shadow of their own ego that they refused to believe any one could be as intelligent or crafty as they were. As a career soldier, Paxton had been burned many times by cryptic men just like Northrop far too many times to trust any of them.

Paxton did not trust Northrop.

CHAPTER SIX

Sergeant J.P. Kaye was sitting cross-legged on the floor, just six inches from the large door that entombed the five men, sealing them away from the outside world in a dungeon. To the men, the door itself was like a gatekeeper from freedom. To some extent the door seemed to taunt Kaye. Kaye studied and studied the door, but the door would not reveal its secrets to Kaye. The door grew stronger and larger, the walls grew closer, and Kaye grew frustrated.

Special Agent Hal Northrop, Sergeant Michael Paxton, and Captain Bradley Pell were sitting at the table, watching Kaye watch the door. They were mesmerized by Kaye, partly because nothing ever changed in the cell, and so there was nothing other than Kaye's obsession for the men to focus on, and partly because the men were very hungry and very thirsty, and with that came very low energy and a strong psychological need for mental distractions. Kaye's obsessive-compulsive tendencies were the best distraction the men had available to them.

When Lieutenant Kelley Pike finally emerged from his sleeping area that day, he stepped out from behind his curtain and scanned the cell from right to left and back again. It was an instinct developed from a lifetime spent in the darkest shadows of the world. Satisfied there were no new dangers in the room, Pike elected to join the group at the table.

Pike walked to the table, and then circled all the way around the table and selected his seat, the seat that put his back to Kaye's sleeping area and allowed Pike to see his own. Pike enjoyed having his back to Kaye; Kaye was the smallest one in the room, and the least physically threatening, but mostly Pike enjoyed insulting the sniper.

Pike had claimed this chair early on, when he was alone in the cell, because it allowed him to watch his own sleeping quarters, to protect his territory. As more men entered the cell, Pike continued to lay claim to his chair, and he had made it clear that it was indeed his chair. At one point, Northrop tried to take the chair, as part of his manipulation, but it was Paxton that warned him off, telling him in very few words and very matter-of-fact, that if Pike caught him in that chair, he would kill him. *Does Pike know?* Northrop had thought, and asked Paxton why Pike would use that excuse. Paxton had simply laughed and explained it was not personal, that was simply Pike's chair and if anyone sat in it, they were probably going to be beaten to death. *Pike does not know*, Northrop had decided. The way the others respected that one chair as Pike's, the more evident it became to Northrop that Pike was a pure alpha, and even if Northrop was successful in securing the allegiance of the others, he would never find a way to make

Pike submissive. Northrop had observed this sort of thing many times. *Pike will have to die*, he had thought.

As soon as Pike sat down, Paxton produced his cigarettes, put one between his lips and passed one to Northrop. Paxton held the pack out, stretching out towards the center of table to meet Pike's outstretched hands; Pike reached into the pack and selected a nail. Pike produced his lighter, and held it over the centre of the table. Pike flipped the lid open, and then he sparked the lighter, produced a flame, and all three men leaned in and lit their nails. Pike leaned back as he snapped the lighter closed and took a good, long drag, inhaling the smoke, and then after a pause he exhaled the smoke with satisfaction. "Breakfast of champions," he said.

Northrop took a pull of his nail, then held it between his thumb and forefinger, staring at it and thinking before he finally looked towards Pike. "So...Pike...what time do you think it is?"

"Six a.m." Pike responded with some degree of annoyance in his voice.

"And why do you say that?" Northrop pressed.

"Because I always get up at six a.m." There was pure contempt in Pike's tone.

Pike, Paxton and Northrop continued to smoke, Pell continued to sit, and Kaye continued to be Kaye and stare at the door.

It was Paxton who decided to voice what was on everybody's mind, which is what Northrop had been waiting for: "So what the hell is it you're doing with your pulse? What is that all about?" Paxton's question had broken Kaye's trance, and he turned from the door to face the table. Kaye uncrossed his legs, pulled his knees into his chest, and began to watch and listen.

"In a minute." Northrop had an audience, and Northrop needed an audience to move his agenda forward. "First I want to do a round table. Names, rank, branch. I want to see who all the players are."

"Control the situation, eh, Company?" By now the contempt in Pike's voice had been replaced by insubordination.

"That's right, Pike." Northrop needed to sound authoritative.

"All right, Company. You think you have a chip in the game, be my guest, but I still don't see no damned cards." Pike swung his foot up onto the table, sank into his chair, leaned his head back, and closed his eyes.

"You're an ass," said Northrop, growing frustrated.

"It's pronounced 'arse' where I come from, Company." Pike was amused.

"Okay, here is what we are going to do," Northrop said, as if he truly were in charge of a situation none of them had any control over. "We are going to go around the table, state who we are and the last place you remember being before we got here. Understood?"

"I don't like conversation during breakfast," Pike

challenged, still leaning back with his eyes closed, and his cigarette burning low in his mouth.

"And I want to know what your obsession with that clock is before we go any further," Paxton added defiantly. Northrop was not gaining the respect he was after. This might have been the end of it if Pell was not such an affable man, but he unwittingly kept the door open for Northrop.

"Relax, guys. Northrop is just trying to figure things out. I am Captain Bradley Pell, United States Air Force. I am currently stationed at the US Navy base Diego Garcia. I don't recall how I came to be here. Last thing I do remember is dinner at the mess. I had a hamburger."

"Good, Captain Pell, good." It may have sounded as if Northrop was praising Pell for getting involved in the solution process, but he was really talking to himself: *good, good*, he thought, *now I have my opening.* "What about you, Paxton?"

Paxton was annoyed, but Paxton was a soldier first and foremost, and so he played ball. "Well, like I already told you, sir, I am Sergeant Michael Paxton, United States Army, Special Forces. As for the rest, I was last stationed at Fort Irwin in California. I was on leave in Cabo, swimming in a pitcher of margaritas, and now I'm here. Sir."

"What about you, Pike?" Northrop's voice had caught slightly, and he hoped no one noticed. It had caught because this could be the moment of truth. *I know how you got here, Pike,* he had thought, *but do you? And if you do, how much do you know?* Pike's reply came, a reply that only made Northrop more

41

nervous.

"If you're so damned bright, Company, why not guess, eh?"

Damnit! Northrop had thought, *is Pike playing with me? Does he know? Pike, do you fucking know?* Northrop screamed in his head while remaining outwardly cool and trying to think of a reply. "Well, saying 'eh' all the time makes you a Canadian, and since you're a jackass, you must be Joint Task Force 2. That's home to all the rejected Canucks that like to play soldier." *Did I go too far?* Northrop wondered. He needed to show aggression towards Pike if he was going to manipulate the others, but he had to be careful not push Pike too far; it was delicate work.

For a moment Pike did not react to the barb, and everyone waited. Pike sat there, leaning back, eyes closed, leg up on the table...then he spoke. "Spooky, but what else would you expect from a spook, eh?" There was pure Canadian sarcasm in his tone.

"Right." Northrop filled the silence. Pike inhaled the last drag left on his cigarette, then slung his foot off the table and onto the floor, opened his eyes, sat up, and exhaled the smoke. Next, Pike flicked his butt towards Kaye.

"Small team, five men, in Colombia. Off books." That was all the explanation Pike offered; he then motioned to Paxton for another cigarette. Paxton took out his pack and slid it across the table to Pike. Pike selected a nail from the pack, put it between his lips and fished out his lighter.

"Last memory?" Northrop asked.

"Ain't got none," Pike said as he opened the top of his lighter and sparked the flame.

"Good soldiers forget, or something like that?" Northrop pressed him. *Does he fucking know?*

"Something like that," Pike responded as he sucked the flame towards the cigarette. Once his nail was lit, Pike snapped the lighter closed, placed it on the pack of cigarettes and slid them over to Paxton, who in turn selected a nail and lit it, before putting his pack away and sliding the lighter back to Pike. This time neither man offered Northrop a cigarette. In that moment, Northrop thought, *I need to drive a wedge between these two.*

"All right Sergeant Kaye, you're up." Northrop spoke more like it was an order than a request. Northrop already had rationalized he had Pell and Kaye in his hip pocket.

Kaye leaped to his feet, almost to a state of attention, and he spoke with pride. "Sergeant J.P. Kaye, United States Marine Corps, Sniper division. I was in South Korea on stand-by, ready to move into North Korea."

"They were going to send you into North Korea?" Pell did not mean to sound shocked, but he was. Pell was not alone in thinking that Kaye was not the real deal, but now, if this was true, perhaps he really was. There was a pause, a moment of silence when they all just looked at Kaye, and then Pell broke the silence by addressing Northrop. "So what about you, Northrop?"

"Special Agent Hal Northrop. Gitmo." *If Pike can be vague, I can be vague*, thought Northrop.

"Figure it out yet, Company?" Pike knew Northrop had it figured the moment he stepped out from behind the curtain to his sleeping area his first morning in the cell; Paxton had realized it shortly after.

"I hope not," Northrop lied. "Paxton, could I get another one of those nails?"

Paxton studied Northrop a moment, and then he fished out his pack, removed a cigarette, and slid it down the table to Northrop. Northrop picked it up and put it in his mouth. As he did, Paxton went back to the question that had started this conversation.

"So what's the deal with you and that clock?"

"Got a light, Pike?" Northrop ignored Paxton. Pike took out his lighter, then gripped it tight inside his fist and leaned in to Northrop, face to face, with just inches between them.

"Answer the man's question, Company." It was clearly an order and a threat. Pike stared hard into Northrop's eyes and Northrop knew he had to back down and answer the question if he wanted a light, and that if he did not want a light, then he was in for a fight. *Fuck!* Northrop thought, *he knows.*

"Blinkey," Pike said, addressing Kaye without moving his face out of Northrop's or breaking his stare. "Stop looking at Pell like that. It's creepy." Northrop turned to look at Kaye, and saw he was staring right at Pell with the same intensity he used to study the door to the cell. Kaye had a strange, far-off look

44

in his face, and Northrop realized Kaye must have been staring at Pell ever since Pell questioned his skill by displaying shock that Kaye was on stand-by for Korea. Kaye snapped back to reality and changed the direction of his gaze.

When Northrop turned his head back to the table, he found Pike was still in the same place, still staring at him, waiting for him to answer Paxton's question. Northrop cleared his throat, and Pike sat back, expecting an answer. "Let me ask you guys this: do you think that clock is working? Other than Pike, do you believe it is running properly?"

Kaye leapt at the chance to answer first, stepping into the table and claiming the empty seat as he did. "Yes. It may not have the right hour on it...like they set it that way to screw with us, but it keeps ticking, so it's working." Kaye moved his finger back and forth making a ticking noise for a few seconds before he calmed down.

"All right, Kaye," Northrop answered, "it is ticking, but it is not ticking right. The clock is not working properly. Well, it is in the sense that it is doing what they want it to do, but it is not running as it should. It is not keeping time like a regular clock." *I have them now*, Northrop had thought. He was about to provide the group with what he thought the others would believe was critical, tactical intelligence.

"What exactly do you mean by that, Northrop?" Pell asked.

"The second hand on that clock," Northrop answered, "is ticking only once for every four seconds that pass."

CHAPTER SEVEN

As the days progressed in the heptagon-shaped cell, the five men aged, and time stood still. Kaye continued to study the large, ominous steel door in the corner of the cell opposite the large wall clock. Kaye would sit cross-legged on the floor, sometimes just inches from the door; other times he would be several feet away from the door, and other times still, Kaye would study the door from the opposite side of the room, sitting cross-legged on the floor beneath the giant clock, just staring straight ahead at the door, studying it. Some days, Kaye would sit in different spots still to study the door. Sometimes Kaye would sit in the corner where his sleeping area was located, and other times he would sit in front of the sleeping areas of the other men, systematically studying the door from all angles available to him. There were days when Kaye even sat on the table and studied the door, but this only happened if Pike were sleeping. Other days still, Kaye would stand right in front of the door, and sometimes he would even touch it, running his fingers over the door again and again, tracing every inch of it, as though he expected to somehow unlock the door's secret and discover where they were and who had imprisoned them there. Centimeter by centimeter, Kaye would incrementally make his way over the entire surface of it with his eyes, or his fingers, or both, with great meticulous detail, taking hours to complete the task. Kaye knew every inch of that large steel door, and he was proud of that.

Kaye was not the only one to develop some outwardly strange behaviors. Pike and Paxton had developed a habit of engaging in daily exercise routines. Generally, they focused on hand to hand combat drills; the first man would hold up his hands, palms facing outward, and move them about indicating targets and drilling combinations. Then the men would switch roles and the second man would hold his palms out for the first man to punch. The two soldiers would also go through wrestling and judo drills, engage in calisthenics, and incorporate stretching into their regimen.

Pell had not developed any unusual behavior patterns per se, but he had noted the habits of the others and observed them daily from his chair at the table. In this regard he was similar to Kaye; both men were observing and studying what interested them. In Pell's case, he was interested in observing the others through the lens of social anthropology, and with Kaye, it was the observation of the inanimate door. With no other source of entertainment in the cell, these were the only pastimes the incarcerated five had to occupy their minds.

When Northrop was not staring at the clock and pretending to take his pulse as he plotted, he had taken to sitting with Pell and watching. Kaye seldom moved, so by default, the bulk of their attention was on Pike and Paxton; bodies in motion naturally attracted the eye with their movement.

"What is it those two are doing?" Northrop eventually asked Pell as they watched Pike and Paxton exercise.

"Every day, for as long as I have been here, Pike and Paxton take time for P.T.," Pell offered by way of explanation.

"We don't get much food or water in this place. They should conserve themselves," Northrop said with mild derision.

"Maybe," Pell agreed. "But then again," he continued, "maybe this is what is keeping them from going nutty in here. It may be the only thing keeping them grounded."

"God help us all if this is what they are like before they go nutty." Northrop was partly making a joke, but more importantly he was engaging Pell, trying to trace out Pell's loyalties. Northrop had already determined there was a bond between Pike and Paxton, which likely meant they felt loyalty towards each other. Kaye, Northrop had surmised, would be loyal to anyone who was against Pike, his tormentor, and that left Pell as the unidentified. Northrop studied Pell's reactions, his body language, and he wanted to see if he could develop a plan to manipulate Pell's loyalties towards him.

Pike and Paxton were focused on their physical training, and as a result they were also occupying their minds. Pell was as comfortable as he could be in his stiff wooden chair, and he continued to occupy his mind by observing Pike and Paxton.

Northrop continued to stay occupied by pretending to watch Pike and Paxton with Pell, though he was actually focusing on observing Pell. Kaye, unobserved by anyone, had ceased studying the door and subtly changed his body position so he could continue to pretend to study the door even though he was in fact now studying Northrop.

CHAPTER EIGHT

Hal Northrop emerged from his sleeping area, and made his way to the table and selected a chair next to Captain Pell. Pell was watching Sergeant Kaye, and Kaye was again watching the door. This particular time, Kaye was standing at the door, tracing it with his forefinger. There was no other activity to observe, and there had been no one else to talk to, so Pell had become oddly mesmerized by Kaye's behavior, as he ran his finger over the door again and again. Before long, Northrop was as mesmerized by Kaye as Pell, and the two men at the table observed Kaye in silence for quite some time before Northrop spoke.

"What is Squirrelly up to now?" Northrop inquired.

"Same old thing with him. He never stops with that door. He's sort of a spaz, focusing on one thing all the time…like an obsession." Pell and Northrop became as intent on Kaye as Kaye was on the door.

Pell and Northrop had lost themselves in the activity of watching of Kaye for quite some time, and when Sergeant Paxton rose from his cot and entered the main cell from behind his curtain, he looked at the table and saw how focused

Pell and Northrop were on Kaye. After a few minutes, he was equally mesmerized by the sniper. After several long minutes, Paxton walked to the table and sat down, joining Pell and Northrop, but never taking his eyes off Kaye. The three men sat at the table and studied Kaye for some time before Northrop noticed that Lieutenant Pike was not among them.

"Where is Pike?" Northrop asked aloud, still focused on Kaye.

"Sleeping, I think," Pell replied, still watching Kaye.

"Does he always sleep this late?" Northrop was trying to force his mind to focus on the conversation, but Kaye still held his gaze.

"It...varies," Paxton explained.

"Varies?" asked Northrop.

"Yeah," added Pell. "The lights go darker at night, we think, and they follow the clock, so we all sleep based on that rotation, but Pike seems to just go with his own rhythm. He calls it his *internal clock*."

"And he calls me stir crazy," Paxton said lightly.

"Yeah," added Pell. "He must be off his gourd."

"Maybe," answered Northrop, "or maybe he is running as smooth as a train." Northrop secretly knew what this meant, and he still wondered if Pike knew where they were and why. Everything about Pike made Northrop uneasy. Pike being here alone made Northrop uneasy, mostly because Northrop was the one who had put Pike in this place. Northrop needed to solidify his place at the top of the pecking order just in case

Pike knew. Northrop wanted distance and protection from Pike's grasp, figuratively at least, and by escaping the cell at best.

"Well you could be right, Northrop." It was Pell that broke Northrop's internal musings. "He never does seem to be quite as tired as the rest of us." As Pell spoke, Northrop realized it was a well defined soldier's instinct in Pike that was keeping him on schedule, but that still did not tell Northrop what, if anything, Pike knew.

The first man to move his eyes away from Kaye was the first man to begin to focus on him, Pell. Pell leaned back, rubbed his eyes, and stretched in his chair. As Pell was stretching he turned to see Pike was now standing behind the three men at the table, looking at them and not at Kaye. "Well, speak of the devil, and Pike shall appear," Pell said with amusement.

Paxton and Northrop broke their stare off Kaye and turned to see Pike. Pike was standing closest to Northrop, and after a cold hard look at Northrop, Pike sat down in his chair and Paxton passed out some cigarettes. Pike produced his lighter, and first he lit his own cigarette, and then he leaned in to the centre of the table so Paxton could lean into the flame and spark his own. Pike stared deep into Northrop's eyes the whole time with the icy stare of a man who had long ago sacrificed his soul.

Does he know? Fuck! Northrop thought anxiously as he tried to remain calm outwardly and meet Pike's stare. After

Paxton had drawn sufficient flame, Pike pulled the lighter into his cupped hands and it looked for a moment that he was going to close the lid, then he moved his arms, stretching his hands towards Northrop, so he could light the cigarette Paxton had given him. *He doesn't know*, Northrop though to himself, but Pike's eyes were still fixed on Northrop's.

As soon as Northrop's cigarette had a red glow, Pike snapped the lighter closed and held his stare a moment longer before giving up on it and putting his lighter away. *No way he knows*, thought Northrop, and then he took a slow, relaxing drag. *He doesn't know.*

CHAPTER NINE

The five had grown shaggy, sweaty, smelly, and hungry over the course of their time together. Living conditions in the cell were not good, and that was of course by design; the cell was meant to prolong a state of existence, not a state of living.

Some days the five spoke very little, if at all. This was not because of animosity or malice, but more the result of having nothing left to say, and no energy or inclination towards small talk. Pike and Paxton continued to exercise and smoke, which was a contradiction in itself; Kaye continued to study the door, an obsession bordering on the insane, as if he was expecting something to change from one day to the next. Northrop continued to stare towards the clock and mimic the actions of a man in thought, though he was losing focus and at times even he was beginning to wonder what good it would do to become the alpha in the cell. Pell continued to collect the meals and say a prayer over the gruel, and pass the time affably at the table. They were five men in solitary confinement together. They existed, but nothing more.

Perhaps it was because he was growing stir crazy, or perhaps it was just his nature, but on an occasion when all five men were sitting at the table, Pell decided it was time to generate a real conversation. For Pell, it would be a welcome, perhaps sanity-saving diversion, and so he asked a question. "So what's out there for you guys? In the real world, beyond...this...place?"

"Don't do that, Pell," Pike growled.

"Do what?" Pell asked.

"In the joint we liked to pretend there was no out there. Trust me, it is easier."

"Well I am not like you, Pike. I need to think about what's out there. I can't sit here in silent denial. I need something beyond this room to focus on." Pell's tone was cheery enough, but just the same, Pike threw his leg over the table, sunk into his chair, leaned back, and closed his eyes.

"Angelo's," Paxton said, breaking the awkward silence Pike had created.

"Angelo's? What's that?" Pell asked, noticeably pleased, almost excited, to have a real conversation developing.

"It's this little hole in the wall spot back home," Paxton replied. "It's so greasy and dirty the rats don't want to eat there...or the health inspector...but the pizza...ohhh, the pizza." Paxton's belly began to rumble with the memory of Angelo's, and Northrop took that as his cue.

"Softball Saturdays," the company man stated.

"You play softball, Agent Northrop?" Pell asked.

"No, but right up the road from me there is a softball field and they play every Saturday all summer. I get a little six pack of beer, leave my life at home, and I sit in the bleachers and I sip my beer and I cheer for both teams and let the sins of democracy fade away." Northrop appeared genuinely nostalgic thinking of his softball Saturdays. "What about you, Pell? What do you have out there?" Despite his history, his training, and the number of times he had been through this on the other side, Northrop found himself genuinely concerned about the lives of the men – well, most of the men – in the room. It was becoming less clinical and more real on this side of the experiment. Northrop realized that could turn into a liability, and he focused to look for leverage as Pell began to speak.

"Oh, I have a good life waiting for me," Pell smiled. "I have been waiting to get back to it ever since I got sent to Diego Garcia." Pell became very nostalgic as he spoke. "I play bass in a cover band... we never had a gig, but we practice every Tuesday at six p.m. sharp. We are terrible. I have a 1976 Mustang I was just beginning to restore when they shipped me to Diego Garcia. I have a Thursday night bowling league, a hound dog, and most importantly, I have an angel."

"No fooling," Paxton asked, "an honest to God angel?" Paxton had never married and it was his biggest regret.

"That's right." There was a great deal of pride in Pell's voice now. "An angel. Five foot five inches, 110 lbs, blue eyes, blonde hair, and tanned legs. And when the time is right we are going to have a family."

"Well that," Paxton replied, "is real nice."

"Thank you." Pell was smiling, and so were Paxton and

Northrop. Kaye remained stone faced. "It really is. It keeps me going knowing I have her to go back to, that she will be there. I am really blessed to have my wife."

As the other men enjoyed he moment, Pike threw his leg off the table to the floor, opened his eyes, and stood up. "I had a wife once," he said, and then walked away, retreating to his sleeping area. The men watched, and the moment was ruined. After Pike was gone from sight, it was Northrop who spoke first.

"He really is an asshole." Northrop was hoping this moment would be the one he needed to wedge Paxton's loyalty away from Pike.

"Funny you should say that," chimed Paxton, "considering how highly he thinks of you." *Paxton did not trust Northrop.*

CHAPTER TEN

Lieutenant Kelley Pike was an exceptionally hard man to get along with. Captain Bradley Pell, however, was an exceptionally easy man to get along with, and this was not lost on Northrop. Northrop planned to use Pell's affable nature to his advantage; he was just not sure how yet. Northrop was pondering this very task as he stared at the clock. He routinely did this, often pretending to check his pulse so he could claim that was how he knew the clock was ticking wrong. The ruse gave him time to think about his situation and re-evaluate the parameters around Experiment FIVE as he searched for loopholes and flaws in the experiment's execution. Northrop knew the timetable inside out; he had been through the experiment many times on the outside of the cell. Unable to find an immediate opening to manipulate the experiment, Northrop placed a great deal of importance on observing the other four prisoners and knowing all he could about their habits and weaknesses, in case the opportunity to exploit them and save himself were presented. Northrop very much resembled Kaye in this respect, always studying the other men; both Northrop and Kaye were falling back on their training, and both saw their cellmates as possible targets and clear obstacles. It was during one of Northrop's strategic reflection sessions when Pell approached him by the clock.

"So, how are you adjusting, Special Agent Northrop?" Pell asked Northrop.

"Captain Pell, I think you are about the only one here I would let call me Hal." It was a small gesture, but it was bait.

"Well, Hal, in that case you can call me Bradley." Northrop knew his key to gaining control of the group was Pell, and he was a step closer. As long as Pell was not the catalyst, Northrop could make this work, he was sure of it; Northrop still did not know what he would do when he gained control, but it would be his.

Northrop walked towards the table, and Pell followed. Kaye and Paxton were already sitting there, filling in time the way the men had come to expect, Kaye staring at the door and Paxton staring at his pack of smokes, waiting for Pike and his lighter.

As Northrop and Pell sat down, Northrop decided to engage Pell directly in front of the others with an open question, establishing the beginning of a pecking order that would begin at Northrop and then step down to Pell; he would do this by initiating a first name protocol between the two of them, and only the two of them.

"So Bradley, exactly what was our order of arrival?" There it was, a relevant, tactical question, displaying trust in Pell's abilities, while creating familiarity with Pell and displaying the dynamic in front of the others. No one else had used a first name to address anyone in all the time Northrop had been in the cell.

"Pike was here first, Hal," Pell responded, using the same familiarity, and thus Northrop created, his pecking order. If things continued smoothly, his plan would work. "We think he was here alone a long time before anyone else popped up."

"Why is that, Bradley?" Northrop was working out a timeline in his head; he knew exactly when Pike was put in here.

"Well, he never really talked about being here alone, but we figure it is the only way to explain his sunny disposition…sort of went off the deep end being alone." Pell was answering as honestly as he could.

"Plausible as anything," Northrop interjected, knowing that Pike was mentally questionable long before he was ever put in this cell.

"Next came Kaye," Pell continued to report.

"That's right." Kaye popped up out of his seat, eager to speak, as though he was chasing validation. "That's when we became friends. We were two peas in a pod… literally and metaphorically. We are pretty well in sync. Buddies."

"The hell we are, Blinkey!" Pike was behind Kaye, and he looked ornery. Northrop realized he did not know how long Pike had been there. He was not at the table when Northrop had asked Pell who had been there in the cell first. Northrop was sure Pike was not there when they walked to the table, but

Kaye had been sitting with his back to Pike's sleeping area. Northrop thought to himself, *What had Pike heard? And does it matter?*

Pike walked in very close to Kaye and he put his forefinger right to Kaye's face as he began to snarl aggressively: "I want to make this crystal. We are not buddies. Call us buddies again and I will beat you. Clear?"

"Cr...cr...crystal." Kaye turned his eyes toward the floor and sat down. Pike circled the table and took his seat. Alpha.

"Relax Pike, cool down." Paxton was calming Pike. Northrop had noticed that although Pike was clearly violent, clearly hard, and a clear alpha, he had a great respect for Paxton, and that Paxton could control Pike, so Northrop knew he needed to control Paxton...but how?

"I was next, Northrop." Paxton interrupted Northrop's thoughts. "Me and my cigarettes and Pike and his lighter got along real good. Some time later Pell showed up, and a very short time after that, you." Paxton thought for moment, and then continued. "Does all of this mean anything? The order of our arrival?"

"To someone, but not to me," Northrop lied. "Not yet anyway." Northrop was more insulted than confused. Protocol was to put the most dangerous man in the cell first, and that was Pike. Northrop had put Pike here and knew exactly who Pike was, and he did not agree with the assessment that Pike was the most dangerous man here; Northrop believed he was the most dangerous man in the room, not

Pike. Northrop also believed Paxton was more dangerous than both Pike and Kaye, and Northrop was sure his judgment was far superior to whomever had set the experiment in motion. Furthermore, Northrop did not believe Kaye or Pell were dangerous at all...somehow, Northrop thought, a variable was changed. *But why?* he wondered; *why was the variable changed* and *why did they do this to him?*

CHAPTER ELEVEN

The old man could not recall exactly how long the five men had been in the cell before they experienced their first major stress test, but he recalled that it was far longer than any other group. The first major test was designed to manipulate feelings of hostility, insecurity, anxiety, fear and paranoia, the very emotions that life in the cell had been intensifying in the five subjects.

It was Northrop who would first discover it, and once he saw it, he began to worry, not because he did not know what it meant, but rather because he did.

Northrop rose that morning, stretched and shook out the cobwebs, pulled back his curtain and emerged from his sleeping area to the main cell. He stepped up to the table and once he arrived at it, Northrop stopped dead and just stood there, staring at it as it laid there on the table, shocked and in a surreal state of disbelief. Northrop had never really accepted that he was in the cell for the experiment; he had always held out a sense of hope, or denial, and had on some level expected that he would be removed before the real tests began. Northrop had expected that he would be rescued, and that someone would explain the mistake that happened and why he was in the cell, and that whoever made the mistake would take his place, here in the cell, in Experiment FIVE. Northrop now realized that he had been wrong; Northrop now feared that he was damned.

The items on the table, the items that told Northrop this was not a nightmare, but rather a much darker reality than any nightmare, were a handgun, a single-action Colt revolver six-shooter, and beside the gun, four single bullets. Northrop was lost in a haze, unable to force his thoughts through the fog and deal with what he was seeing. Northrop was so wrapped up in the fear that came with his knowledge of the revolver and what it meant, that he did not notice the shadow that overtook him. It was not until he heard the low, gravelly voice that his focus was broken and he regained a sense of his surroundings.

"What's with the hardware, Company?" It was Pike's voice.

"How should I know?" Northrop was turned to face Pike, and his voice and body language were defensive. *Did he know?* Northrop thought to himself with panic. *Did Pike know?*

"Because you're a spook," Pike responded in a hostile tone, "and this hardware showing up all of a sudden is spooky." Pike and Northrop were locked in on each other's eyes, hatred staring into fear, and fear staring into hatred.

As if they had felt the increased level of tension in the room, Pell and Paxton both emerged from their sleeping areas and began walking towards the table. Pell was first to the table, and stopped dead beside Northrop, his eyes fixed on the stare-down between Pike and Northrop.

"Whoa...why so tense looking?" Pell asked as he approached the table.

"Look on the table," Northrop instructed, still locked in a staring contest with Pike.

Pell looked at the table and fell silent as Paxton walked up to his side and looked down at the table a split second after Pell.

"The math is wrong. It's a bullet short." Paxton was thinking out loud, calmly, tactically, like a soldier.

"The math is right," Northrop assured him

"Where do you suppose all this hardware came from?" Paxton asked to no one in particular.

"Well, you have the floor, Company," Pike said with derision.

"It's a mind game," Northrop said quickly, trying to flex his knowledge, and hoping to mask it as deductive reasoning. "Like the slow ticking clock. It's a trick, a stress test." Northrop had turned back towards the table and his eyes were darting between Paxton and Pell and back as he tried to explain it all. As he was speaking, Kaye emerged from his sleeping area and casually strolled up to the table. "Think it through. It is a test, just a test."

"A deadly one." Paxton stated what they were all thinking. Kaye began to move his hand towards the gun, and

Northrop was the first to notice, and when he saw Kaye's hands were only inches from the revolver, he barked.

"Kaye!" Kaye stopped short. "Leave the gun and the bullets where they are, Kaye. Everyone, leave the gun and the bullets right there, right where they are."

"Control the situation, eh, Company?" Pike's hatred hung in the air and fueled his words.

"That's right, Canuck," Northrop shot back. "As long as the gun and bullets are there, where we can all see no one has taken them, we are in control of the situation. If they go missing we have a problem. Understood?" Then after a pause for effect, Northrop continued. "Everybody, is that understood?"

Paxton, Pell, Kaye and Northrop stared down at the gun in silence, but Northrop could feel Pike's eyes on the back of his head. *Fuck! Does he know? Does Pike know?* Northrop thought, his mind panicking, his body seemingly calm.

CHAPTER TWELVE

The old man said the five men had gone a long time, many days, with the gun on the table, and that this was not typical of the Experiment. Generally, there was a fight for the gun; sometimes they all agreed to leave it, but within hours someone had taken the gun. With this group of five, the revolver remained on the table for more days than the old man could recall.

Even with the stress of the gun in the room, many of the other rituals that the men had developed remained as constants; the five men were not allowing disruption or change to their lives in the cell. Kaye still studied the door almost every moment of every day. Pike and Paxton continued with their physical training regimen. Pell continued to collect and distribute the food in the same manner, and Northrop continued to pretend to be testing the speed of the clock.

As the days went by, the five men almost seemed to forget about the gun, giving it no more thought than one would a desk lamp. Northrop continued to observe the others and look for leverage to exploit through their behavior. More than any of them, Northrop saw an opportunity to do that with Pell's ritual around collecting and distributing the food.

Every morning, when the men rose, there was a tray with five bowls of gruel and just slightly less than enough water for five, left on a tray, on the floor beside the door. Every morning Pell would go to the door, kneel beside the tray, and pray over the food before picking it up and bringing it over to the table and dispensing it for the group of men. As Pell brought the tray to the table on this day, Northrop decided to probe Pell's ritual.

"Are you looking for Mecca when you do that?" Northrop asked the Captain.

"I'm not a Muslim, so I can pray in any direction I like," Pell replied in good humor, "though I do prefer to pray up." Pell shot his eyes upward to emphasize his point.

"Bradley, you say a prayer over there, kneeling on the concrete, every morning before you bring the food over. Why? Why not say grace at the table?" Northrop asked.

"Well, Hal," Pell said as he started putting the bowls in front of the chairs, "I won't say who, but one of the others here is not too thrilled when I say grace at the table, so I do it over there, by the door, before I bring the food to the table." As Pell finished his explanation, and set out the last bowl of gruel, Paxton came to the table, followed by Kaye.

"Mmmmm, gruel," Paxton started, "my favorite." Paxton grinned wide as he took his seat.

"Are you going to say that every time they feed us, soldier?" Northrop asked him.

"Yes." Paxton replied as a matter-of-fact.

"Why?" Northrop pressed.

"Because," Paxton said in all sincerity, "I actually do mean it." Paxton assaulted his bowl.

"We all believe him, Hal," Pell said, seeing the confusion on Northrop's face. "To Paxton here, if it is edible, it's food."

"So why do you say grace for this...food?" Northrop turned his attention back to Pell. "Are you thankful for the gruel, Bradley?"

"Well, Hal, it is better than the alternative." Pell dug into his bowl, and after a pause, Northrop and Kaye did the same.

Chapter Thirteen

The tension in the cell was getting higher, and the cigarettes were getting low, very low. Paxton was sitting at the table, staring into the cigarette pack and waiting. There were only two left, and Paxton had been sitting there, with those two cigarettes, for several hours.

Pike emerged from his sleeping area, and he saw Paxton sitting at the table. Paxton was the closest thing that Pike had ever had to a friend, and Pike was the only other man in the cell that Paxton considered a real soldier, so through circumstance, they became close. Pike stretched and yawned, made his way to the table, and sat down in his regular chair.

Paxton pulled the two final cigarettes out of the pack with his right hand and crumpled the package with his left. He held the two cigarettes up, spaced out to look like a peace sign. "Last two," he said. "I've been waiting for you to smoke 'em." Paxton put one cigarette between his lips and passed one to Pike. Pike produced his lighter, flipped open the lid, struck the wheel with his thumb, and produced a flame; Pike lit Paxton's smoke first, then his own.

The two men, Sergeant Paxton and Lieutenant Pike, sat at the table and smoked the final two cigarettes in reverent silence as the other three men stood near the clock and watched. As the smoke rose towards the ceiling and evaporated, so did the last semblances of hope in the room, and as the cigarettes turned to ash, so too did any remaining hope, anywhere in the cell.

Chapter Fourteen

As the tensions in the cell grew, so too did Northrop's desperation. Northrop was struggling to appear in control, though on the inside his anxiety was escalating and his fears were growing. Northrop's biggest fear had been realized the moment that the gun appeared in the cell: he was a prisoner, and it was not a mistake. Until now, Northrop had truly believed it was a mistake and that he would be rescued. Northrop had put a lot of effort into devising a scheme to manipulate the others and become the leader, but that was less related to his long-term fears and more closely rooted in the immediacy of his situation, and his fear of Pike.

As Northrop became more and more desperate, he spent more and more time staring at the clock. The clock was a very interesting clock. Instead of numbers, the clock had faces, and as the faces changed from the one o'clock face to the twelve o'clock face, they grew more and more grotesque, representing a descent into madness. The clock itself had been built by a man in an insane asylum as he drifted further into his own madness, and as he stared at the clock, Northrop began to question his own sanity. He began to hope the whole ordeal was a mere hallucination. It was not.

Despite his inward turmoil, Northrop did his best to remain outwardly cool. As much time as he may have spent staring at the sinister clock and becoming a victim of his own thoughts, he was always composed enough to go through the motions of checking his pulse, pretending he was using his pulse rate to track the clock. That was impossible, though, as his pulse was racing to match his ever-vigilant fear. The pistol weighed heavy on Northrop and he was very much afraid.

As long as no one in the room took the gun, Northrop knew he had time, but what he didn't know was how he would get out of this. It was about this moment that it dawned on his efforts to gain control of the other prisoners had been busy work at best, and he could no longer remember why he ever thought that crusade had mattered. All that mattered was escaping the cell, but no one ever had. Northrop needed a bargaining chip, and the only bargaining chip he could imagine was the leverage of the gun. If Northrop took it, he could control the men in the room and he could control his fears, but mostly, he could control Experiment FIVE, and they would need to remove him from the cell and reset.

Northrop was lost in his thoughts when Pike approached him. "Expecting that clock to speed up?" Pike asked from behind.

"No, slow down." Northrop turned to face Pike and he saw no need to manipulate his answers anymore. "Of course, if they know I know, then all bets are off. They might change the variable."

"What do you mean by that, eh?" Pike challenged Northrop.

"Company secret," Northrop replied as Pell came over to the clock. That was when Northrop realized if they were following protocol, the clock was slowed the instant the revolver was planted in the cell, and that was days ago. *Damnit! The clock should be slowed, and I didn't say anything,* Northrop thought to himself. *Fuck! Did Pike notice? Does he know?*

"Come on, Hal," Pell interjected, "what happens if the clock slows down?"

Northrop changed gears. He did not want to tell them the truth: that nothing happened. The clock slowed, time crawled, and whoever had the gun would turn on the group. That was the predictable outcome, the one that always happened and was always studied, and the reason he did not want one of the others to take the gun. *No,* Northrop thought, *the only safe place for the Colt is with me.* As he was searching his mind for an answer, Northrop noticed Kaye pacing about near Paxton's sleeping area. "What is Kaye doing over there?"

"Looking for another exit, I guess." Pell answered. "He keeps saying there has to be a back way out."

"His training is telling him that," Northrop explained. "But there is not. That is the stressor. Snipers do not operate in enclosed spaces like this. He is out of his element." Northrop came to a realization, and it almost put a look of

panic on his face. *Why didn't I think about the speed of the clock?*
Damn! he thought as he watched Kaye. "Where is Paxton? Is
he still sleeping?"

Before anyone could answer, Kaye spoke loud enough for
the other men to hear him.

"This isn't right," Kaye said, staring at Paxton's curtain.

"What's not right?" Northrop asked.

"It's damaged." Kaye raised his hand and pointed a finger
at the corner of Paxton's curtain. The top corner, closest to
the large door, was torn. Northrop and Pell walked over to
join Kaye. As Northrop, Pell, and Kaye all stood there,
looking up at the damaged corner of Paxton's curtain, Pike
pushed past them and pulled the curtain down. They all
looked into the exposed area and saw that Paxton's cot was
empty.

CHAPTER FIFTEEN

The cell was dark. Northrop was alone at the table, picking at cigarette butts, his mind racing and his fear growing. They had taken Paxton, so he did not need to check his pulse to know the clock had slowed again. *The second hand should be moving once for every six seconds now,* he thought, *that happens with the first abduction, but Paxton?* That is not who Northrop would have expected. The variables had been changed, or someone was operating off a different a playbook. Northrop also had to accept the fact that he was here, locked in this cell with the other men, because he had been making mistakes, and that was an unforgivable sin. No matter how he spun it, the prognosis was not good. Northrop was growing more desperate, and he did not expect to see Paxton again.

Northrop looked at the gun on the table. It was a single-action Colt revolver, identical in every way to the firearm he normally carried. It might have actually been his gun. It was definitely not the weapon used in past studies of Experiment FIVE.

Finally, after Northrop had stared at the gun enough, it was time to give in to his need for sleep. Northrop stood up, looked at the gun one last time, and then walked off to his sleeping area, entered it, and pulled his curtain shut. He had not noticed Kaye.

Kaye had been sitting on the floor inside of his sleeping area with the curtain pulled back just enough for him to peer out and see the whole of the main area of the cell. Kaye watched Northrop, and then, after Northrop was securely behind his curtain, Kaye noticed movement; it was the curtain around Pike's sleeping area. It opened and Pike emerged.

Pike took a long look towards the gun and bullets that were still atop the table. Pike then turned his head and went into Paxton's sleeping area. The curtain was still half pulled down, but it was dark enough where Pike disappeared into the shadows, out of Kaye's view. After several minutes, Pike emerged from the shadows and then returned to his sleeping area.

Kaye continued to stare at the table and memorize the placement of the gun and the bullets. Kaye now studied the Colt with the same ferocity that he had applied to his study of the door.

After a time, when Kaye was sure no one else was awake, he skulked out to the door and he stood inches from it, tracing it with his eyes, up one side, down the other. Kaye ran his fingers along the door, and then he stood back and stared at it some more. When Kaye had learned all there was to learn about the door that night, he walked back to his sleeping area, unaware that as he walked past Northrop's sleeping area,

Northrop pulled his curtain back slightly, no more than an inch, and watched Kaye return to his area, then Northrop looked back to the table to make sure the revolver and the bullets were still where they belonged. They were. *The only safe place for that weapon is with me*, Northrop thought to himself.

CHAPTER SIXTEEN

Time felt slower in the cell after Paxton was abducted. Life went on, but it felt slower, like the speed of a bug desperately moving through the fresh, wet, concrete of a new sidewalk; time was moving forward, the men went through their motions, but it felt slower and somehow more hopeless.

Pike continued to exercise, though without a sparring partner it was simply push-ups, sits-ups and shadow boxing, but he was staying active. Pike insisted he was exercising at the same time every day, and Pell and Kaye did not believe it, because it was at odds with the changing patterns of the light, but Northrop figured it was true to the best of his math.

Northrop watched Pike exercise and though about how thick his beard was getting, and then he would rub his own and determined it was at least as thick. They had been in the cell a very long time now.

Pell continued to collect the food, whenever the food was made available, and he continued to say grace. Pell even added a prayer for Paxton's safe return, though Pike would tell him that if he really wanted to end Paxton's pain, he would pray that God had taken mercy on the Special Forces soldier and had called him home. Only once, when Pell and Pike were alone, Pell challenged Pike on this, but to his challenge, Pike said, "You should pray for death to come sooner for us all. I do," Pike confessed to Pell. "I say those prayers each night, kneeling beside Paxton's cot."

Pell continued to pray for Paxton's safe return, refusing to be as cynical as Pike; even in this cell, Pike was more cynical than the rest. Pell's spirits were high enough to be functional only because he refused to give up hope, even if Pike was choosing to live a hopeless existence on this occasion in hell.

Kaye continued to sit cross-legged in the cell, and he generally squared his shoulders to the door so he would appear to be looking at it, but he no longer was. Now Kaye spent his time looking at his cellmates, studying them: the way they moved, the way they spoke, how they behaved when they thought they were alone. And he continuously looked to the gun and bullets, and they remained untouched on the table just the way they were when Northrop discovered them.

This particular day, Northrop was sitting at the table, alone, Pike was sleeping, and Pell pacing; Kaye was pretending to look at the door as he secretly studied Northrop. Kaye finally decided to get up off the floor and walk to the table to make his move. Kaye pulled out the chair closest to Northrop and sat down.

"Door lose its appeal?" Northrop asked dryly.

"We have a problem," Kaye stated.

"Evidently." Northrop managed a slight grin and motioned around the room with his hand.

"I mean a new one. With Pike." Kaye was being assertive with his tone, putting authority behind his words.

"And here I was worried things would get dull in here," Northrop spoke sarcastically. "What's up with Pike?" *I may have an ally*, Northrop thought, *and a scapegoat.*

"I was up late last night...sort of worrying about Paxton," Kaye lied. "I have been worried about him ever since they took him. Anyway, I opened my curtain a bit...to see if anyone was up to talk to...and I saw you just heading to bed so I didn't bother you, but as soon as your curtain closed, Pike came out of his sleeping area."

"So? So what? Who cares? Pike sleeps on his own schedule. The right one, too." Northrop was edgy and it showed.

"So?" Kaye was hurt that he was being dismissed; he had seen many similarities between himself and Northrop, even if Northrop had missed them, and Kaye felt Northrop should respect him more. "So he went into Paxton's ... room, for lack of a better word. After several minutes, he came back out. He has done that every night since we lost Paxton."

"So what does he do in Paxton's spot?" Northrop's interest picked up on that cue.

"I don't know, but..." Kaye stammered, looking for a way to finish his thought.

"...but the guy is off his gourd," Northrop finished the thought for Kaye.

Northrop and Kaye froze instinctively at this point in their conversation. Collectively they felt a chill, a presence, and not a very pleasant one. They both turned their heads and discovered Pike was standing there, nearly over top of them, with his face contorted into a snarl. Pike stared at Northrop and then at Kaye; Kaye and Northrop stared at each other, both wondering what part, if any, of their conversation Pike had heard.

It was then, as if on cue, though that was not the case, that Pell emerged from his sleeping area. Seeing the tension, Pell realized he no longer had it in him to deal with this level of bullshit and posturing, and he made that clear.

"I don't care who did or said what to who or why they did it," Pell said. "Just wait until I go back to bed tonight to settle it."

And with that, Northrop and Kaye looked away from Pike, and Pike, brazenly, strolled into Paxton's spot, pulled the cot down towards the entry point, grabbed the curtain, stood on the cot, and repaired it as best as possible.

CHAPTER SEVENTEEN

Tense. Tense was the only way to describe the atmosphere in the cell, and even that did not do it justice. Perhaps it was the absence of Paxton, or maybe the way in which he had been abducted, or the appearance of the gun, or some sort of combination of it all coming together in a perfect storm, but the dynamic had shifted drastically and there was more animosity hanging thick and heavy in the air. Regardless of why and how, the change had occurred, well behind any projected schedule based on the knowledge gained from previous experiments. Most surprisingly though, the revolver was still on the table, with all four bullets, and there had yet to be any real violence in the cell, despite the fact that the men had been reduced to living like animals. Pike had devolved further than that, having already been an animal when the experiment had first begun.

Northrop, Kaye, and Pell sat at the table that morning, and Pike was stretching, preparing for bed; despite the fact the others were calling it morning, Pike was sure it was evening. Pike did not know it, but his internal clock, which was accurate, had caused a problem for the interactions with the outside; it had slowed the frequency down, meaning it took longer to get the revolver in place, to abduct Paxton, to put the others in the cell. This might not have been a problem if Pike ate with the other men, but he also ate his gruel at the same time every day.

Everyone's sleep, and approximate meal times, needed to overlap for the timeline to stay on track, and so, because they were at a point when Pike's internal clock was so far off the rotation of the others, that decision was made to do something very different. Once again, a variable was changed, changed in a most unexpected way, marked by the sudden blaring of sirens.

The sirens and alarm bells were loud, too loud, and they echoed ferociously, emanating from the door. Northrop, Pell, and Kaye turned towards the door quickly, and Pike, in true Pike-like fashion, turned slower, standing where he was, in the furthest corner from the door. Next, the door opened.

When the door opened, the grey cell was bombarded with light so bright it was blinding. It was impossible for the men to see anything. The door and the entire corner of the room were engulfed by the lights, and then the door closed and the alarms stopped. As the men's eyes adjusted to the light of the cell again, they saw him, crumpled in a heap on the grey concrete floor, beaten and bruised: Sergeant Michael Paxton, United States, Special Forces.

Northrop, Pell, and Kaye ran to Paxton's side, and as Northrop and Pell began to pick him up, Kaye began with the questions: "Paxton, are you all right? Where were you? What did th…"

"Not now, Kaye!" Northrop barked as he and Pell continued to lift Paxton. As soon as Paxton was to his feet, he began to speak, and as he did, Pike began to walk over. "They…they…really put the boots to me. It was a real beat down." As Paxton finished speaking, Pike pushed past Kaye and he examined Paxton; the others stood silent, watching Pike look Paxton over.

"You say they beat you?" Pike said, and he reached into Paxton's shirt pocket and pulled out two of packs of cigarettes.

"Like a rug, man." Paxton tried to smile. Pike looked right into Paxton's mouth.

"It couldn't be all that bad," Pike stated. "You still have all your teeth." Pike opened one of Paxton's cigarette packs and removed three cigarettes before putting the two packs pack back into Paxton's shirt. Pike put two cigarettes between his lips, and one into Northrop's mouth. Next, Pike took out his lighter and lit Northrop's cigarette, then he lit the two in his own mouth, snapped off his lighter and returned it to his pocket, and finally placed one of the cigarettes between Paxton's lips, and gave him a playful slap on the face. "I had all my teeth once," Pike stated as he winked at Paxton, patted him on the chest, and then turned and walked away, retreating into his sleeping area.

After Pike had gone, Paxton spoke. "I'm good, guys." Northrop and Pell slowly let go of Paxton, and he stood freely for a moment, but then began to collapse. Northrop and Pell caught him. "I think I need to lay down. I am having a bad day."

Pell took Paxton's weight from Northrop, and Paxton, leaning heavily on Pell, began to walk towards his cot. "Well, look on the bright side, Paxton," Pell offered; "they may have put the boots to you, but they gave you two new packs for your troubles." Paxton began to laugh, but it quickly turned to a wince and he grabbed his ribs.

"Easy on my ribs, Pell. Easy on my ribs." Pell and Paxton continued, and once they were behind Paxton's curtain, Northrop spoke.

"This is a new variable. A deviation." Northrop was talking more to himself than he was to Kaye, but Kaye responded just the same.

"Yeah," said Kaye, "well, we have another problem."

"What's that?" Northrop asked absently.

"Look." Kaye pointed to the table. Northrop followed his finger, and what he saw sunk his already low spirits – the revolver and the bullets were gone. They had vanished as mysteriously as they had appeared.

CHAPTER EIGHTEEN

The five may have been isolated in their cell, but they were not alone in the facility. The facility was more than secret. It had been built secretly with military money that was unaccountable, despite the fact it was all accounted for on spreadsheets. Construction costs were hidden in the always-perplexing cost overrun structures embedded in government military spending, and kept very exclusive and secret under the convenient guise of Homeland Security.

The most fascinating facts about the secret facility were also the most surprising parts. The first surprising revelation was that the facility was located on a large American military base. Very few of the military personnel stationed there were aware the facility existed, and even fewer had any idea of the true nature of its purpose. The second shocking fact was that there were four more identical facilities hidden away on four other large American military bases. They were the five bases in use for a project code named Experiment FIVE, each one conducting the same experiments on five people as the others, countless times over.

The locations of the facilities were geographically distant from one another, but they were all under the control of one man, and that man had assigned one person to oversee Experiment FIVE at each location. The people selected to administer the duties of the facility assigned to Experiment FIVE were hand-picked, and they were posted to Experiment FIVE through a very confidential recruitment selection process. When they were invited to serve here, they accepted or they disappeared. Refusal was never permitted; refusal was not an option.

The elite of the elite were selected to serve here. The mandate was simple: support the experiment, secure the experiment, and keep the experiment out of the eyes of the public, of spies, and of the very government that was conducting Experiment FIVE. Experiment FIVE was beyond top secret.

For years, the secret facility that housed the five, Northrop, Pell, Paxton, Kaye, and Pike, was under the command of different leader. The former commander of the facility was a company man, not a soldier, and he had been put in his position because he carried favor with the powerful man who authorized Experiment FIVE: Benedict Cain. That man had recently been replaced by a new commanding officer, this one a soldier.

The new commanding officer of the facility was Lieutenant Colonel Samantha "Sam" Braun. Braun was the product of an excellent military pedigree: both her father and maternal grandfather were military men. Braun's father had risen to the rank of General in the United States army, and her maternal grandfather had risen to the rank of Admiral in the British Navy; her paternal grandfather had been a German poet, but Lieutenant Colonel Braun had no use for poetry, the arts, or any right-brained function. She was a type "A" personality bordering on the obsessive, and her only concerns were results.

Braun was one of the most decorated graduates of West Point, with some impeccable scores early on that had helped to frame her legacy. It was also at West Point when one psychiatrist concluded that Braun was a sociopath, and had recommended that she not be moved on; however, his career ended abruptly after writing that report, and the report had been misfiled. This was the power of the invisible hand of Benedict Cain.

It was during her time at West Point when Benedict Cain had first taken notice of Samantha Braun. After Braun had appeared on Benedict Cain's radar, she was monitored to see when and in what capacity she would become an asset to Cain's agenda and Experiment FIVE.

When Braun was approached to run this facility, she did not need convincing or coercing to accept the post. In fact, she accepted very quickly, perhaps too quickly to truly appreciate the task she was undertaking or the role it would play in historical context. To the ambitious Braun, the command opportunity was one more stepping stone. Of course, whether Braun accepted the post too quickly or with too little understanding was a small matter of no consequence, since refusal was never an option and all soldiers were ultimately expendable pawns of Benedict Cain. The old man confessed that once he had met Lieutenant Colonel Braun, and had understood she was in command of the facility, he was able to predict her career trajectory in those dark times.

Lieutenant Colonel Braun was cold, efficient, and even evil, but it was her clerk that truly instilled fear in the soldiers of the facility, and beyond. Master Sergeant Withers was a legend in the military machine, much the same way the Boogie Man is a legend in the dark corners of a child's bedroom. Withers' name was whispered globally, known for his unusually sadistic nature and sinister designs. Withers' legend was so terrifying that most people dismissed the stories as being just that, stories, because it was believed no human could delight in being that cruel. Master Sergeant Withers was a man born without a soul.

Braun was enjoying her ego, looking out of the window in her office, hands clasped behind her back, plotting her career trajectory and growing dangerously more ambitious the further she withdrew into herself. She ran the facility, but she had no patience for the experiment. Stress tests such as revolvers, faulty clocks, and light manipulation were too pedestrian for her. Braun rationalized that if the point of the experiment was information extraction, it could be done more efficiently with force and fear than with manipulation, and so on her own authority, she decided to alter the parameters of Experiment FIVE.

Braun's desire to alter these parameters was directly related to her desire to advance her career in the military; Braun would be satisfied by no less than five stars, but her ultimate ambition was to be appointed to the position of General of the Army, a title no longer in use but maintained. Samantha Braun would never be satisfied in her career simply as the gatekeeper to a secret facility, but she was cunning enough to see how this post could be used to accelerate her military ascension. Lost in her ambitions, it was a knock at the door that brought Lieutenant Colonel Braun back to the moment at hand.

"Come," Braun replied to the knock, without taking her eyes from the window. Braun used the window pane as a mirror to watch her office door, and as it opened, the door revealed Master Sergeant Withers. Withers entered, walked to the desk, and stood at attention.

"At ease, Withers," Braun commanded.

"Yes sir." Withers clasped his hands behind his back and stood at ease.

"Report." Small talk did not become Braun.

"We introduced the Paxton subject to your new parameters," Withers reported with a sinister smile.

"Paxton?" Braun was unconcerned and disinterested in any name that was not leading to her next promotion.

"The Special Forces soldier, sir," Withers clarified.

"Ah…yes. And how long did you have him?" Braun asked.

"A few days, though it would have seemed longer to the men in the cell; at least to the ones sleeping on the Experiment FIVE schedule, sir." Braun paused for a moment and thought about asking Withers to clarify his statement, but after a quick reflection she decided instead to dismiss it as unimportant.

"And did you make my point when you re-introduced him to his habitat?" Braun was referring to the commotion she added when putting Paxton back in the cell. In Experiment FIVE, the protocol was to slip the soldier back into his cot quietly and unobserved. The experiment was designed that way to breed mistrust, but Braun felt terror would be more effective.

"Yes sir. They were all awake this time, even the one with the renegade sleep pattern giving Dr. Reynolds a hard time."

"Speaking of the good doctor," Braun continued, still looking at the windowpane; she had not once looked directly at Withers throughout the entirety of his brief, but rather focused on his reflection, "what time is he due on base today?"

"Dr. Reynolds' flight back will not land until about ten this morning, sir." Withers began to smile very widely, and Braun noted as she watched his reflection, and she chose to dismiss Withers' grin as unimportant, though in reality, Withers was visualizing the look on the doctor's face when he discovered that the new Lieutenant Colonel had altered his experiment. *Reynolds will not like this*, Withers thought quietly.

"That will be all, Withers," Braun said by way of dismissal.

"Very good, sir." Withers turned on his heels, exited the room, and closed the door.

Braun returned to her ambitious daydreams of a future she would never know.

Chapter Nineteen

Hal Northrop was every bit as ambitious and cold as Samantha Braun, but he had much better social skills and the ability to fake empathy flawlessly; these skills had always proved to be among his greatest weapons. Northrop's ability to emulate the expected emotions of a given situation despite his lack of true empathy was a common skill in sociopaths, but even among sociopaths, Northrop was very gifted.

Northrop was able to deduce that the parameters of Experiment FIVE had been altered, and so he began to rationalize that the experiment may no longer be a no-win scenario for the inmates of the cell. Northrop now had hope, hope that he could manipulate the new variables and either escape, or better still, use that manipulation to show that he was still needed in Benedict Cain's circle and reclaim his former position; hope that he could show he was necessary. Northrop was strategizing around these very possibilities as he sat by Paxton's bedside, waiting for Paxton to regain consciousness, hoping to gain some useful intelligence that he could leverage for his own salvation. Northrop was so lost in his own selfish thoughts that he did not realize Paxton had been awake, watching him, trying to gather intelligence of his own. *Paxton did not trust Northrop.*

"Damn," Paxton groaned, putting on a show of waking.

"I'll try not to take that personal." Northrop smiled. Empathy was one of his weapons, and he would use it to manipulate Paxton at every opportunity.

"Sorry, sir. I was just hoping when I woke up, it would not be here," Paxton responded.

"If not here, where?" Northrop replied.

"Fiji would have been all right." The men laughed, neither one sincere in their laughter.

"Be glad you woke up at all," Northrop offered by way of continuing the conversation.

"Special Forces, sir; we don't roll over for nobody." Paxton summed up his words with pride. "Have you been sitting here all night?" He had been, for a long time; Paxton knew that, and he found it creepy.

"We all took shifts. You became a team-building exercise," Northrop lied.

"Did I seem that bad?" Paxton asked.

"Worse," Northrop replied. "You know it wasn't supposed to be this way, soldier."

"It sure ain't what the recruiter and his brochure promised me, sir," Paxton said dryly.

"I mean the variables here are…changing. This whole thing is being altered." Northrop let that hang in the air, testing Paxton. *Paxton did not trust Northrop.*

Paxton began to sit up, and Northrop advised him against it, but Paxton insisted, so Northrop helped him to a sitting position. "Fuck. It hurts like hell to breathe," Paxton offered.

"What exactly did they do to you, Paxton?" Northrop wanted to understand the new variable.

"Not 'they,' sir – 'he.' He really put the boots to me, sir," Paxton responded as he thought back to the silverback of a man that had beaten him and the soldier that had stood there, watching him, laughing, feeding the instructions of where to hit Paxton, what to hit him with, and more.

"How? How did they do it?" There was desperation in Northrop's voice, and Paxton recognized it. Paxton also noted that Northrop did not ask who beat him; his facial reactions were indicating he knew exactly who the silverback must have been.

"Does it matter?" Paxton challenged.

"It might," Northrop said, but never explained why.

"Sir, are there things you are not sharing with the rest of us?" Paxton called Northrop on his behavior.

"Yes," the Special Agent admitted.

"Okay." Paxton decided to bite. "Have you ever been to a meat warehouse? One where the pigs are just hanging there?"

"No," Northrop admitted.

"Well, oink, sir," Paxton stated in a dry, even tone.

"They hung you?" Northrop asked for clarity. "How?"

"They put weights on my ankles...those goofy things runners wear... to counter-weight me, I guess."

"For how long?" Northrop became very clinical in his tone.

"Too long." *Paxton did not trust Northrop.*

"And they just...hung you there?" Northrop asked.

"I was not that lucky, sir," Paxton replied. "But that freak wailing away wasn't the worst of it," Paxton offered. "Eventually my shoulder separated and they cut me down. Then he just shoved it back in place. That is the last thing I remember before this conversation, sir." Paxton did not lie to Northrop about what had happened, but he did not tell him everything. *Paxton did not trust Northrop.*

"That is not good, Paxton," Northrop said, and although it might have sounded sympathetic in tone, what Northrop really meant is that the information was useless to him, and the agent could not see how to leverage it to win his freedom.

"So, are you going to let me in on what you know?" Paxton called Northrop out again.

"No, Paxton," Northrop said. "But I will tell you this much. This variable...your beating...it isn't right...something changed."

"Worst answer possible, sir." Paxton knew he deserved an answer. "I'm going back to sleep, and you can get out. Don't wake me up again unless you're willing to share." *Paxton did not trust Northrop.*

CHAPTER TWENTY

Lieutenant Colonel Samantha Braun was tasked with the command of the secret facility, which was in reality little more than a gatekeeper's job, guarding the gates to hell. However, the security of the facility, and the four others like it, were critical to Benedict Cain because they were the locations for his pet project, Experiment FIVE. The five facilities existed for the purpose of Experiment FIVE, and so did Dr. William Reynolds.

Dr. William Reynolds was a psychiatrist, and he was a manipulator. Reynolds had written many dissertations and papers to support his hypothesis, a hypothesis that stipulated that manipulating men is the most reliable means of information extraction. Reynolds proposed to bind a group of men together through fear and confusion; fear against a common, unseen, enemy, one that they all knew was more powerful than they. As the men formed bonds to unify themselves against the powerful hands of their oppressors, they would share the details of their histories, the most intimate and classified ones, to create a social hierarchy that in turn would become their social structure. Reynolds proposed that the results would be slow in coming, but accurate. It was this research that attracted the attention of Benedict Cain. Cain proposed to fund the doctor's research, but only if he could ensure quicker returns on his investment, and based on the requests of his benefactor, Dr. Reynolds designed Experiment FIVE, which would isolate five men and force them to create a social structure to rebel against their captors. He then introduced variables, such as the anonymity of the captors and the appearance of a revolver without enough bullets for all the men, and many other stressors to accelerate the program. This was meant to extract the information that Benedict Cain wanted with a greater degree of accuracy than physical abuse, which was well documented to be inaccurate and held to only by the severely obtuse, incapable of a paradigm shift.

Dr. Reynolds had not only designed Experiment FIVE, he also personally oversaw the execution of the program across all five secret facilities. Samantha Braun did not realize it, but she was the most irrelevant part of the experiment, and her command authority was not as vast as she liked to believe. Braun was expendable; Reynolds was not.

Once Benedict Cain and Dr. Reynolds had come to an understanding, an unholy alliance had been born and no expense was spared in the construction of the secret facilities. Dr. Reynolds ran the show, period.

When Reynolds arrived at the facility for the first time after Lieutenant Colonel Braun had taken command, he was enraged at what she had done. The research was compromised, and this was the group that he believed would yield the breakthrough he and Benedict Cain had been waiting for due to the unique mixture of men, in particular the volatile relationship they anticipated between Lieutenant Pike and Hal Northrop. The compromise in his research was brought to his attention when Master Sergeant Withers entered the doctor's office with x-rays of Sergeant Michael Paxton and tossed them on to Reynolds' desk.

"What are these?" Reynolds had asked, confused.

"Paxton's ribs," Withers replied with a smile. Next, Withers explained in graphic detail what they had done to Paxton and how they had altered the experiment. Withers explained how he had instructed the silverback named Sergeant Briggs on how to hurt, but not cripple, Paxton as they tried to discover all of his military secrets. Then Withers explained the manner in which Lieutenant Colonel Braun had instructed them to re-introduce Paxton to the cell. Withers was relishing the fact that simply by following his orders he was stirring the pot, and that it would soon boil over.

Reynolds shoved past Withers and made for Braun's office with the speed of a man possessed. When he arrived at her office, Reynolds did not knock, he barged through the door, and Master Sergeant Withers followed closely.

"Blue hell, Colonel!" Reynolds screamed as the door flew open. Braun remained in her place, looking out the window, watching Reynolds in the reflection of the glass pane.

Reynolds went right to her desk and slammed his fists down, loud and hard, and as Braun turned he continued to dress her down. "Have you got a screw loose?

"I'm sorry, sir," Withers offered Braun by way of apology. "He bolted right past me."

"Dismissed, Master Sergeant," Braun ordered.

"Sir?" Withers looked for verification, and he was disappointed to receive it from his commanding officer.

"Dismissed," Braun snapped.

"Yes sir." And with that Withers left the room and closed the door.

"Who do you think you are?" Reynolds challenged the new commanding officer of the facility in their first meeting. "I am the psychologist here. I set the parameters! I control the variables! Just what do you think you are doing?"

"I thought it best to change the parameters." Braun approached the desk and stood face to face with Reynolds, across the desk, locked eye to eye.

"You have not got the authority!" Reynolds barked.

"I am the ranking commanding officer of this facility, Doctor," Braun countered.

"This facility's sole purpose is to support my research, not dictate it." Reynolds was very angry.

"You have been conducting these exact experiments for a very long time, Doctor." Braun was making a challenge.

"What's it to you, Colonel?" Reynolds responded.

"Efficiency, Doctor," Braun replied smugly.

"Efficiency?" Reynolds was not sure where Braun was going. "What are you talking about?"

"I have been a very efficient soldier and commanding officer." Braun was maneuvering for power. "I go where I am needed, where efficiency is needed. I go there because the shit, Doctor, needs to get back on track, and you, Doctor, are the shit."

"Beating a man like Sergeant Paxton is not efficient. It is like trying to empty a bathtub with a teaspoon." There was nothing more infuriating to an academic like Dr. Reynolds than a close-minded individual like Lieutenant Colonel Braun.

"My methods will work, Doctor. We will empty that bathtub." Braun's dismissive nature showed Reynolds exactly what he was dealing with, and it was a close-minded bully. Braun had missed the point.

"The methods *are* the experiment. You cannot change the variables. Especially not by physically torturing, beating, a man. It does not work." Even then, on that first day of their first meeting, Reynolds knew he was wasting his breath, and he began to wait for the end he knew would come.

"It works," Braun stated, proving Reynolds' point, but not knowing she had.

"It cannot be accurate." Reynolds knew the research inside out. He was right.

"Why is that, Doctor?" Braun's tone was sarcastic and dismissive.

"Because when you beat a man he either dies, or guesses at what you want to hear. He wants the beating to stop, and he will say anything. Unreliable."

"Exactly my point. He will say anything. You just made my point." Braun did not address the term *unreliable,* but rather chose to ignore it had even been used.

"No, Colonel. I didn't. You really do not understand any of this." Reynolds was softening a bit, not because he disliked confrontation, but because it does you no good to be angry at a fool who cannot learn and adapt.

"Doctor, I am here because your old commanding officer was inefficient." Braun was making assumptions, and although historically her assumptions had been very accurate, this time that was not the case.

"Not exactly, Colonel," Reynolds replied.

"Oh, it is exactly, Doctor." Braun was proving herself a fool. "The experiment was not yielding the proper result."

"I run the experiment, not him. You are rationalizing an irrational thought," Reynolds said, exhausted by this conversation.

"Nonetheless, we are resetting the parameters and doing this my way now. I will fix your research." Braun's arrogance was unparalleled.

"Colonel, you have ruined the research. Don't you see that? By changing the variables, you have changed the results, the thesis. There will be nothing to substantiate any of this. We may as well go home now," Reynolds responded.

"You can get on board or you can get run over, but I am driving the bus now, Doctor. Your bleeding heart liberal mindset is the real liability," Braun countered.

"Keep your hands off my subjects," Reynolds stated.

"They are my subjects now, Doctor. That will be all." Braun turned her back to the doctor and returned to her window.

Reynolds sighed, and rubbed his neck, and then spoke: "Okay, here is what we will do to salvage this."

"You misunderstand your place, Doctor." Braun was dismissive.

"No Colonel, this is what is best for you, not me. Trust me on that."

Braun turned back to face the doctor: "Interesting. Go on."

"You got one. I will use the others as a control group. We will see how they react with your method and mine in the same mixing bowl." Reynolds continued. "Caveat: you cannot continue with your methods until I have observed the reaction of the subjects in detail, and then use my methods to do the same."

"But I wanted to accelerate the timetable, doctor," Braun argued.

"Colonel, you have already introduced a variable that, if it works as you surmised, will do just that," Reynolds explained.

"All right, Doctor," Braun agreed, "but try not to let your liberal agenda interfere with the experiment."

"Colonel, in our line of work, none of us can ever be accused of having a liberal agenda." And with that, a most unholy alliance was created, and Reynolds exited Braun's office.

As Reynolds left Braun's office, he found Withers waiting by the door. "Relax, Withers. We worked out an agreement."

"Pity." Withers had been hoping for chaos.

"You are a sadistic son of a bitch." Reynolds began to walk down the corridor, and then paused and turned back to address Withers. "She has no idea what happened to the last occupant of that office, does she?"

"Not unless you told her, Doctor," Withers replied with a smile.

CHAPTER TWENTY-ONE

Paxton was on his cot, still suffering from his injuries and willing his body to heal despite the lack of medical attention. Paxton tried to spend as much time asleep as possible because it was during sleep that the body could best heal, but a man can only sleep so long, and as his sleep became dreamless, Paxton grew more and more weary.

When Paxton was not asleep he was awake, and when he was awake, Paxton was in a great deal of pain. Being a soldier's soldier, Paxton chose to ignore the pain, which was difficult when there were so few distractions around. That is why on some level he was glad to see the feet poking under his curtain. He could tell by the size of the boots that it was Kaye standing outside his sleeping area, and desperate for a diversion, Paxton invited Kaye in.

"Well Kaye, are you going to come in or stand there being creepy?" Paxton was only half joking.

Kaye opened the curtain and slipped inside, then looked Paxton over for a moment, studying him the way Kaye studied everyone and everything. "How did you know I was out there?" Kaye asked.

"In the Special Forces they teach us how to sense things," Paxton replied dryly.

"Really?" Kaye asked.

"No." Paxton was truly confused; he was almost certain Kaye had believed him. "I could see your feet under the curtain."

"Oh, right," Kaye replied, sounding hapless. The entire situation struck Paxton as odd. Kaye was observant, but yet...something was simply amiss, and Paxton could not be sure what that something was.

"Is there something I can do for you, Kaye?" Paxton was regretting inviting Kaye into his sleeping area. Paxton had discovered that talking to Kaye was creepier than being watched by Kaye.

"No, but something happened, and I think you need to know about it too." Kaye was setting a hook.

"And what is that?" Paxton bit.

"It's gone." Kaye just made a statement, and without a point of reference, Paxton did not know what Kaye was referencing.

"What's gone?" Paxton asked.

"The revolver," Kaye replied, "and the bullets."

"So they just disappeared? The same way they appeared before?" Paxton asked.

"No. We think Pike took them," Kaye replied.

"We?" Paxton pressed.

"Me and Northrop." Kaye puffed out his chest as he connected himself to the Special Agent, as if it was giving him some sort of authority.

"Why?" Paxton's tone was growing dismissive, and he was growing tired of Kaye. The revolver seemed a useless obsession in the cell.

"Well, they were on the table, we were all looking at them…then you got dumped in the door and we all ran over to help… except Pike. He came over slowly… last." Kaye said it like it should mean something.

"So?" Paxton replied as if it meant nothing.

"Well, after that, Pell helped you to bed, and then I looked up and I saw the gun was gone, and then I pointed out to Northrop that the gun was gone. So Pike had to have taken the gun." Kaye was trying very hard to sell this information to Paxton. Typically Paxton would want to know why someone was pushing him so hard to believe something so insignificant, but right now he was too busted up to care.

"So Pike may have the gun. So what? Who cares?" Paxton was pretty much done with this topic, and he was giving Kaye the hint to drop it, but Kaye was not picking up on the hint, and he pressed on.

"So what?" Kaye repeated with a high pitch. "So he's crazy, that's the so what! He could shoot us all to death in our sleep!" Kaye's sale pitch was laughable, and that is just what Paxton did: he laughed. Kaye grew a bit annoyed, but never quite came unglued. "What's so funny?"

"Do you really think," Paxton explained, "that we will all sleep through the first shot? Let alone three more? Whoever has the gun – Pike, me, you, Pell, whatever – we aren't going to be able to kill guys in their sleep. It is just not practical. There was no silencer on that thing."

"Well, what if he just pulls it out because he's nuts and WHAM!, he shoots us all at the table?"

"Relax. Pike is no killer." Paxton spoke to Kaye in a calm tone just in case Kaye was worried about Pike, though Paxton was still not convinced Kaye was on the level.

"He's JTF2," Kaye shot back.

"Okay, let me rephrase. Pike would not murder anyone in cold blood for no reason," Paxton lied. Paxton, and every man in the cell, knew Pike was perfectly capable of murder.

"Are you sure about that?" Kaye pressed.

"No, but I am sure that I am not going to waste my time worrying over stupid shit like that locked up in here." Paxton was done with the conversation, and his tone made that clear. Kaye took the hint and began to slip out the curtain before adding a last thought.

"Yeah. Me neither."

CHAPTER TWENTY-TWO

Kelley Pike continued to follow the rhythm of his internal clock, sleeping when his body told him it was night and rising when his body told him it was morning, regardless of how bright or dim the lights in the room were set; soldier's instinct. During those hours when both Kelley Pike and Michael Paxton were awake, Pike spent the time sitting with the wounded Special Forces soldier. Pike had moved a chair from the table in the center of the main cell area into Paxton's sleeping area, placing it beside his bed. It was a cramped fit, but it was a fit nonetheless; soldiers in a foxhole, holdover from the horrors of an invisible war. The two passed the days that way, sitting in Paxton's sleeping area waiting for nothing and experiencing nothing; really, it was no different than the way the other men were passing the time in the main cell, or any different, for the most part, of what had gone on the cell most days before Paxton's abduction. The only real change to the routine of life for the five was Paxton's body.

As the days passed on by, Paxton sat up on his cot more often, and he seemed to be healing at a good pace. Pike once told Paxton that he knew exactly how many days had gone by since Paxton had been injured at the hands of the large silverback named Briggs, and that he was healing very fast; Paxton did not know if this was true, but he chose to believe it was.

As the two soldiers with the most in common sat in Paxton's sleeping area smoking, day in and day out, they found that they engaged in more meaningful conversations, conversations that revolved around their histories. Some of their conversations were about the horrors they had witnessed in the field, and about the horrors they had inflicted in the field. The price a soldier paid for having an exceptional skill set at a level above all others was a tattered soul, and somewhere in the dark cell, the dark sins of their military careers came to the surface in a setting where the men were free of judgment and were perhaps laying some of the burdens and guilt to rest, as if setting their affairs in order. This was not typical of subjects in Experiment FIVE, but nothing about this group seemed to fit the patterns already established in the research of Experiment FIVE.

Pike and Paxton had both spent many hours, days, nights, and years collectively being dropped in one jungle or another, or a desert, or the capital region of unfriendly nations; these men had seen more action, and more tragedy, than any man ought to see in a lifetime, and very little of it known to history. They were covert black ops and false flag assignments. They did not discuss the missions. The men held their bond of silence well, with honor and dignity, and the missions were in fact irrelevant into them. Along the way the missions came to mean nothing to them; they had turned to digressions of a larger story. Their larger stories had started out as the digressions to support the stories of their missions, but it was never the missions that changed a man, it was the unintended consequences that carried the weight and became the narrative. Pike and Paxton were burdened with the narratives created through the digressions of their lives, very different lives and very similar narratives. Pike and Paxton were brothers in arms, and brothers in captivity.

When Pike first joined Paxton at his bedside, the men were not smoking; that tradition began again after Paxton's ribs seemed to improve and the thought of a coughing fit becoming too painful to breathe had alleviated to an extent. Once Pike had surmised it was time to return to smoking, he reached into Paxton's shirt pocket and retrieved a pack of cigarettes. "You still too busted up to smoke?"

"You help yourself, Pike," Paxton offered with a smile, and as he did, Pike put two cigarettes between his lips, then fished out his lighter, sparked the flame and leaned in as he replied.

"I planned to." Pike drew on the nails and they both lit. Then Pike reached over and put one of the cigarettes in Paxton's mouth. "Try not to cough…I have a feeling it might hurt a bit."

"Smartass," Paxton replied as he half laughed and half coughed, and fully winced.

"If I was so smart, why the hell did I join the military, eh?"

"For adventure," Paxton mocked. "And look at it this way, Pike – your plan worked."

"Adventure? Nah, not me. I had planned on a nice, long, safe career peeling potatoes."

"Bullshit," Paxton challenged.

"Bullshit," Pike admitted.

"So why did you enlist?" Paxton asked.

"Not a whole lot of jobs out there for ex-cons with anger issues and bloody hands," Pike said.

"So you really have been in the joint?"

"Two of them, and in two different countries. Possibly three depending on where we are now."

"Well, not me. I did sign up for adventure. I bought right into the recruiting videos. Make a difference, be a hero, save the world." Paxton looked down as he spoke.

"And?" Pike asked.

"And they lied. I have taken more lives than I saved, and most of the time I don't even understand why anymore." Paxton drew on his smoke and then exhaled, and the two men sat in collective smoke and silence for a few moments. "They think you have the gun." Paxton finally broke the silence and then looked up at Pike.

"Who? Company?" There was derision in Pike's voice.

"Him and Kaye. Or at least that's the way Kaye tells it, so take that for what it's worth. He never did say if Pell thought you took it."

Pike inhaled from his cigarette and replied, "A lot of good a gun would do a fellow in here. What would you do with it? Shoot everyone and be all alone." Pike exhaled smoke.

"At least it would be quiet." Paxton unexpectedly laughed at his own joke, and then winced and grabbed his ribs.

"Don't do that man, it hurts," Pike offered.

"Yeah, my ribs were not ready for that," Paxton agreed.

"No, I mean the puns. They hurt my delicate sensibilities," Pike said sarcastically.

"Bullshit," Paxton challenged as he laughed. "You ain't that delicate of a bastard."

"Bullshit," Pike admitted as he laughed. "I ain't that delicate of a bastard."

Pike and Paxton finished their cigarettes in silence, and then they sat a few moments longer, and the air in the cell grew heavier, as it often did in moments of silence. Finally, Paxton asked the question that had been swimming around his mind since his first day in the cell: a question he had avoided asking, because he knew having the answer would be worse than not having the answer.

"What's going on here, man?" Paxton asked Pike. "Really? What is this all about?"

"I don't know," Pike admitted, "but…" Pike trailed off.

"But?" Paxton pressed him.

"Whatever it is that's going on here, this it for all of us…end of the line." Pike slid his hand out in the air, slicing it right to left in front of himself.

"What do you mean?" Paxton asked.

"We're all going to die," Pike said flatly.

CHAPTER TWENTY-THREE

Life in the cell was slowly killing the five men, in body and, even more quickly, in spirit; and in the case of Kelley Pike and Michael Paxton, the hard men, the cigarettes were also killing them – and all the assaults on the soldiers were slow-moving in their processes.

Pike and Paxton had sat quietly for some time after Pike had answered Paxton's fears: *We're all going to die.* Pike's voice echoed with horror in Paxton's mind because he knew Pike was most likely right. Paxton had faced many dangers, and death was always a real possibility for him, but he had never been afraid of it before. Perhaps that was because he had always assumed if it happened in the line of duty, it would be quick, and he would know where he was and why he was dying. Paxton was not comfortable dying slowly in a sensory deprivation chamber with four strangers, and never knowing why they were dying, only that their deaths would be empty. Meaningless. An empty, meaningless death, Paxton realized, was the source of most of his fear.

Pike was more at peace with the prospect of a pointless death, because Pike had always figured he led a pointless life. Two prisons, one in Canada and one in Russia, a body full of scars, a liver that had to be half destroyed a decade ago through self-loathing and abuse, probably some stage of cancer or another somewhere in his body, and false teeth; he got those during his second stint in a prison, a prison most men never leave: the Russian Gulag.

Pike had realized within moments of waking up alone in this dark, evil prison that he was going to die here, and that he would have to answer for his many sins to a higher power sooner rather than later. Pike never questioned the existence of a deity but he had abandoned hope of his own salvation years ago. To Pike, the real irony is that it was not until he was a middle-aged man, locked in a secret prison, that he had made his first real friend, and a friend earlier in life might have changed the course of his life, and made him into a redeemable soul. Before life in Experiment FIVE, Pike had always smoked alone.

The silence in Paxton's sleeping area was growing too loud, so they decided to fill it with another cigarette. Pike lit them the way he had before, and he passed Paxton one, the way he had before, and they smoked. In their minds, they could still both hear their earlier exchange:

"What do you mean?" Paxton asked.
"We're all going to die," Pike said flatly.

They could hear their words in the sound of the burning cigarette paper, and they knew the truth of those words was as absolute as the flames of damnation awaiting Pike.

When Paxton's cigarette was done, he tossed it on the floor, and Pike took the last drag off his. As he did, he knew someone had entered the sleeping area; his back was to the curtain, but the entrance of another man was unmistakable, and without looking up, Pike knew who it was. "Funny, we put the nails out and the air quality got worse," Pike said, and then he exhaled his smoke into the air.

"Give it a rest, Pike." It was Northrop's voice, and pushed up beside Pike's chair and took a knee. "How are you holding up, Paxton?"

"It ain't nothing in the grand scheme, sir." Paxton did not trust Northrop, so Paxton did not share his real emotions, not like he had with Pike.

"I want to talk about your beating." It sounded more like an order than anything else, but Northrop's mind was in overdrive, looking for leverage with the new variables in Experiment FIVE.

"Cold, Company." Pike called him on it.

"It's okay, Pike," Paxton said, adding, "I don't know what I can tell you other than what I already have." *Paxton did not trust Northrop.*

"I am more interested in why they beat you than how they beat you," Northrop said, as if Paxton was nothing more than a pawn to him.

"We didn't really discuss that, sir." Paxton put a sharp tone to his reply. *Paxton did not trust Northrop.*

"But what did they want? They were looking for information. You do not beat and torture someone unless you want to find out something. That would make no sense. What did they ask you?" Northrop knew they wanted information; he just did not know if they wanted Paxton's information, and did not understand this new variable. Northrop was not making any assumptions. Assumptions were dangerous, and in Northrop's line of work, often deadly.

"That's just it, sir. No one even spoke to me. Thinking about it now, that seems creepy. No one said hello, good-bye, kiss my ass… nothing. It was a creepy feeling." Paxton began to shift about in his cot, anticipating the next question.

"So no one spoke at all? The whole time you were…there?" Northrop's voice was frustrated and confused; this did not make sense.

"Well," Paxton began, "I didn't say that."

"Then who spoke?" Pike asked, finally taking interest and leaning in close, appearing concerned, something that did not happen often with the Lieutenant.

"Me," Paxton admitted. "Pike, will you light me up again?" Pike took a cigarette and his lighter. Pike put the cigarette in Paxton's mouth and sparked the flame. As Paxton was drawing the flame, Northrop pressed onward.

"What are you saying, Paxton?" Northrop asked.

"I am saying I shamed myself." Paxton turned to Pike. "I'm sorry, man."

"Bullshit," Pike said with a smile, but really he was telling Paxton he had nothing to apologize for. "Ain't no shame, not with the beating you took."

"Bullshit," Paxton said, and smiled himself. The balance was restored and Paxton continued. "They were beating me pretty good. At one point I was screaming...just screaming... not noise, but screaming things like 'what do you want to know' and 'please tell me what you want to know.' It was right when my shoulder popped out and I was hanging there that I told them."

"Told them what?" Pike asked.

"We were on a mission...to take out one of the bad guys...a wanted terrorist type." Paxton took a drag, exhaled the smoke, and then he continued. "Thing is, the guy was already dead, had been for years. The government didn't want the world to know, so they propped it up. Used a double, fooled the world... kept him in position for public relations...political grandstanding. Then one day it changed." Paxton looked at Pike, then Northrop, then back to Pike. "We were sent to assassinate the guy we put there... and we did... we carried out the mission as if he was the real guy...and the public still believes he was the bad guy. I told them all of that."

Pike and Northrop were silent a moment, and they traded a look. Pike waited for Northrop to respond, and he did:

"Well, Paxton," Northrop said, "one thing we can say for sure is if that is the worst secret you have, it is not why you are here…they were not trying to get that out of you."

"And how do you know that, sir?" Paxton asked, confused.

"Because that was not that big of a secret," Northrop said as he stood back to his feet.

"What do you mean?" Paxton asked Northrop.

"Well, I already knew. It was fairly high profile, but far from a real secret for the people that matter." Northrop was not sure how to leverage this, but he knew the leverage was in the room.

"What? No way! It was a big deal….Pike, did you know about that? That it was all a fake-out?" Paxton asked.

"I had an inkling," Pike admitted, "but they say I'm a cynic."

"Then what am I here for?" Paxton almost sounded hurt.

"To be a rat in a maze," Northrop answered, honestly, but more honestly than he thought they knew. Then Northrop began to think, *What does Pike know?* "Now Paxton, there is some world class gruel out there at the table. Are you strong enough to come eat with us, or do you want me to bring it in?"

Paxton decided it was time to leave his sleeping area, and gruel was a powerful motivator for a starving man. "The family that eats together stays together."

Chapter Twenty-Four

Pike would have helped Paxton move to the table, and frankly Paxton would have preferred it, but Northrop was quick to lean in and be the human crutch; it was a management trick. Northrop wanted the other men in the cell, Pell and Kaye, to see him doing this; Northrop understood the importance of building an image. Northrop was also very happy that Paxton had accepted his invitation to come to the table; it would make his plan to appear as an authentic authority more natural.

Pike followed Northrop and Paxton, bringing the chair from Paxton's sleeping area with him. When Northrop and Paxton reached the table, Pike set the chair down directly behind Paxton, and Paxton gingerly set himself down into the chair, and then his mouth began to water when he saw the gruel. Paxton was ready to eat.

Pike pushed Paxton and his chair right up to the table, and as soon as he was close enough, Paxton grabbed his spoon and went to work on his gruel. Paxton devoured his gruel quicker than Northrop could have hoped; in fact, Paxton's gruel was gone before Pike made it to his chair.

Northrop was sitting next to Paxton, and as soon as the last spoonful of gruel was out of Paxton's bowl, Northrop slid his own bowl over in front of the Special Forces soldier. "Here you are, Paxton. I think you need this more than me."

"Well, if you insist," Paxton responded as he dug into Northrop's bowl.

Northrop was watching Paxton eat, but he was wondering who in that group would be the key to his leverage. Who had a secret that Dr. Reynolds needed, and how would he get that secret first?

Pike was watching Northrop, disliking him more and more all the time.

Kaye was studying Pike, wishing it had been him, not Paxton, who was suffering with broken ribs.

CHAPTER TWENTY-FIVE

The light had dimmed for the night cycle, and the twilight hours of the grey cell found Pike and Paxton sitting at the round wooden table, with the soft red glow at the ends of their cigarettes burning noticeably; the smoke escaped the nails, but like the men in the cell, remained in the coffin.

The air around them was heavy. Paxton was struggling to understand why he was beaten so badly when it turned out he only had worthless information; if the information was of no value, Paxton began to question if any of his service in the military had held any tangible value. Paxton had always thought that the only reason anybody ever tortured someone was for information that the captor wanted and the captive possessed, but if Paxton's was worthless and already well known to his captors, then what was the point? And if nothing Paxton knew was of value, then how could he continue to believe anything he ever did in his career had any value? What had been the point of his military career if nothing he had ever done really mattered?

"It's built on war," Pike said, out of the blue.

"What?" Paxton asked, confused.

"The economy. Has been since Rome and Greece and Persia." Pike turned to look at Paxton. "Modern western economies are no different. The sun never sets on the British Empire, the manifest destiny of the United States, Saudi oil fields. Border expansions, colonialism, invasions, all the same, and always for the same reasons. Greed."

"You lost me," Paxton said.

"You're thinking about the point of false flag operations, right?" Pike asked.

"Well, yeah," Paxton admitted. "And the point of my entire career, my life. How did you know?"

"You were nearly beaten to death for something you just found out didn't matter," Pike replied.

"I don't get it. Why set up false flags like that one? They had to put the guy in power, put years into his cover, lie to the whole world, and they had to have known someday they would execute him. It doesn't make sense." Paxton shook his head.

"It's all about money," Pike said.

"Money? What money?" Paxton asked.

"Well, ever wonder why governments sell off military surplus or leave tanks behind after a conflict?" Pike asked.

"Logistics. Cost reduction, some sort of business bullshit," Paxton responded.

"Maybe. I never bought that," Pike replied.

"Why not?" Paxton asked. "It's the first thing anyone else would think."

"Because if the governments really wanted to stop

uprisings, cartels, terrorists, they would just stop leaving their toys laying around and selling off excess hardware. Wars exist because the people who could stop them don't; they fuel them," Pike said.

"You really are cynical," Paxton said with a smile.

"I thought I was the ray of sunshine in here," Pike responded sarcastically.

"Bullshit," Paxton said.

"Bullshit," Pike agreed.

The soldiers sat in silence a few more moments and then stubbed out their cigarettes.

"What time is it?" Paxton asked Pike.

"Just about ten," Pike answered.

"Isn't that when you always go to bed?" Paxton said sarcastically.

"Yes." Pike stood up and then helped Paxton struggled to his feet. After Paxton was standing, Pike then helped Paxton to his sleeping area.

"I feel twice as tired tonight," Paxton yawned.

"You had a busy few days," Pike answered him. Pike helped Paxton in past the curtain, and then down onto his cot. After Paxton was down, Pike retreated out of Paxton's sleeping area, stepped back into the main cell area, and then slipped into his own sleeping area.

On the other side of the cell, Northrop's curtain was pulled back slightly as he watched the two soldiers. Once they were both in their cots, he knew it would not be much longer.

CHAPTER TWENTY-SIX

The gruel that sustained the five men in the cell also served a sinister purpose. The gruel was laced with a sedative designed to enhance sleep; with this experimental sedative in their systems, the men would fall into a deep sleep once they went to bed, but they would never feel drugged when they were awake. The sedative was the product of military science.

When all the men went to sleep and the sedative went to work, it allowed Master Sergeant Withers to enter the cell and do what he needed to do unobserved without waking anyone. Sometimes Withers' needs were quick, like delivering the gruel, and other times he adjusted the clock, or entered with other soldiers to abduct inmates away in the night, as they had done with Paxton. The idea was to create both a fear of and a dependency on an unknown and unseen force that could manipulate the environment and nourish the men; it was a means of manipulating the five, and controlling their lowest needs: nourishment and shelter. Typically the experiment moved more quickly, but Pike's internal clock was an unexpected variable for Dr. Reynolds. With Pike's schedule remaining true to real time, the changes from light to dark that were used to manipulate the perceptions of night and day did not work, and that meant that some of the times scheduled for Withers to enter the cell needed to be pushed back or altered. The only other option was a sedative that made the men feel drowsy, but if they knew the food was drugged, then another variable would be altered, and that would jeopardize the scientific accuracy of Dr. Reynolds' findings.

Ultimately, Dr. Reynolds had concluded that the Pike variable itself was not a big issue, and that the impact of limited and erratic food and water, food and water that was never available in substantial quantities, was correctable. However, another variable was about to change, one Dr. Reynolds knew would change, as soon as Benedict Cain had informed him that Hal Northrop would be among the five: Northrop would lift the veil.

The five, or four, of them may not have known exactly where they were being held or by whom, but the contact was made with their captors, violently; first with Paxton's abduction, and then later with a show of putting him back in place. Reynolds believed the way Paxton had been re-introduced to the environment of Experiment FIVE was the factor that had completely compromised the research and made it unreliable. This variable could work against the experiment; by putting a face on the unseen force controlling the lives of the men in the cell, the subjects might react by banding together against a mutual, unseen, enemy; a tactic as old as time.

Despite the fact that Lieutenant Colonel Braun had compromised the research, Dr. Reynolds was insisting the experiment parameters be returned to normal. Late one night, on a night that really was night, and Lieutenant Pike was asleep, Master Sergeant Withers slipped into the room. He opened the door only enough to slide in, with no alarms to announce his presence and no lights to blind the men, all of whom should have been sleeping, and four of them were.

Northrop had been waiting for the right day to do this, and now the time had come. He went without food that day so that he would be awake when the Master Sergeant entered the cell. Northrop had sat at the foot of his cot all evening, listening intently. When he heard the door, which was very quiet considering the size of the door and the hollow nature of the cell, he stood and pulled his curtain back enough to peek through. He watched Withers step inside, and waited until he had squatted down with the tray of gruel, only inches into the cell. As soon as the tray was on the ground, Northrop stepped out from behind his curtain.

"Master Sergeant Withers, who altered the experiment?" Northrop asked. "Who is the stunned soldier now in charge of this facility that introduced the new variable?" Northrop's posturing was a bluff. Northrop spoke as if he was part of the experiment, covertly, and that he was outraged. Withers knew who Northrop was, and Northrop doubted that Withers' clearance was high enough for him to be fully aware of the parameters of Experiment FIVE; he had never kept Withers in the loop. Withers did not take the bait.

"I really can't say, sir." Withers stood to his feet, squared his shoulders to Northrop, clasped his hands behind his back and looked the Special Agent dead in his eyes, defiantly. "How did you manage to stay awake?" It was more curiosity than shock.

"I didn't eat the gruel today," Northrop replied, with more pride than he should have used.

"Really?" Withers raised an eyebrow.

"I wrote the book, Master Sergeant," Northrop barked. "I have been around this block more than any man."

"That is exactly why I am surprised you didn't eat the gruel," Withers responded. "You have been around the block enough to know this road is a dead end."

Northrop tried to take the Master Sergeant's words in stride, doing his best not to show the weakness in his knees, but he was losing focus. Northrop needed to convince Withers he had retained his authority and that this was part of some larger plan. This might have worked had they sent a soldier he did not know in with the gruel. Northrop's gambit would have had a much better chance of success on an ambitious and unseasoned soldier, but Withers was well seasoned.

"Now tell me, soldier, is it really nighttime or is this the middle of the day?" Northrop was fishing for a life preserver.

He desperately needed Withers to believe Northrop was still connected.

"Ask Pike, sir." Withers smiled wide and Northrop became angry. No one had ever questioned or spoken to him that way before...except Pike.

"You are very by-the-book, soldier. I'll remember that. It will look favorable in my report. But now," Northrop continued to bluff, "I need to know who altered the experiment and why. I am the only one who can fix it."

"It is highly irregular for me to be talking to you, sir." Withers was dismissing the Special Agent, and as he turned his back on Northrop to exit, the company man knew he had only one trick left.

"He'll be coming now. You know that."

"Who will be coming, sir?" Withers paused, and half turned his head back, but kept his shoulders squared to the door.

"Benedict Cain. And he will be riding in on a sickly green horse."

"And why, sir," Withers asked, "why would Benedict Cain be coming back here?"

"Because someone here changed the variables, before I could conduct the new experiment. Benedict will not like that and you know it. He will be coming, and he will not be happy."

Chapter Twenty-Seven

Benedict Cain would be coming, there was absolutely no doubt; it was a fact. Special Agent Hal Northrop knew it, and Dr. William Reynolds knew it as well. In fact, it was the realization that Benedict Cain would soon be coming, and that he would be angry, that had actually calmed Dr. Reynolds in the days following his first meeting with Lieutenant Colonel Braun. Braun had tried to usurp the doctor's authority, but that authority was given to him by none other than Benedict Cain himself.

When Samantha Braun chose to alter the parameters of Experiment FIVE, the very instant she conceived of the idea to have Sergeant Paxton hung and beaten like a stuck pig in a meat warehouse, she had sealed her fate; even before she gave the order, Lieutenant Colonel Braun had made a grave and unforgivable error in judgment. Benedict Cain did not like deviations; he liked meticulous planning and flawless execution, and accepted no less than perfection. Benedict Cain did not tolerate insubordination or alterations to his instructions. Benedict Cain was an absolute authority unto himself.

Dr. Reynolds was beginning to feel better and better not only knowing that Benedict Cain was going to come to the facility, but Reynolds took delight in the fact that he would not even have to contact Benedict Cain and tell him what was going on. Cain already knew; Cain always knew. In fact, Benedict Cain probably knew before Dr. Reynolds had, and Dr. Reynolds was on the base. The corrupted research and failed results would not be put on Dr. Reynolds; the doctor would not need to fall on his sword. With that in mind, Reynolds began to review the cell recordings from the night before; just because Benedict Cain was coming to cleanse the facility did not mean that the doctor could stop working, and truthfully he would not want to. Experiment FIVE was the culmination of his life's work in the field of psychology, and it would indeed change the world.

The cell was full of hidden cameras and microphones; nothing was ever done or said in the grey tomb of the five subjects that Dr. Reynolds did not know about. This particular day, Dr. Reynolds was most interested in the previous night's exchange between Master Sergeant Withers and Special Agent Hal Northrop, an exchange that Reynolds could have predicted word for word once Benedict Cain had told him Northrop would be the fifth in the group this time. Dr. Reynolds smiled widely when he heard Northrop remark, plain as day, that Benedict Cain would be coming.

"He'll be coming now, you know that," Northrop had said.
"Who will be coming, sir?" Withers had asked back.

"Benedict Cain," Northrop had said.

"And why, sir?" Withers had asked.

"Because someone here changed the variables," Northrop had said.

Reynolds smiled, because he knew what Northrop knew, and what everyone else would soon know – you do not want Benedict Cain coming to visit. **Ever.**

CHAPTER TWENTY-EIGHT

Lieutenant Colonel Braun was standing in her office, staring out her window, smiling, and watching the reflection of the door in her window. Braun was amused by her own power and she was relishing the opportunity ahead of her, to use her power to demoralize and humiliate her rival, Dr. William Reynolds.

Samantha Braun enjoyed bullying those in her command, and in her view that included Dr. Reynolds. When she heard a knock on the door, Lieutenant Colonel Braun began to salivate as she visualized the way her visit with the doctor would go, but when Reynolds opened the door and entered the room, Braun's smirk quickly changed. Braun's eyes popped out, her jaw opened slightly, and her face turned red; she had expected an irate psychologist that she would make grovel before her, but instead what she got was a middle-aged man with a cup of coffee.

Dr. Reynolds tried hard not to react to the change in Braun's features as he watched them in the reflection of the windowpane, but despite all his best efforts not to, he smiled wider. Reynolds lifted his coffee mug to his face and took a sip. Dr. Reynolds knew Braun was expecting a defeated man, not a cavalier one, showing her little to no respect; Dr. Reynolds was not even showing enough respect, or fear, to seem upset, uneasy, or angry. In fact, Reynolds was amused, and reveling in the knowledge that Benedict Cain would soon be here. No one had to tell him that Cain was coming, any more than anyone had to tell that to Hal Northrop. Anyone who knew Benedict Cain – really, really, knew him – would expect nothing less. Dr. William Reynolds and Special Agent Hal Northrop both knew Benedict Cain very well.

After Dr. Reynolds finished his sip of coffee, he smacked his lips, lowered his mug, and then strolled to Lieutenant Colonel Braun's desk. Braun had struggled to regain her composure, and she nearly had, when she turned to face the doctor; however, Braun remained at the window. Enjoying the moment, Dr. Reynolds chose to soliloquize, or ramble, as academics often do:

"You know, Colonel Braun, the last occupant of this office and I, we got along great. Real great. Mutual respect." Pausing for effect, Reynolds took a sip of coffee before continuing. "As a matter of fact, if he wanted to see me, instead of sending for me, he would walk out of this office, travel west for about eight feet, and then walk on into mine and say hello. And if I wanted to see him, well I came east, all the way here to his office. Usually one of us brought coffee." Reynolds raised his mug in a salute, and then enjoyed another sip of coffee, and then continued. "Maybe we were the victims of polite upbringing."

Dr. William Reynolds was enjoying himself, and in a facility like this one, heavy with death and pain, it was a rare occasion to find joy. Reynolds sat down in one of chairs facing the front of Braun's desk, without having been invited to do so, took another sip of his coffee as if to emphasize his point, and then continued, adding, "I did not bring you coffee."

"We are not friends, Doctor." It was the first thing Braun could think to say and she did not want the room to go silent; silence showed weakness, and Braun was a soldier. She refused to be weaker than an academic. "I run this facility, but you work here. I will send for you when I want you." Braun stepped closer to the desk.

"Your facility, but my experiment, and my experiment is the reason this facility exists. Your purpose is to be my support mechanism, nothing more." Reynolds was being very cavalier, and he took another sip of his coffee, and watched Braun through the rising steam coming off his coffee mug as he did so. "You have a post because of me. Though really, with your new variables, you can have all the credit for this group."

"As you wish, good Doctor." Braun stepped right up to the desk now, sensing a shift in power could occur if she could indeed get the doctor to relinquish his authority of Experiment FIVE. "Where you have failed, doctor, I will succeed, and you will then learn your place." Braun sat down in her chair, opposite Reynolds, and now, feeling her sense of power return, she continued, expecting to drop a bomb on Dr. Reynolds that would devastate his cavalier attitude. "I had Withers type up a report, along with all of the findings from the interview with the Paxton subject."

"Interview. Quaint." Reynolds said dismissively.

"I think you will see that we had tremendous success. We were able to assemble some interesting information – classified information. My methods are working very well, Doctor." Braun reached into the top drawer of her desk and retrieved a file, placed it on the desk, and pressed directly down on it with her forefinger and slid it in front of Reynolds.

"Colonel," Reynolds said, almost with a laugh, "I don't need to read that file to know that it is worthless." Reynolds left the file where it was and leaned back in his chair.

"Your arrogance is embarrassing you, Doctor." Braun's tone was smug. "We uncovered military secrets of a classified nature from this man that are important. This proves my methods do work. And they work fast."

"Colonel, my clearance is higher than yours. You may not believe it, but it's true. This experiment requires it." Reynolds paused a moment, then decided to go ahead and give Braun the background on Experiment FIVE, which was within his discretion. "You were not meant to know this, but I will enlighten you nonetheless. The project is codenamed Experiment FIVE. There are five facilities all running

Experiment FIVE: this one and four more. The five facilities all follow my experiments under my supervision, and all of these facilities house five men in five different but identical dark, grey cells." Reynolds paused briefly and looked at Braun's expression, and then he continued. "There are five subjects in the cell beneath this office, and they all have what some would call military secrets or shames. I know four of them; they are at the level of no consequence, though above your pay grade. You can beat those sorts of secrets out of men…they don't matter."

"And the other secret, Doctor?" Braun asked. "The one you do not know?"

"That is the point of this research, Colonel." Reynolds looked Braun dead in her eyes; he wanted to see if she was capable of a paradigm shift. The doctor had his doubts. "There are people out there with very special skills, or talents. Or maybe they just have no souls or stronger wills. In any event, people like that, elite soldiers or masochistic fools, whatever you prefer to call them, will never break under physical torture. It is a proven fact."

"I do not believe that." Braun's response confirmed Reynolds' hypothesis; she was not capable of a paradigm shift.

"You are thinking intuitively. The fact is if you beat a man enough, eventually he will tell you what you want to hear. The truly elite are made of sterner stuff. They will have real secrets, and they will never tell them to tormentors; they just wait to die, they wait until you kill them. Some are fueled by

loyalty, some by pride, and the nastiest ones, by spite."
Reynolds drank the last of his coffee. "No, Colonel, you didn't
uncover anything here. Assassinating staged doubles and fake
terrorists is a very low-level secret. A public relations issue at
worst." Reynolds took a moment to enjoy the blank look on
Braun's face. The file was still on her desk, untouched, yet
Reynolds had known exactly what was in it. The doctor stood
up and began to leave. "I'll be eight feet to the west of your
office if you need me, Colonel."

"Wait!" Braun sounded desperate to Reynolds, and he
liked it.

"Yes?" Reynolds relied.

"The secret, the one we need to discover," Braun started.
"Who wants it?"

"Colonel, when you were transferred here, did they tell
who this research was for? Who was backing Experiment
FIVE?"

"No. I was told I didn't need to know," Braun admitted.

"Well, Colonel, it is the man you ultimately work for, the
man who knows all the secrets of all the men recruited to
Experiment FIVE. You work for Benedict Cain." Reynolds
watched shock, horror, and surprise flood into Braun's face,
and then he smiled. "It's best not to think about that."

CHAPTER TWENTY-NINE

After Special Agent Northrop's interaction with Master Sergeant Withers, Dr. Reynolds decided there was no longer a reason to go through the motions of the unseen force; first contact had been established and the five men had seen the enemy, meaning they now had something to unite against. Technically, Withers was second contact, but the interaction between Withers and Northrop was more profound and spoke directly to the parameters of the experiment, so Dr. Reynolds decided it was time to begin phase two of Experiment FIVE: the reveal.

The reveal was one of Dr. Reynolds' favorite parts of Experiment FIVE. It was theatrical, which appealed to the doctor, and the reactions were unique with every group, and he enjoyed that about the experience very much.

Just outside of the cell door, on the side nearest freedom, there was a large monitor. Dr. Reynolds stood in front of it, waiting for the perfect time to execute the reveal to the men in the tomb. Standing to the left of Dr. Reynolds, waiting to take part in the reveal, was the doctor's favorite prop, one that always created a strong reaction, and this time he was preceded by his reputation: Sergeant Briggs would enter the cell with the doctor.

Sergeant Briggs was a hulking silverback of a man. Briggs stood six feet, five inches and weighed two hundred and sixty pounds of pure muscle. Briggs was a very intimidating sight. Briggs was also that man that had hung Sergeant Michael Paxton, a Special Forces soldier, like a stuck pig and beat him half to death, and Paxton would not have forgotten that. The other men in the cell were now well aware of the reputation of Sergeant Briggs.

The monitor was not the only device outside the cell doors. The large steel doors were controlled by a computerized panel on the wall on that allowed the operator to control the speed with which the door opened, as well as the berth; Master Sergeant Withers stood at the controls, ready to open the door on Dr. Reynolds' command.

This is going to be a very interesting reveal, Reynolds thought to himself. The doctor checked over the notes in his leather pad-folio, and then made sure his pen had plenty of ink, just in case he wanted to make a note. Reynolds returned his attention to the monitor, and then when all five men were sitting at the table, the doctor signaled Withers to open the door.

CHAPTER THIRTY

There was little for the five men to do in the heptagon-shaped cell. Lieutenant Pike and Sergeant Paxton sat at the table and smoked their way towards an escape, either by fantasy or cancer; Special Agent Northrop also sat at the table, and he flicked cigarettes off the tabletop towards the ground. Captain Pell occasionally engaged the other men in small talk, but as the cell had no windows and the men had no yard time, the topic of the day's weather was unavailable, and with current weather always being the basis of most small talk, Pell had fewer and fewer things to say to the others with each passing day. Sergeant Kaye kept to himself, often sitting in some odd corner of the room on his haunches and still very much acting like Kaye except for one crucial distinction: Kaye no longer stared at the door, silently studying it. Kaye now studied the other four men with every moment of every day. Kaye studied Pike the most because Kaye decided Pike was the man he hated most, and he studied Northrop nearly as much because that was the man whom Kaye felt he could somehow best exploit. Kaye studied Paxton and Pell as well, but not as intensely. Sometimes Kaye would join the other men at the table and study them close-up, and on this day Kaye opted to do just that. As soon as he joined the others at the table, the door to the cell opened, and Dr. Reynolds walked in purposefully, flanked by the hulking Briggs.

When Dr. Reynolds walked in, the room fell silent, and Reynolds walked right up to the table with Briggs in tow. The five inmates of the mysterious cell were horseshoed around the round table, which meant than they all had a bit of table between them and Dr. Reynolds. It also meant that each man had a clear view of the doctor as well as his silverback, Briggs. When Paxton caught sight of the monster, the beast who had nearly killed the Special Forces soldier with just the force of his fists, Paxton turned white and instinctively recoiled. When Paxton recoiled, Pike stood up quickly and defensively, slamming his hands on the table and locking eyes with Briggs. *I will kill you,* Pike thought to himself. *You hurt my friend. I will kill you.* The sole thought running through Pike's mind was killing Briggs. Pike had killed men for far less than what Briggs had done to Paxton, and now he vowed silently that he would kill the giant.

Pike and Briggs had locked eyes, and the intensity was beyond anything Reynolds had expected or ever experienced in one of these cells during one of these reveals; the doctor was fascinated by the Pike subject and scribbled a note in his pad-folio very quickly. After he had made his note on Pike, the doctor then looked to the table and scanned the men from one end to the other. From right to left around the table were

Kaye, then Northrop, then Paxton, recoiled and slightly behind the man next to him, Pike. Pike was on his feet and the others were sitting. Finally the doctor's eyes rested on Captain Bradley Pell, in the final chair. Reynolds broke the silence:

"Captain Bradley Pell?" Even though Reynolds was asking Pell to identify himself, he already was fully aware of which man he was; the doctor knew all the men. In the brief moments before Pell replied, Reynolds studies the Captain's face and once again opened his pad-folio and made notes on Pell's reaction: *sheer terror.*

"Sir?" Pell managed to stammer.

"Ah, excellent. Captain Pell, would you kindly follow Sergeant Briggs?" The doctor's question was formal, but rhetorical.

"The hell he will." Pike's voice was solid and steady, and his eyes wide and focused right on Briggs. *You hurt my friend. I will kill you.*

"And you must be Lieutenant Pike," Reynolds said smugly, already knowing the answer.

"How do you know he's Pike?" Paxton asked Reynolds.

"Because," Reynolds responded with a challenging tone, "my files say Pike is an asshole." Reynolds stared a Pike.

"Damn straight," Pike replied to the doctor's challenge, never taking his eyes off of Briggs. *You hurt my friend. I will kill you.*

"Now, Captain Pell, if you will kindly come with me," Reynolds instructed.

"You ain't got to go nowhere, Pell," Pike said, still locked on Briggs. "You stand behind me and I'll handle the ape."

"You misunderstand, Lieutenant. This is not a request. The Captain has no choice in the matter," Reynolds informed them.

"There is always a choice." Pike was still staring at Briggs, still thinking: *You hurt my friend. I will kill you.*

"All right, Lieutenant," Reynolds conceded, "I will give the Captain a choice." Then turning his gaze back to Pell, the doctor laid out Pell's choice. "Captain Pell, you can follow the Sergeant and sit with me for a nice chat all on your own, or I will have everyone in the room killed except you. I will see to it you live a long time, in perfect health, with the guilty knowledge that your cowardice is what killed these men."

"Forget him, Pell," Pike said, still locked in a staring contest with Briggs. "He will kill us all soon enough anyway."

"Not Pell." Dr. Reynolds spoke clearly. "Not if he resists. I will see to it the Captain lives a long life, here in this cell, and I will see to it that he is reminded constantly that he is the reason you are all dead and he is alive. The Captain will live a long time, and the rest of you will have very, very unpleasant deaths, and I will see to it that Pell knows every detail of every death."

"All deaths are unpleasant." Pike was defiant.

"No, Pike." Pell finally spoke. Then Captain Pell rose to his feet, squared himself to the doctor, and said, "Sir," before lowering his head. Dr. Reynolds nodded to Briggs, and Briggs

146

silently turned to escort Pell out of the cell. Before Briggs walked away from the table he winked at Pike, then turned his back. Pike called out to him, causing Briggs to look back.

"Hey! Briggs! I'll be seeing you, Sunshine," Pike said, but he was thinking: *You hurt my friend. I will kill you.*

Reynolds stayed for a moment and made eye contact with Northrop.

"Benedict's coming. You know that, right?" Northrop said.

"Yes, I know, Hal," Reynolds replied. They held each other's gaze for a moment, and then Dr. Reynolds showed himself out of the cell, and the door closed.

Pike was still standing when he turned to Northrop and said, "Who the hell is Benedict?"

"Cain," Northrop replied. "Benedict Cain." Pike sat down, and the men fell silent under the weight of the most feared name in their world: **Benedict Cain**.

CHAPTER THIRTY-ONE

The door to the cell led Captain Bradley Pell into a long corridor, constructed entirely out of reinforced concrete, with no windows, no pictures, no wallpaper, and no paint; it was grey and lonely. The floor, the walls, the ceiling: all grey concrete, creating a very dark atmosphere. There were dim lights illuminating the way, although typically they were bright and appropriate; for this occasion, Dr. Reynolds had had the lights lowered to enhance his mission and create a feeling of isolation in Captain Pell. The corridor was darker than the cell now.

Pell stepped out of the cell into the long corridor that seemed to stretch on forever into an abyss of despair. Pell looked down the long corridor in front of him, unable to see anything else, just the abyss created by Dr. Reynolds' lighting; as far as Pell could see, the corridor appeared to have no end. As he looked along the walls, he could not find any ductwork, outlets – nothing. Captain Pell was feeling defeated and intimidated. Pell was scared.

Pell paused briefly once he was clear of the steel door that separated the cold cell from the Faustian corridor, and he felt more dread in his bones then he had ever felt. He shivered with trepidation as his soul became as cold as an open grave

Pell had become somewhat institutionalized in the holding cell, and being separated from his surrogate family so abruptly was a jarring experience for the Captain. It took Pell several minutes to collect enough composure to begin to walk down the corridor, trembling with fear of the unknown and fear of the all-too-well known. Pell did not need to be ordered to march; he knew he was going someplace and there was only one possible route in front of him.

Briggs had stepped out of the cell right behind Pell and slightly to his left. Briggs remained silent, and began to march half a step behind Pell as soon as Pell began to march. Brigg's muscular frame was so heavy that his footfalls sounded like thunder echoing down the hall, and Pell was more afraid of the sound of Briggs walking than he would have been if he could see the silverback; fear of an unknown.

Captain Pell, who had spent more time than he cared to guess in the small cell of the secret facility wishing he could walk right out through the steel door and back into the world, suddenly found himself wishing he could turn around and run back in to the very same cell.

CHAPTER THIRTY-TWO

The cold interview room of the diabolical facility was very similar to the interview rooms found in most military or police facilities. The room was a perfect rectangle with a perfectly rectangular table in the center. On side of the table there was one chair, and on the other side of the table there was another chair. Behind the first chair was a solid, cold, grey, concrete wall, and in front of the chair was the table, and atop the table directly in front of the first chair was a closed manila file folder, and laying atop of the manila file folder was a pen loaded with ink.

Behind the second chair was a solid, cold, grey, concrete wall, and in front of the chair was the table, and atop the table directly in front of the second chair was nothing; this visual cue, the distinction between a place at the table with a manila folder and the place at the table with nothing, established a power dynamic.

Access to the interview room was through a steel door located in the southern corner of the western wall. The west and east walls ran the length of the room, and the south and north walls ran the width. All four walls were bare, unpainted and undecorated with no windows or mirrors; there was only the one access point. Hanging from the corner of the ceiling where the west wall met the south wall was a camera that pointed to the table, capturing primary focus on whomever should be the occupant of the second chair, but allowing for a view of the first chair's occupant. In the opposite corner of the room, hanging from the ceiling at the point where the east wall met the north wall, was a second camera with a tight focus for whomever the occupant of the second chair should be, capturing nothing else except the face of that individual.

Hanging from the ceiling in the corner of the room where the west wall met the north wall was a speaker, plain, grey, and military in appearance. Hanging from the ceiling in the corner of the room where the east wall met the south wall was an identical speaker. The speakers were playing traditional Christmas carols.

On the same side of the rectangular table as the first chair, but further to the east end of the table, or to the right of the first chair, there were four bottles of rum, all of which had little red Santa hats sitting down over the neck, and a ribbon tied around the center of each bottle in a the shape of a decorative bow; the bottles had the appearance of Christmas gifts. There were also two coffee mugs on the table next to the bottles of rum; the first mug was a red Santa mug, and the second a green reindeer.

The steel door to the interview room opened, and Captain Bradley Pell was ushered into the room by the monstrous

Sergeant Briggs. After Pell had fully penetrated his way into the room he stopped dead in his tracks for a moment as his ears were assaulted by the Christmas carols. Pell became terrified all over again trying to reason out just how long he had been locked up in the cell. After Pell digested the new sounds, he took a moment to scan the room and he noticed the chairs, the folder, the pen, the Christmas coffee mugs, and the rum. Pell was in recovery.

Briggs simultaneously pointed to the second chair and shoved Pell towards it; Pell complied silently, shuffling his way to his seat and then slowly setting himself into it, never taking his eyes off the rum. Briggs stood at ease at the door and the men remained there silently, Pell looking at the rum and Briggs looking at Pell.

After what seemed like an eternity to Captain Pell, but in reality less than ten minutes, Dr. Reynolds opened the steel door and stepped into the interrogation room. Reynolds was carrying two large bottles of cola. He stood beside Briggs for a moment and observed Pell, who continued to look at the rum. Without taking his eyes off the bottles of rum, Pell spoke to Dr. Reynolds.

"Is it Christmas?" Pell asked.

"Dismissed, Sergeant Briggs," Reynolds said.

"Sir, yes sir," the silverback replied in a very crisp, soldier-like fashion, before exiting the room and closing the steel door behind him, leaving the pilot alone with the doctor. Reynolds did not yet acknowledge Captain Pell's question.

"Good soldier, that Briggs," the doctor said once the door had closed, "but as far up the chain as he will ever go. Limited potential for strategic thinking. That is my professional opinion." Reynolds began to walk towards the first chair, the one opposite where Pell was sitting, and Pell turned his attention from the rum to the doctor. "Of course, I also believe he has found the path he is best suited for here, and most of us are not so lucky as he in that regard." Reynolds stared right into Pell's eyes for a few moments, not in a confrontational way; it was purely as a means of observation. Reynolds set the cola on the table and he watched as Pell's eyes darted from the cola to the rum before settling back on Reynolds; the doctor's approach was on target. To the doctor the Captain was just a subject, and Pell realized that at once, which in turn further demoralized him.

"Yes, Captain, it is Christmas," Reynolds finally said, answering the pilot's question as he sat down in his chair opposite Pell. "Well, Christmas Eve to be precise. The timing is part of why you were selected for this conversation." Dr. Reynolds added some cheer to his voice to create a more comfortable atmosphere to relax Captain Pell. "Please Captain, relax, and be comfortable." Dr. Reynolds opened the first bottle of cola, and then pulled the Santa hat off the first bottle of rum.

"You keep calling me Captain." Pell's interest was not uncommon in this situation; perhaps, Reynolds had always surmised, it is because the minds of the interview subjects are desperately trying to re-organize after all of the emotional disruptions, and so the most elementary questions always came first.

"Well, of course I do, Captain," Reynolds replied in a cheery tone. "It is your rank, you earned it, and you deserve the respect that goes along with that accomplishment. Or at the very least, the rank itself deserves the respect."

"Are you a military man?" Pell asked Reynolds.

"A military man? No, no. I am a scientist." Dr. Reynolds continued to look at Pell and smile in a friendly manner. "I have advanced degrees in psychiatry, psychology and sociology. No, Captain Pell, I am a civilian, technically, but I am not at all unfamiliar with military culture, military life." Reynolds smiled amicably and continued. "I am intimately acquainted with the stressors and the rewards, the cultural hierarchy, and much more.

"Please, Captain, allow me to fix you a drink. After all, it is Christmas Eve, and traditionally rum and eggnog would be the convention, but you will have to bear with me, as we have no eggnog." Dr. Reynolds retrieved the reindeer mug, then he opened the first bottle of cola and poured some of it into the mug, and then, slowly and deliberately, Reynolds reached to his right, selected a bottle of rum, the one closest to Pell's side of the table, opened it, and added it to the reindeer mug. Reynolds slid the reindeer mug in front of the air force pilot. Pell's eyes grew wide and he began to lick his lips.

"I have not had a drink in close to three years," Pell said.

"Actually, it is closer to four now. You have been with us quite a while," Dr. Reynolds said. Then, by way of temptation, he added, "It's not like a drink will get you into trouble in here, Captain. Really, how much trouble can you get into in your large, nearly empty, room anyway?" Reynolds reached for the second mug, the Santa mug, and began to mix a second drink, though he mixed it considerably weaker. "Here, I will have one with you." After his drink was mixed, Reynolds raised his mug towards Pell: "To as merry a Christmas as we two can manage." Reynolds held his mug in the air as Pell struggled with temptation before finally lifting his drink up and touching it to the doctor's mug. "That's more like the Christmas spirit, Captain. Gin gin." Dr. Reynolds watched as Pell slammed his entire drink back in one gulp; Reynolds then took a sip of his own drink.

"So why me?" Pell asked, with his nerves somewhat calmed.

"Why you what, Captain?" the doctor replied coyly.

"You said you chose me for this because of the timing," Pell responded.

"Yes, yes. I did indeed, Captain," Reynolds replied.

"Why?" Pell pressed.

"I think Christmas meant more to you than the others, so you would enjoy the timing," Reynolds explained.

"How come?" Pell asked, clearly confused.

"Because you used to be a family man, and it is a family-centered celebration." Reynolds took another sip from his mug as he watched Pell's face register what he had just been told.

"Used to be? I still am a family man. My wife and I are still married and we are planning to have children," Pell said.

"No, Captain," Reynolds replied simply.

"Why? What happened to my wife, my family?" There was horror in the Captain's voice.

"Oh, nothing happened to them, Captain. They are fine, in perfect health. Safe." Reynolds began pouring some more rum into Pell's mug. "However, they are no longer your family," Reynolds said. "You see, when you were selected for this experiment, they were informed of your death. If it is any consolation, you died a hero and made them very proud. I believe some sort of medal was awarded." Reynolds poured the slightest bit of cola into Pell's mug. "But don't worry, Captain, you are still very much alive." Reynolds slid Pell's mug closer to him with the new drink mixed inside.

"You told my family that I died?" Pell was shocked.

"Oh, no, not me, Captain. I would never do that," Reynolds said with a cheerful tone. "The Air Force did that." The doctor motioned to Pell to drink, and without thinking, Pell drank.

After downing his second drink, and staring at the empty mug for a few long moments to process, Pell simply asked, "Why?"

"It seemed kinder to give them closure instead of having them suffer with your lengthy disappearance. Your mother has a hero for a son; your wife's late husband is a local legend." The doctor was using his best sympathetic tone to manipulate Pell's emotions now. "Captain, we can discuss your family and bravery at great length, for as long as you like, once we have taken care of some minor housekeeping issues regarding the information in your file." Reynolds tapped the file in front of him with his forefinger as he spoke, and then he began flipping through the pages. "You see, Captain, I need your help with some psychological profiling. There is a connection between your past and a...shall we say... off books, assignment you were given." Dr. Reynolds watched as Pell reached for the rum. "Yes, Captain, by all means help yourself. It is Christmas, after all." Reynolds gave Pell the permission to indulge that the captain had been waiting for, and Pell pulled a bottle of rum close to him. He took off the cap and took a long drink of the rum.

"You see, there was a reason you were posted at Diego Garcia when you were," Reynolds then continued. "A retired Air Force colonel named Fredericks had some influence, and he insisted on it. You see, he wanted to run for the senate...actually I think he may have won, but don't quote me... but before he retired from the Air Force a few years ago he had done some things. Things you helped him cover up. Under orders, I am sure." Reynolds was doing his best to sound sympathetic.

"Orders and blackmail!" Pell said defiantly, and then he took a long pull from the bottle of rum.

"Ah, well, that explains it all," Reynolds said in cheerful tones. "It is all becoming clear. We are almost done, and then we can go back to discussing Christmas and family. Don't worry, Captain Pell, none of this ever reached them...as I said, you had a hero's death in the public eye." Reynolds watched as Pell took another drink straight from the bottle.

"I didn't do anything." Denial.

"Well, maybe not with Fredericks, but regardless, you never reported him, you never protected the children, and you provided alibis and transportation and cover-up assistance. Fredericks did some terrible things... terrible things involving young children...you helped cover it up. You were complicit, therefore, in his actions." Pell's face contorted into a sinister caricature of itself as Reynolds spoke.

"I was ordered to..." Pell began in protest.

"And blackmailed," Reynolds interrupted the Captain. "You just told me you were blackmailed. You know, I have often wondered how it is people like you always manage to find each other." Dr. Reynolds flipped another page over in the file. "Your father was a military man too, was he not?"

"Yes, but he never..." Pell protested.

"Well no, not that we are aware of, but Fredericks served under him for many, many years. One could argue that Colonel Pell made the career of Colonel Fredericks. Interesting." Dr. Reynolds flipped about the file some more, a gesture that was surely for effect; Reynolds knew Captain Pell's file inside out. "Ah, here it is. When you enlisted, your father was retired from service, but serving as a congressman. Hrm…looks like he had a fair bit of influence in his day." The doctor looked Pell right in the eye as he continued. "So you were only 21 when you were picked up by the police…went to the district attorney's office, but they never followed through and you entered the Air Force. Is that about right?"

"Listen here," Pell protested further. "I may have made some mistakes when I was young, but I have been a good man ever since and I am nothing like Fredericks." Captain Pell was defending himself to the doctor. "I have learned my lesson, changed my ways, and I have never gone down that road again."

"Ignorance is no excuse, Captain." Reynolds corrected him. "And you did indeed go down that road once, and then you helped Fredericks walk it many, many times, and according to you he knew about your indiscretions, so it was blackmail…but interesting that he knew." Reynolds stared hard at Pell, and Pell took another drink, then Reynolds, in a softer tone, continued. "You joined the Air Force to get out of the community – thank your father for that. Then Fredericks used his influence to move you to Diego Garcia to run his campaign without any chance of a scandal. It just leaves two questions." Reynolds closed the file. "First, how come your father had influence over Fredericks? And second, just how many perverts are in the damned Air Force?"

It had been a tough, and sinister, interview about a dark subject targeting a very nefarious end. Dr. Reynolds reached into his pocket and produced a small capsule. The doctor held it up between his thumb and his forefinger. "Captain, Christmas is a tough time of year. I want you to consider this a Christmas gift. Take it, and tuck it away…just in case." Reynolds put the capsule in front of Pell, and after a few moments of indecision, Pell picked it up and put it in his pocket, and as soon as he did so, Reynolds knew he had the Captain. "Now," Reynolds said, filling his mug with only cola and leaning back in his chair, "let's chat about Christmas and family…holiday traditions, turkey dinners, and so forth." Dr. Reynolds smiled and Captain Pell took a long drink.

CHAPTER THIRTY-THREE

Life in the cell continued to endure during Captain Pell's absence. Lieutenant Pike and Sergeant Paxton sat at the round table in the centre of the heptagon shaped room and smoked cigarettes as they swapped war stories; internally Paxton was trying to forget they were all going to die, whereas Pike was wishing their captors would get on with it already.

Sergeant Kaye continued to be Sergeant Kaye, sitting cross-legged on the floor and alternating his stares between the door and the other men in the room.

Special Agent Northrop continued to pretend to track the accuracy of the clock against his pulse, using it as a cover to his real purpose of observing the other men, trying desperately to develop a plan to leverage them for his own escape. Northrop was standing under the clock going through his motions when Kaye approached him.

"What are you doing, Hal? Timing how long Pell is gone?" Kaye said, interrupting Northrop. Paxton and Pike had heard the question and exchanged looks, Paxton raising an eyebrow as if to ask *he can't be that hapless, can he?* And Pike in turn shaking his head from side to side as if to say *no.* And although Pike and Paxton had come to the realization that Kaye was putting on some sort of act, Northrop still thought of him as a harmless and foolish annoyance.

"No, Kaye," Northrop responded. "I am timing the clock. The second hand is now moving once for every six seconds that pass."

"Why?" Kaye asked. And before Northrop could answer, Christmas music began to play in the cell, creating a very unholy atmosphere.

"Merry Christmas, Kaye," became Northrop's response.

"Now this," Pike said, waving his hand through the air as if to indicate the music traveling through the air, "gives me a bad feeling."

"Now you have a bad feeling?" Paxton responded. "Just what the hell kind of prison where you in?"

"First one was Renous, back in Canada, but the second was the Russian Gulag," Pike stated flatly, and the three other men all stared at him, unsure if he was telling the truth.

CHAPTER THIRTY-FOUR

Captain Pell's breath smelled heavily of rum; Dr. Reynolds had stayed on the cola, but Captain Pell had been drinking the rum straight, talking about his wife and his parents, family memories, and Christmas traditions. He also spoke of his personal demons, how he had fought hard to keep his demons repressed, and that he was in reality no better than a monster.

Pell had confessed in detail the horrible acts of his early life and the extent of his involvement in covering up Fredericks' transgressions. Pell even began to talk darkly about his father, and he became angry when he realized it was these men, these perverts he had protected, that sent him to Diego Garcia. Pell blamed these men for transforming him into a monster at a young age, and causing this fate to befall him, and Pell reasoned that if he had not been posted in Diego Garcia, he would have never been a target for Dr. Reynolds' experiment. Reynolds corrected Pell, and explained it did not matter where the Captain was stationed; Pell was selected for his sins, not theirs, and Reynolds would have collected Pell from any corner of the earth to bring him here for their chat.

Pell swallowed the last drops of liquid from the rum bottle in his hand, and then slammed it on the table hard and reached for a new bottle, which he opened aggressively and began to drink. Dr. Reynolds calmly picked up the empty bottle and moved it off the table, setting it on the floor beside the table leg.

"In Russia," Reynolds told Pell, "it is considered a bad omen to leave an empty bottle on the table."

CHAPTER THIRTY-FIVE

There is something inherently disturbing about waking disoriented in a cold, grey cell with a group of strangers, and that disturbing sensation degenerates into something far more creepy and sinister with the abrupt and unexpected introduction of Christmas music. This sensation became even darker when, amidst the sounds of Christmas carols, it was discovered that one of the men in the room had survived the Russian Gulag, but announced it was only now that he had developed a bad feeling about their situation.

Silently, both Paxton and Northrop had come to the conclusion that Pike was telling the truth about Russia. For Paxton it was simple: Pike was a man of action, and although he had done many despicable things in his life, men like Pike simply did not lie. Lies were excuses, and excuses did not become such men. For Northrop it was different. Northrop did not have the firsthand experiences with men like Pike the way Paxton had, nor had he and Pike formed a bond that would allow Northrop the luxury of personal insight, but Northrop knew most of Pike's file inside out, and he knew what Pike was capable of. Even if at first he had not believed it, he had changed his assessment during his time in the heptagonal cell. There were some things that Pike had done that were beyond Northrop's clearance, but based on what he did know about Pike, both from his file and from his firsthand observation, Northrop had no problem picturing Pike in the gulag.

Kaye dismissed the idea as fiction. Kaye had made his mind up some time ago that Pike was not nearly as dangerous or dark as he appeared; Kaye believed it was an act; that Pike was trying to intimidate the rest of them to achieve a state of dominance in the pack. Kaye hated Pike, and he had no respect for him, so he assumed everything Pike said was a lie. Kaye and Paxton had very different opinions of the Canadian.

Northrop made his way to the table, and after a last glance at the clock, more out of reflex than anything else, Northrop took a seat at the round wooden table. Kaye followed Northrop and sat down next to the Special Agent. Pike sucked back on his cigarette, then he swung his foot up on to the table and spoke:

"So Company, what's with the Kringle Chorus, eh?" Pike asked.

"I have never seen this one," Northrop answered honestly; it worried Northrop that another new variable had been introduced, and it was one that did not seem like the work of a new facility commander. When the other variables changed, it was clear that someone was over-stepping, but this variable had to be a result of Dr. Reynolds alone. Then

Northrop found he had grown silent with fear when he realized every other variable that had been changed might not have actually been changed, but rather that Reynolds may have had different parameters at each facility. If the variables here were not deviations, then Northrop had no hope of leverage, and he could no longer be sure that Benedict Cain was coming. *Dr. Reynolds had admitted Benedict was coming*, Northrop thought. *But did he lie?* In Northrop's line of work, lies and truths were blended so seamlessly it was almost impossible to separate them most times. His mind spiraling deeper and deeper into anxiety, Northrop had another thought: *Could the variables had been changed because I am now a subject? Could all these small changes have been for me?*

Before Northrop could give it much more thought, the door to the cell opened and the men were shocked to see Captain Bradley Pell stumble back in to the cell, very drunk and carrying two bottles of rum, one full, one nearly half empty.

Pell staggered to the table as the cell door closed behind him, and then when he reached the table, the Captain fought to remain upright as he swayed right to left while standing still. He slammed the two bottles down on the table, and then looked at the four men, right to left and back again.

"Merry fucking Christmas!" Pell barked at the others, and then he staggered off to his sleeping area and pulled the curtain tight behind him.

"What's wrong with Pell?" It would be Kaye who would speak first. As much as Kaye hated Pike, he liked Pell.

"He's drunk, Blinkey," Pike snapped at the foolish question.

"But what if he's been drugged, or..." Kaye insisted.

"He is drugged. With alcohol. Christ, you're dumb," Pike snapped, cutting Kaye off.

"But..." Kaye stammered.

"I'm a real soldier," Paxton interrupted, "and I know when a man is swimming. Trust me, Kaye, he's drunk and needs to sleep. If we hear him throwing up, someone go look and make sure he's not on his back. The rum has him now." Then after a pause, Paxton added, "And we have the rum." Paxton, Pike, and Northrop smiled as Paxton reached for the half empty bottle, un-capped it and took a long pull. Some of the rum burned its way down the wrong pipe and Paxton coughed, then he winced, with his ribs still clearly badly damaged.

"What's wrong, real soldier?" Northrop taunted as he grabbed the bottle. "Not smooth enough for you?" And Northrop took a shot.

"Too smooth, sir. Only a pencil pusher could put that back without hacking." And Northrop did just that.

Pike, Paxton, and Northrop began to pass the first bottle of rum around the table; Kaye refused to take a single drink, but the others were not heartbroken that they did not need to share their Christmas spirit with the sniper. For the most part

168

they drank in silence, until they neared the bottom of the first bottle, at which point Kaye began to speak.

"At least this is the worst Christmas any of us will ever have," Kaye said to the group of imprisoned men.

"We can only hope," Northrop agreed.

"My worst Christmas before this was in Korea," Kaye stated. "I had to sit out in the cold for seventy-two hours waiting for an order to shoot. It was so cold my snots froze to my nostrils so badly that I almost suffocated. Worst of all, I never even got the order to shoot." Kaye really seemed to place a high value on taking the shot, and really saw it as a great hardship he did not get to kill a man at Christmas. There was something unholy about those implications, and so Paxton decided to challenge him with a worse Christmas story, one that was far worse as it had threads of humanity attached.

"Well, boo hoo, you were chilly. I can top that. It was the last Christmas before we came here, so it was between one and twenty years ago, I guess. I was minutes from going on leave when we were ordered out to a crash site. A small aircraft went down near Irwin. We deployed: orders were to look over the wreckage, check for survivors, try to locate the black box. Standard orders, really."

"Routine crash duty in California is not worse than freezing in Korea," Kaye challenged Paxton right back, and that was when Paxton dropped the bomb.

"Except for what I pulled out." Pike could see where Paxton's story was going, so he grabbed the second bottle of rum, the full one, pulled off the cap and put it right into Paxton's hand, and then put his other hand on Paxton's shoulder as a show of support. "Little fella never even made it to his first Christmas...missed it by hours."

There was a thick, heavy feeling in the air, and Northrop noticed that three of them, himself, Paxton and even Pike had felt the emotional impact of the infant's death, but Kaye looked unimpressed; Kaye lacked empathy, and as cold as Northrop was, the death of the infant had triggered empathy even in him. Northrop decided the best way to change the mood of the cell was for him to tell his Christmas story. It wasn't true, but it would create a better atmosphere for Christmas Eve. Northrop reached over, picked up the bottle, took a drink, and began to talk:

"Well, you guys never went to college, but if you had, you would understand why this is the story of a terrible, terrible Christmas." Northrop smiled and continued. "I was second year at Yale, and she was very, very, pretty. I could have gone home to Syracuse, but she was from Idaho and so, because I believed I was Don Juan and playing the long game of love, I drove her all the way to Idaho so she could see her family, meaning I would not get home to mine."

"A long drive with a pretty girl," Paxton began with a sarcastic humor. "What a terrible Christmas burden that must have been."

"Well, let me finish," Northrop said. "When I got her home, I helped her take her bags to the door, and when I got to the door her husband opened it. She said, 'Hey Honey, surprise, I made it home.' Then she turned to me and said, 'Thanks Hank, I'll see you on campus.' Then she went inside and closed the door and then it started to snow." Pike, Paxton, and Northrop began to laugh, but Kaye just looked confused.

"But your name is Hal, not Hank," Kaye stated.

"Exactly!" Northrop exclaimed, and the laughter rose to a new level. And it was at that moment, just after the laughter had crested, that Kaye decided to engage Pike.

"How about you, Pike? What was your worst Christmas?"

"Yeah, Pike, how about it?" Northrop added.

"Leave it alone." Pike's laughter began to trail off, and Paxton knew that it would be best to let this one go; whatever Pike's story was, it had to be bad.

"Are you sure?" Northrop asked. "It won't be as funny as mine, but it can't possibly be as bad as Paxton's."

"Leave it alone, guys," Pike replied, and Northrop came to the same realization as Paxton, and decided to drop it, but Kaye kept going.

"Don't be like that, Pike," Kaye sneered.

"Like what, Blinkey?" Pike was no longer laughing.

"Like some Christmas-storytelling coward," Kaye stated.

"Shit," Paxton said.

"Fuck," Northrop said.

Paxton and Northrop were expecting Pike to sail across the table and beat the life out of Kaye, but what they got instead was much, much worse. Pike grabbed the rum, and he took a long drink, then he locked eyes with Kaye.

"I come from a small town, Blinkey," Pike started, his voice heavy and raspy. "A very dirty one. We had a man in our town. He was involved with children's groups, sat on the town council. He had a lot of influence. And he hurt small children. It was no secret." Pike's eyes grew more and more intense, but his voice remained level. "The heat came on, and the police covered things up really good and he was never prosecuted. But he kept on hurting kids. Then he hurt one that mattered to me." Pike lifted the bottle and drank again, never taking his eyes off Kaye. "I sat with him at the hospital for a couple days, then finally I had to get some rest. I went home. I had a shower, a drink, and a sleep. When I woke up I had another shower and another drink, and it was just a couple hours before the Children's mass, Christmas Eve. The little guy was supposed to be in the pageant, so I made up my mind. I went to this man's house."

"Why?" Kaye asked, but Paxton and Northrop already knew the answer.

"To kill him, Blinkey." Pike took another drink, and then passed the bottle to Paxton who took a long pull before passing it to Northrop, who did the same. Pike continued his story. "I went to his house, walked to the door to bust it down, but the door wasn't even locked. I walked through the house. No sign of him in the living room, or the bedrooms. Then I made it to the kitchen. There was a pitcher of some sort of kids' juice and some mickey bottles. I stopped dead and I scanned the room. Then I saw a little light sneaking out past a door. I went down the stairs, and they creaked and creaked, and for some reason as loud as each creak and crack seemed to me, he never heard me coming. I turned the corner and there he was, on top of another kid. I grabbed him around his neck and I threw him with a twist and as he moved past my ear I heard his neck snap... quick, quicker than he deserved. For the second time in one week I was sitting in the hospital waiting for a kid to come out of surgery at the hands of this monster. Merry Christmas. I never regretted going to kill him; I only regretted the bastard lived. He got paralyzed for Christmas and I got a nickel in the pen."

The room fell silent, and Pike took a quick pull from the bottle of rum, then leaned into the table, setting his elbow on it and beckoning Kaye to lean in with his finger. Kaye leaned in and Pike grabbed him by the scruff of the neck and pulled Kaye's face right into his own, and barked, "I was a virgin once too. Do you want to talk about that too, Blinkey?!" Pike screamed it, and then let Kaye go. Kaye lowered his eyes, humiliated, rose from the table, and disappeared.

Pike also felt humiliated, and was looking down, and Northrop was at a loss, so Paxton started to sing. Paxton began slow and low. He had selected a sea shanty from deep within his memory, a song as far removed from Christmas as these men truly were and always would be, and he began to sing. Northrop recognized the song, and by the chorus, he had joined in. By the time that Paxton and Northrop were halfway through, Pike's spirits had improved and he joined in.

CHAPTER THIRTY-SIX

Sergeant Kaye felt beyond humiliated after Pike's story, yet he felt nothing for the children, or for Pike. Kaye perceived himself as the sole victim of Pike's story, even though he was not a part of the narrative. Kaye rationalized that Pike had told his story simply to humiliate him, and that was not acceptable to Kaye. Kaye had left the table for those reasons.

The other men at the table, Lieutenant Pike, Sergeant Paxton, and Special Agent Northrop, would have assumed that Kaye went to his sleeping area if they had thought about him at all, but they would have been wrong. Kaye believed he and Pell were kindred spirits, and so he went to Pell's sleeping area, but what he found surprised him.

Kaye stepped through the curtain and called Pell's name. "Pell. Hey, Pell. Are you awake, Pell?" There was no response. Kaye looked at Pell's cot, and he saw Pell was laying on his side, with his face turned away from the side of the cot where Kaye was standing, so Kaye sat on the edge of Pell's cot, listening to the others sing, and waiting, thinking the singing would wake Pell, but then he noticed that something was very wrong. Pell's body was not rising and falling the way it should with his breath. Kaye looked closer, and he realized that Pell was not breathing.

When Kaye realized Pell was not breathing, more from curiosity than concern, Kaye rolled him over on to his side and discovered that Pell's mouth had foamed over, and his eyes were staring outward in a haunting fashion. As Kaye continued to look Pell over, he discovered a paper, crumpled in Pell's hand. Kaye removed it and looked it over. There was writing on both sides of the paper. On the first side, the writing was typed, and it was a summary from Pell's file that explained the horrible things he had done; on the reverse side, the words were handwritten.

The handwritten side of the paper was a suicide note. It was addressed by name to the four other men who occupied the cell. In the note, Pell pleaded with his cellmates that if they were survive this facility and go free, that they would keep his secret and let the lie the Air Force had told his family remain intact; not for his sake, but for his wife's. There was also a plea to the men, and to God, to forgive him, and there was nothing else.

Kaye went to take off Pell's wedding ring, with every intention of taking it, but it was not on his hand; Pell had swallowed it directly ahead of the tiny capsule Dr. Reynolds had given him. Kaye listened to the others sing as he thought, and then when he made up his mind what to do, he screamed Northrop's name.

CHAPTER THIRTY-SEVEN

Kelley Pike, Michael Paxton, and Hal Northrop were finally pulling themselves up out of the darkness of Pike's story and building a sense of camaraderie when they were jarred back to the reality of their existence as Kaye's voice hit their ears, screaming. "Northrop! Northrop!"

"What?" Northrop yelled back.

"Pell's dead!" Kaye replied.

It took a few moments for this to register in the minds of the drunken men, but once it did, Northrop sprang to his feet and ran. Pike took another drink, and after exchanging a look with Paxton, rose to his feet and walked off to Pell's sleeping area.

When Pike stepped into Pell's sleeping area, Kaye was standing at the head of the cot and Northrop was on one knee, looking at Pell and holding his wrist as if he were looking for a pulse in spite of the fact that Pell was clearly dead. Northrop looked up to Pike, and stated the obvious: "He's dead, all right." Northrop let go of Pell's wrist and stood up.

"Lucky guy," Pike responded.

"What was that, soldier?" Northrop said.

"Oh, I'm sorry, Company. I didn't realize you liked in here so much." Pike turned his back to Northrop and walked out of Pell's sleeping area. Kaye waited a moment and then spoke.

"So what do you think happened?"

"Poison," Northrop replied. "Cyanide. They got him drunk, gave him a pill, and sent him back here. I guess he could not take living in the cell any longer." Northrop stood at the foot of the cot for a long time, staring, after Pike left the room. Northrop really did not know what to make of Pike. He wondered many things: *Is Pike picking a fight? Does Pike know what is really going on here? If so, how? Is Pike part of the group? Does he know I put him here? Is Pike one of them?* Northrop just stared, growing more and more concerned that he had misread the entire scenario. *Maybe the parameters were altered for me,* he thought once again. *Damn,* he thought. *Does Pike know?*

Northrop's mind snapped back to more practical theorizing. The cyanide was pretty standard in espionage. Northrop carried one when he went into the field to avoid ever being in a hell-hole like this one. Northrop also knew that most of the men Reynolds offered the capsule to had left it on the table in the interview room, at least the first time they had a chat, and this made Northrop curious about the late Bradley Pell.

Northrop knew Reynolds tended to research histories, find some trauma; he then chose the subject that way, and approached them under the guise of friendship, not animosity.

Dr. Reynolds was a master of psychological warfare and an expert manipulator. One thing was for certain: the horrible demons haunting Pell had given Reynolds all the leverage he needed to push Pell over the limit. Northrop thought about what might have existed in Pell's past to lead Reynolds to select him. Northrop never would have selected Pell; he would have chosen Kaye. Kaye was the furthest one outside the social hierarchy that they had established, and that should have made him the most vulnerable. Kaye was also highly anti-social and maybe diminished, and all of these factors would have led Northrop to give the capsule to the sniper.

As Northrop was staring after Pike, Kaye was studying Northrop. Kaye thought his best opportunity to survive was to leverage Northrop against the other two men. Kaye knew Northrop knew more than he was letting on, and Kaye wanted to know exactly what that information was. He now thought he had something to leverage over Northrop to manipulate that information out of him: Pell's suicide note.

CHAPTER THIRTY-EIGHT

Pike emerged from Pell's sleeping area, returned to the round table, and sat back down the same chair he had been seated in when the men were drinking the rum. Paxton, who had remained in his chair because of his injuries, looked to Pike inquisitively. Pike responded to Paxton's unspoken question by nodding his head, as if to say to Paxton, *yes, Pell is dead.* Men like Pike and Paxton did not needs words to communicate about death; they had both seen too much death and words were simply no longer needed.

Paxton reached into his pocket and took out the second pack of cigarettes he had been given after his beating, opened them, and passed one to Pike and put one between his own lips. Pike produced his lighter and used the flame to first light Paxton's cigarette, then his own. After the smokes were burning, Pike snapped the lighter closed, slid it into his pocket, and threw his leg up on the table as he slunk back into his chair and closed his eyes.

"How?" Paxton finally asked after a moment of silence; not because it really mattered in the end, but because it seemed like he should.

180

"Poison." Pike replied.

"Reaction to the alcohol?" Paxton asked

"His mouth was foamed over," Pike answered.

"Cyanide," Paxton said aloud. "At least he is at peace."

"I'm Catholic, Paxton. Suicide is the unredeemable sin."

"Are you saying you think Pell will be suffering hellfire and brimstone because he committed suicide?" Paxton knew Pike was the most religious sinner in the world, and so he was curious to learn Pike's thoughts about the late Bradley Pell.

"I'm saying, from where I sit, the sons of bitches murdered him," Pike said and he took a long drag.

Pike and Paxton continued to smoke, and it was when they were halfway through their cigarettes that Northrop emerged from Pell's sleeping area.

Northrop walked to the table, circled it, and took the seat opposite Pike. For a few seconds, Northrop just stared at Pike, and when he realized Pike was never going to acknowledge him, Northrop barked,

"Just who in the hell do you think you are, Pike? A man is dead in there and you disrespect him like that! What have you got to say for yourself, you son of a bitch?" Northrop's voice was loud, and met with a few beats of silence before Pike spoke softly.

"You, Company," Pike replied. "I disrespected you." Pike took a long drag that burned his cigarette into the filter, and then he tossed it in Northrop's general direction before pulling his leg of the table, sitting up straight, and finally opening his eyes. Pike squared off, looked Northrop in the eye, and pointed his forefinger right at the Special Agent. "That's what you really think, isn't it?"

"That man is dead!" Northrop fired back.

"And so are we!" Pike's tone rose slightly before coming back down. "Pell is free now and the rest of us are all trapped in this cell, dying slowly. And you know it."

"You do not get to talk to me like that. This is about Pell's life!"

"No, it's not. It is about your ego. You're not barking at me because Pell is dead, you're barking because I just do not give a shit about you. You're not in charge and it is pissing you off."

"Who the hell made you an expert on me?" Northrop's temper was flaring.

"You did," Pike said coolly, and Northrop's face turned white. *Fuck! Does he know?* Northrop thought.

Pike stood up, turned his back to Northrop and began to walk towards Pell's sleeping area. As he approached it, Kaye stepped out through the curtain, and Pike shouldered him to the ground. From the ground, Kaye watched Pike step over him and go into Pell's sleeping area; it was not until the curtain to Pell's area closed that Kaye rose to his feet.

Once he was up on his feet, Kaye looked towards the table at Paxton and Northrop. Kaye began to think about Pell's suicide note and decided he would keep it tucked away for now; Kaye did not want Paxton to know about the note.

Once Kaye had made up his mind not to share the note with Northrop in front of Paxton, he went to his own sleeping area and disappeared behind the curtain.

Paxton watched Kaye disappear behind his curtain, and then he turned his attention to Northrop. Northrop seemed deflated; his posturing was gone and he seemed lost in his thoughts.

"Let me ask you something, Northrop," Paxton said.

"Sure," Northrop replied in a defeated tone.

"When you were in there, with Pell's body, did you make a sign of the cross over his body like a blessing? Or cross yourself?" Paxton asked.

"No," Northrop said. "Why?"

"Believe it or not, Pike is a religious man and he takes death very serious. Right now, in there, he is probably performing the last rites on Pell's body," Paxton said matter-of-factly.

"Pike?" Northrop replied, raising his head. "Pike is religious? A God-fearing man?"

"Yes. Very," Paxton stated.

"But he is a black-hearted son of a bitch."

"Yes, he is that too," Paxton agreed. "Pike is the sort of man that would kill you as soon as look at you, but after he did, he would be sure to give you a decent burial."

"That makes no sense," Northrop said.

"That's Pike," Paxton replied. "He is a man greatly complicated by great simplicity."

"No. You are wrong," Northrop insisted. "Pell told me that he couldn't say grace at the table because of Pike."

"Did he, now?" Michael Paxton raised an eyebrow and looked right at Hal Northrop.

"Well no, not exactly, but he said someone had a problem with it," Northrop said, realizing he had made an assumption, and Northrop had learned a long time ago that assumptions were dangerous.

"Well, sir, someone did have a problem with it, but it certainly was not Pike." Paxton struggled to his feet and made his way over towards the late Captain Pell's sleeping area, gingerly and wincing, and then disappeared behind the curtain, and Northrop again hung his head.

CHAPTER THIRTY-NINE

Lieutenant Pike was kneeling over Captain Pell's body, and Sergeant Paxton was standing behind the lieutenant, his hands folded in front of him and his head slightly bowed. Paxton was not religious; he had been at one time, before the day he pulled the body of an infant out of a plane crash on Christmas Eve, but not after. Paxton knew, though, that Pike was religious, and like all good soldiers, he had respect for the dead. Paxton had joined Pike over Pell's body partly out of respect for Pike and what he was doing, and partly out of respect for the dead. Paxton was a soldier's soldier.

Pike had performed a modest last-rites blessing over Pell, and selected an Irish blessing for his final words; Pike was as Irish as he was Catholic. As Pike performed the blessing, he made the sign of the cross over Pell's body: "May the wind be ever at your back."

"Amen," Paxton said softly.

Pike and Paxton remained silent for a few moments. When Pike rose to his feet, Paxton concluded the last rites were over and that he could break the tense silence.

"Wouldn't that prayer really work better if Captain Pell had been a sailor?" Paxton asked.

"Tail winds and turbulence," Pike said with a wink.

"Amen, again," Paxton replied.

CHAPTER FORTY

Bradley Pell was dead. There was no doubt about that, and there was no way to properly care for his body; the others could neither bury nor cremate the air force pilot, nor could they set him adrift at sea like in a Norse funeral, or even commend him to the sea like a mariner. Bradley Pell remained on the cot where he had died, with his pillow under his head, and his dog tags upon his eyes, holding the lids shut in place of the pennies that were set to that task at one time and used to pay the ferryman; the curtain from Pell's cell had been pulled down and draped over him to cover his body in the most respectful way the remaining four could manage in their cold, grey tomb.

Heavy with the death of his cellmate and with thoughts about the eventual fate of his own mortal soul, Pike was sitting on his cot, twirling his lighter around in his hands, when he heard Kaye whispering to him from outside his curtain.

"Pike....hey Pike," Kaye whispered.

"What, Blinkey?" Pike answered, and Kaye slipped around the curtain.

"I was wondering..." Kaye trailed off, and he shuffled his

feet around nervously. Kaye hated Pike, and he was afraid of the more ornery man, but he saw Pike as a pawn, something to be sacrificed to strategy, and that is what had brought Kaye to Pike's sleeping area.

"Spit it out, Blinkey," Pike said impatiently.

"Do think it is really Christmas?" The question was partly genuine. Kaye knew Pike would have a better idea than the rest of them because of his internal clock, but the question was also designed to study Pike, to see if the Canadian was rattled by Pell's death, and if he could manipulate the Lieutenant.

"No," Pike said flatly, and then he laid down on his cot, and Kaye got the message: dismissed. Kaye did not see any change in Pike's behavior; he was still a hard man, and that is what Kaye had hoped.

"Pike, do you trust Northrop?" Kaye knew the answer, but he wanted to expand the distrust between the other men.

"No," Pike said, and then he closed his eyes on Kaye, dismissing him despite the fact the sniper was still standing there. Kaye felt insulted and angry.

CHAPTER FORTY-ONE

Michael Paxton was sitting on his cot with feet on the floor, and he was waiting. Over the years Paxton had spent in the field with men like Kelley Pike, and in the time he had spent in the heptagon-shaped cell with Pike, Paxton had come to develop a good sense of the man, so despite the fact it was late and he was growing more and more tired, Paxton decided to wait for the visit he knew would be coming once the other men, Hal Northrop and J.P. Kaye, had fallen asleep. Trading sleep for mission results in tensely hostile conditions was nothing new to Special Forces soldiers; Paxton had done it many times over many years.

Paxton waited on into the night, and eventually he heard the footsteps he had been anticipating approach. When the footfalls stopped silent outside his curtain, Paxton spoke:

"I'm up, Pike," Paxton announced, and then Pike entered his friend's sleeping area.

Pike let the curtain fall into place behind him, and he then went to Paxton's cot and sat down beside the Sergeant. The men were silent for a long while before Pike spoke.

"I have done...things," Pike said.

"It shows," Paxton responded.

"I used to think the scales always balanced, you know what I mean? I did a nickel in Renous for crippling a man."

"Bastard deserved worse," Paxton said it, and he meant it.

"Yeah," Pike agreed. "And it was worth it. Things need to balance though." Pike paused, then continued. "After prison I came the Armed Forces. It was the only place a guy like me could go, other than back to Renous."

"Certain skills," Paxton said.

"Certain skills," Pike agreed. "I was doing something for the military, on behalf of a few friendly nations. Doesn't matter what, but it was wrong. I did it, I was caught, and I ended up in the Russian Gulag." Pike stopped and looked up at his friend. "Things need to balance." Pike looked down towards his boots.

"Must have been a tough spot," Paxton stated.

"Makes this look like cabin on a lake," Pike agreed. "Scales were balanced. But I was too good at what I did. After Russia, well, everything escalated. Eventually I realized something."

"What's that?" Paxton asked.

"The scales didn't balance. Before Renous, before the Gulag, before JTF2, I was overweighting one side of the scale and nothing, no penance, was going to balance it. And then things got worse. It escalated." Pike picked his eyes up off his boots and looked Paxton in his eyes again. "At first you rationalize, but then one day you realize there is too much blood on your soul." Pike paused. "I realized a long time ago, I couldn't balance the things I have done. It is doesn't matter why I did them; it only matters that I can't balance it out."

Paxton dug out the cigarettes, and Pike fished out the lighter; they lit two.

"After the last few days," Paxton agreed, "I think I really understand that. This thing here, this is a false flag. We are a small part of something large and terrible."

"Yeah," Pike agreed. "It is dirty, and we are here because we are dirty."

"Worst of all, we don't know why we are even here." Paxton inhaled.

"I know why I'm here." Pike shocked Paxton.

"What? You know what they want from you?" Paxton asked in disbelief.

"Yup." Pike inhaled his cigarette.

"How can you be sure?" Paxton asked.

"I remember my abduction." Pike exhaled smoke.

"Do I want to know?" Paxton was quite serious with his apprehension.

"No," Pike said flatly. The two men sat in silence for a long time, thinking about the scales they could never balance. Finally, Paxton re-started the conversation.

"But?" Paxton said. "If there wasn't a 'but,' you would not be here getting all metaphysical on me."

"The 'but' is easy. I still want to balance the scales," Pike said.

"Confession?" Paxton asked.

"Something like that," Pike admitted. "I know I am going to hell. You can't balance a life like mine, even with confessions, penance, but if I could get one thing off my soul before they laid me to rest, it would be this one."

"I'm no priest, but..." Paxton began to offer.

"Can't," Pike said. "We both know this place has to be bugged."

"And you want to keep this from them? You want to do something noble, before you die?" Paxton asked Pike.

"Screw nobility," Pike said. "I want to spite the motherfuckers."

CHAPTER FORTY-TWO

Master Sergeant Withers walked the long corridor through the secret facility that led to the heptagon-shaped cell that now housed four men. Withers was flanked on either side by two soldiers. The soldier on his left was a fairly generic-looking soldier named Patterson, easily dismissed when contrasted with the soldier on his left, the silverback known as Sergeant Briggs.

As the three sinister men walked the corridor, Withers enjoyed the echoes of their footfalls: the sound of men marching for the sole purpose of spreading fear. Withers began to smile.

Master Sergeant Withers was sadistic, and he had been waiting a very long time for today. Withers would finally get a shot at the greatest challenge of his career: Pike. As Withers planned what he would do to Pike, he began to grin wider and wider.

When they arrived at the door to the main cell, Withers stopped, and turned to face his men. "Do not kill him." Withers reached into his holster and removed a dart gun. Next, he pulled out a dart and loaded the gun.

"You don't need that, sir. You have a silverback," Briggs

boomed with confidence.

"You'll get your chance, Briggs, but I have seen his file." Withers turned back to face the door. "Remember, we can't kill him yet, but everything else is optional." Withers adjusted his posture. "Open the door," he ordered, and Patterson hit the controls on the wall.

CHAPTER FORTY-THREE

Sergeant Paxton was at a loss for words after what Lieutenant Pike had told him: *I know I am going to hell. You can't balance a life like mine.* Paxton was fascinated by the unbreakable faith of a man who believed himself to be damned. Pike was a paradox.

To Pike, the real torture was not confinement, as he had been confined before; it was not the food, as he had been hungry before; it was not the suffering, because he had suffered before. To Pike, the real torture was dying without the sacrament of confession. This further fascinated Paxton; Paxton did not believe a confession could save his soul, but he still needed to confess, and would if he had the opportunity. Even a confession to Paxton would have eased Pike's burden, but then their captors would have what they wanted, and that was simply not an option.

"You Catholics sure do like to make it hard on yourselves," Paxton finally said.

"Amen," Pike agreed.

Paxton went into his pocket and produced the cigarettes; he put one in between his lips and passed one to Pike. As Pike was fishing out his lighter, they heard the door to the cell open, and both men froze.

"Life is all about timing," Paxton said, and both men knew what was about to happen. Pike and Paxton had been in hostile territory too much not have figured out the pattern.

Pike took his unlit cigarette from his lips and tucked it behind his ear. Pike then flicked open his lighter, sparked the flame, and leaned in to light Paxton's nail.

"I got to go," Pike said. "My ride's here." Pike snapped his lighter shut and put it in his pocket, straightened up, and walked over to the curtain, then exited Paxton's sleeping area and entered the heptagon-shaped cell.

As Pike emerged from behind the curtain to Paxton's sleeping area, he took in the room. Kaye and Northrop were sitting at the table facing the door, and a few feet from them was Withers, with a soldier named Patterson on his right, and a gorilla named Briggs on his left. Pike stepped up, standing next to the closest man to him, Briggs, but looking Withers right in the eye.

"Well, let's get on with it, then," Pike said.

"What makes you think we came for you?" Withers said mockingly.

"Lucky guess." Pike began to walk past them towards the cell door, and then he turned towards Briggs. "Oh, I forgot. I have something for you, Sunshine."

Briggs smiled widely. "What is that, now?"

Pike threw a devastating right cross up and into Briggs' face, breaking his nose and causing blood to fill the air. Briggs' head snapped back and he dropped to one knee. As Briggs went to one knee, Pike swarmed in, reaching out and grabbing the back of Briggs' head and then throwing his knee up towards Briggs' face. The impact would have been devastating, but just as Pike's knee was about to make contact with Briggs, Withers' dart went deep into the flesh of the lieutenant's trapezius muscle.

Pike stopped short, and recoiled his knee, putting his foot back on the ground. As he did, Briggs scrambled to his feet and hit Pike with a left hook that sent Pike to the ground. Pike was out before his body had even found the concrete. Effortlessly, Briggs pulled Pike to his feet, and along with the other, Patterson, they grabbed his arms and dragged the Canadian soldier off like a rag doll.

After his soldiers had left the room dragging the unconscious Pike, Withers turned to Northrop. "Thank you, Special Agent Northrop." Withers' grin was nearly ear-to-ear.

"For what, Master Sergeant?" Northrop asked.

"Your very detailed report, sir. The best way to deal with Pike was in your notes." Withers spoke loudly, hoping that Paxton would hear him from his cot.

"The dart," Northrop said, and as he spoke, Northrop felt Kaye's eyes on him, and he hoped Paxton had not heard Withers.

"Yes, the dart. I never would have thought of that, sir." Withers began to walk to the door, and then he turned back and looked at the blood on the concrete. "You know, he really is a tough bastard. I think most of that blood is from Briggs." With that, Withers turned and exited the cell, and the cell door closed behind him.

Northrop stared at the cold metal door.

Kaye stared at Northrop.

Paxton had heard every word.

CHAPTER FORTY-FOUR

Hal Northrop and J.P. Kaye sat at the round table in the center of the heptagon-shaped cell in silence for a long time. After more than an hour, Northrop would begin pacing, or studying the clock against his pulse, or going through any number of rituals he had developed to pass the time in the cell. Northrop continued to think, desperate to find a way to leverage his position, but he was growing anxious. Northrop was developing serious doubts about whether or not Benedict Cain was coming, or if Reynolds had set him up to believe Benedict was coming, even though he was not. *Were the parameters different here?* Northrop kept asking himself. *Did Reynolds customize them for me?*

Northrop also wondered about Pike. Northrop was not concerned for Pike or curious about what sort of hell Pike was enduring; Northrop had a very strong concept of what Withers would be doing with Pike. Northrop was more interested in trying to determine what Pike may or may not know, asking himself silently: *Does Pike know? If Pike does not know, will they tell him?* Those questions always lead to one more: *Did Paxton hear Withers? Does Paxton know what I did to Pike?*

As Northrop thought, he went deeper into his own mind, losing track of the time as he gave in to his anxiety. Northrop was desperately trying to retain a cool outward appearance, but Kaye was studying him intently, and whereas Northrop might have been able to fool most people, Kaye was very detailed in his observations, and he had been studying Northrop for hours now.

Kaye noticed the subtle changes in Northrop: the way the special agent was breathing, the way he stood, and smaller mannerisms. Kaye studied the change in speed with which he paced or pretended to be checking his pulse. Kaye noticed Northrop's eyes no longer focused in the areas of the cell he typically pretended to watch, but instead were unfocused. Northrop was coming unglued, and Kaye could see it, and he knew it would soon be time to make his move.

Suddenly, abruptly, Northrop turned sharply from the clock and went directly to Paxton's curtain, paused, took a deep breath, and then entered Paxton's sleeping area.

CHAPTER FORTY-FIVE

Pike's eyes came into focus and he realized he was in a very bad spot. Pike was lying in a heap on a cement floor in a small room. The room was a perfect square, with concrete walls and high ceilings. Along the wall, there was a wooden chair, exactly like the ones in the cell. Pike looked up and he saw a bar running between two walls, and below the centre of the span was a dried-up bloodstain: Paxton's blood.

Pike thought about the time. He figured had been in the room thirty minutes. There could not have been a huge dose of sedative in the dart, but Pike was still very groggy. Thirty more minutes passed before the door opened, and Briggs entered. Briggs had stitches along the side of his nose and bruises around his eyes that made him resemble a raccoon. Briggs was wearing a fresh, clean shirt.

Next, Withers strolled into the room, walking casually, followed by Patterson. Patterson closed the door.

Withers turned to face Pike, with his hands clasped in front of him. "Get him to his feet, Briggs," Withers ordered.

Pike shot Briggs a look and held up his hand to signal him to stop. Pike then lifted himself to his feet, wiped the dust off his bloody pants, and reached behind his ear; miraculously, the cigarette was still there. Pike took the nail from behind his ear and moved it between his lips. Next, he fished out his lighter and flicked open the top.

"Mind if I smoke?" Pike asked Withers.

As Pike struck his lighter and produced a flame, Briggs backhanded him, and Pike dropped the cigarette from his mouth. Pike squared his face back to Briggs.

"Really?" Pike said to Briggs defiantly. Pike squatted down, picked up his cigarette, and put it back in his mouth, and sparked his lighter to create a flame. As Pike was drawing the flame into the cigarette, he looked to Withers. "Tell your ape that was rhetorical."

"Your attitude is very strange, Lieutenant Pike," Withers stated as he held a hand up to Briggs, indicating that he was to let Pike have his cigarette. "This is not at all what I expected from you."

"I've been disappointing ever since 1976," Pike responded as he drew smoke in from his cigarette.

"I don't think you realize what's going on here, Lieutenant," Withers said, partly confused by Pike and partly fascinated.

"You don't, eh?" Pike closed the top of his lighter and exhaled the cigarette smoke in his lungs.

"Maybe I should explain something here," Withers offered. "We want information, and we will get it."

"Let me know how that works out for you." Pike drew

some smoke as he put his lighter back into his pocket.

Withers began to laugh, and then he nodded to Briggs and Patterson. Patterson grabbed the chair from the wall, and then slammed it down behind Pike, and Briggs manhandled Pike into the chair. Patterson used cable ties to restrain Pike's wrists and ankles to the chair as Briggs held the soldier down; Patterson pulled the cable ties so tight around Pike's wrists that he began to bleed.

"Now, Lieutenant Pike," Withers said, as he leaned in and sneered, "that was rhetorical."

Withers leaned into Pike until the two men's faces were only inches apart, their eyes locked. Pike caught movement out of the corner of his eye, and adjusted his stare to see the mammoth Briggs removing his shirt. Withers kept his eyes focused on Pike.

"Don't mind Briggs," he said. "The sergeant just does not want your blood to get all over another one of his shirts."

"I'm not too thrilled about it either," Pike replied as he drew more smoke from his cigarette.

Withers then took the cigarette out of Pike's mouth and began to smoke the nail. Withers inhaled a large amount of smoke, and then he blew the smoke into Pike's face, and Pike began to smile at Withers.

"If I was ever going to walk out of here alive," Pike said to Withers with defiance, "I would come back and kill you. You know that, eh?"

"I do, Lieutenant Pike," Withers responded as he stood

back up to his full height and looked down at the man strapped to the chair. "Believe me, I know you would do exactly that." Withers' tone began to transition to mockery. "JTF2. But I am not too worried." After a pause, Withers leaned back into Pike's face and he continued. "You will never leave this facility alive. You know that, *eh*?" Withers backhanded Pike, and then after Pike's face snapped back to looking forward at Withers, the sadistic Master Sergeant put the cigarette out on Pike's neck. Withers stood and looked to Briggs. "Briggs, come get me once you have broken him."

"Yes sir," Briggs replied as he moved in close to Pike. Withers and Patterson left the room, leaving Pike alone with Briggs.

"I am going to knock each and every one of your teeth out, Lieutenant Tough Guy," Briggs threatened Pike as he balled his fists and prepared an assault to break his prey.

"Go ahead," Pike replied. "The damned things are false anyway."

Chapter Forty-Six

Paxton did not trust Northrop.

Paxton had remained in his sleeping area after Withers had come and abducted Pike. When Pike was abducted, Paxton had heard everything. Paxton heard Pike attack Briggs, and he heard the unmistakable sound of bones breaking when Pike struck Briggs, and he heard Withers' dart gun fire, and Pike's body fall. Paxton heard the soldiers drag Pike's body away. Paxton also heard what Withers and Northrop had said at the end:

"Thank you, Special Agent Northrop," Withers had said.

"For what, Master Sergeant?" Northrop had replied.

"The best way to deal with Pike was in your notes," Withers had said.

"The dart," Northrop had said.

"Yes, the dart," Withers had said.

Paxton did not trust Northrop.

Paxton understood everything he had heard. There was no need to think it through and analyze the information; it was not Paxton's first go-round. Northrop and Pike had history, and Northrop was the one responsible for Pike being locked up in the heptagon-shaped cell. As Paxton was digesting these thoughts, Northrop came in through the curtain.

Paxton did not talk first; he waited. Northrop walked over and sat down on the cot beside Paxton.

"You haven't come out today." Northrop began his fishing expedition.

"Pike and I heard the door," Paxton said.

"Do you know what happened?" Northrop asked.

"No," Paxton lied.

"Your friend gave the big one hell, broke his damned nose, but there were three of them, and a tranquilizer gun. They took him down pretty quickly," Northrop explained.

"What do you know about this place?" Paxton asked.

"A lot," Northrop said. Northrop knew Paxton was not going to accept a lie; he had given the soldier too much information when they had their talk after Paxton's beating.

"Tell me," Paxton said.

"I can't do that, soldier," Northrop responded.

"You mean you won't," Paxton responded.

"All the same, Sergeant," Northrop lied.

"No," Paxton stated. "I am calling you out." Paxton turned his head to face Northrop with his challenge.

"Soldier?" Northrop asked him.

"It's like this, sir. We are all locked in this cell together. We are all in this together. If you have intelligence, you need to share it so we can all use it to try and save our lives. If you're not sharing it, then you're planning to double-cross the rest of us…screw us over to save your own life at our expense."

"Now listen here. It is not like that, Paxton," Northrop lied emphatically.

"Sure it is. You forget, guys like me and Pike and Kaye, we do cloak and dagger all day. We execute the false flag operations and we fix your plans on the fly, because you pencil pushers don't have a clue," Paxton said angrily.

"Paxton, if we work together, we can leverage this situation," Northrop said.

"That is exactly my point. So now, tell me what you know about this place," Paxton ordered the special agent.

"I can't do that, soldier," Northrop replied.

"We have nothing more to talk about." Paxton dismissed Northrop, and with nothing left to say, Northrop lowered his head and stood up and walked out through the curtain.

Paxton did not trust Northrop.

CHAPTER FORTY-SEVEN

When Sergeant Briggs heard the door to the torture chamber open, he stopped, turned towards it, and watched as Master Sergeant Withers re-entered the room. Withers stepped into the chamber expecting to discover that Pike was either talking or dead, but instead was shocked to see him slumped in the chair, silent and alive. Pike was bleeding from his mouth, nose, and wrists. Briggs was sweating and breathing hard; Pike was gurgling and spitting up on himself.

"Briggs, report," Withers said crisply as his smile grew, anticipating what the future would hold for Lieutenant Pike.

"This son of a bitch ain't talking." Briggs kicked Pike in the chest and sent the captive man and the chair to the floor.

"Impressive," Withers said as he walked towards Pike. Withers squatted down over Pike and stared at the battered Canadian soldier. "Take him back to the cell." Withers stood back up and stepped away from Pike

"Yes, sir." Briggs squatted down, took his knife out of its sheath, and began to cut the cable ties off Pike's wrists. Withers walked to the door and turned back to interrupt Briggs.

"And Briggs," Withers said.

"Yes sir?" Briggs responded professionally.

"Don't be gentle." Withers smiled.

Briggs smiled back.

CHAPTER FORTY-EIGHT

Sergeant Kaye was sitting alone at the round table in the center of the heptagon-shaped room. Northrop had disappeared into Paxton's sleeping area a few minutes earlier, and Kaye elected to wait rather than to follow; it was obvious to Kaye that Northrop wanted to learn if the Special Forces soldier had heard his conversation with Master Sergeant Withers. There was no doubt in Kaye's mind that Withers had wanted both Kaye and Paxton to hear what he had said, to expose Northrop's position. It was clear to Kaye that Northrop knew more about this facility than he had admitted to the others. Northrop's behavior had indicated that he knew a lot. The Special Agent had been hinting about knowing more than the others, but at this point it was becoming quite obvious that his level of firsthand knowledge was quite extensive.

When Northrop did emerge from Paxton's sleeping area, only a few minutes had passed and Kaye was not sure how to read that against the existing narrative. Kaye wanted to know if Paxton had heard Withers as badly as Northrop did, likely for similar reasons: to use this knowledge to manipulate and leverage a position with the others and escape the cell. Kaye watched Northrop, looking for clues in the agent's body language. Northrop walked briskly to the clock and stared at it as he took his pulse, but he did not take his pulse long enough, so Kaye figured it was a cover, and that Northrop himself was unsure of what Paxton knew. Kaye deduced that meant that Paxton had heard everything, and Northrop was trying to plan a way to control the situation.

Kaye waited as Northrop went through his motions and thought his plan through, watching the Special Agent silently. When Northrop began to regain his composure, he made eye contact with Kaye for a few seconds, and then joined the sniper at the table, taking the same seat he had been in when Withers was in the cell.

"How is Paxton?" Kaye asked, although he was less concerned with Paxton and more concerned with how to leverage Northrop and form an alliance he could control.

"He is still in rough shape," Northrop replied, and it was true, but it was not the full story.

"Listen, Hal," Kaye said, "there is something going on here." The sniper decided it was time to make his move, as right then there was no one at the table but him and Northrop.

"What do you mean?" Northrop asked cautiously. It had not occurred to Northrop that Kaye might have pieced together that he had put Pike in this tomb; Northrop had never given Kaye much credit.

"I mean Pike," Kaye stated flatly, and for the briefest second, Northrop held his breath, but was relieved when Kaye continued. "We need to figure out what to do about him before he returns," Kaye whispered. "He's going to kill us."

"What are you talking about, Kaye?" Northrop asked, unsure of Kaye's logic but quite relieved that Kaye saw Pike as a threat.

"You know he is a loose cannon. You even had a file on him. That soldier said so when they took him. When they abducted you, they must have gone through your files," Kaye reasoned, and although Kaye knew there was more to it than that, he did not want to tip his hand to Northrop.

"Pike is a dangerous man, but why do you think he is going to kill us in here, in this cell?" Northrop prodded.

"Why else would he steal the gun?" Kaye responded.

"That doesn't make sense, Kaye." Northrop was trying to read Kaye and Kaye was trying to read Northrop.

"There is more," Kaye said. "I have a note." Kaye produced Pell's suicide note from his pocket and passed it to Northrop.

"Pike gave you a note?" Northrop asked.

"No," Kaye said. "It's Pell's suicide note."

Northrop read the note carefully, both the side of the paper with Reynolds' notes on Pell and the handwritten message Pell had left on the back side of the page.

"I thought it was best to hide it from Pike," Kaye continued. "If he had seen this, after what he told us about...Christmas..."

"Wouldn't have mattered," Northrop said. "Pell was already dead."

"But Pike's rage would have set him off. He would have wasted us all." Northrop thought about what Kaye was saying, and he decided that Kaye really believed this. Knowing a great deal about Pike, Northrop also knew it was actually a very plausible conclusion.

"So what are you driving at, Kaye?" Northrop asked.

"Well, we need a plan before Pike gets back, one that could get us all out of here together."

"And how would we manage that?" Northrop asked.

"The way I see it, we are all here for a reason. We were picked for some reason. We don't know each other. We don't know why we are here. We need to figure out what connects us," Kaye said in earnest. "Once we know that, we can bargain. We can get ourselves out of here."

"Okay," Northrop said. "What connects us?" Northrop knew Kaye was partially right; they were all chosen for a reason, and Northrop had already figured out why he was here, and he knew what they wanted from Pike. Even if he did not know the particulars, he knew the question.

"Three of us are the same – Americans – but Pike, he's a Canadian. Why a Canadian?" Kaye asked the Special Agent.

"They make good neighbors?" Northrop said sarcastically.

"You don't see it?" Kaye asked, and without waiting for an answer, continued. "This has got to be a Canadian facility. The Canadians are pulling the strings here."

"The Canadians?" Northrop asked.

"Yes. Pike is some sort of plant, and they are trying to figure out our military secrets." Kaye continued talking, and Northrop was beginning to believe that Kaye really did think he had it all figured out. "Look at the secrets. We know Paxton's team was taking out phony targets; that is pretty big. We now know Pell was covering up for a senator hurting kids. International embarrassments. So what do we know?"

"You think we should trade confidential information?" Northrop asked Kaye, sensing a trap.

"Yes. Once we know all of each other's secrets, we have scope. We can figure out what they want and look for leverage. We can make a deal," Kaye responded.

"So, what do you know, Kaye?" Northrop asked. "What do you think the Canadians want from you?"

"If they are looking for embarrassments, then they want my information to expose the sniper corps," Kaye said flatly.

"Expose the sniper corps?" Northrop repeated.

"Yes," Kaye said. "People think snipers are used for control situations, but that is a mistake. Sometimes we are sent out to the field to take out targets."

"I think people have already figured that one out, Kaye," Northrop responded.

"But sometimes, our targets are our own people." Kaye paused and looked right into Northrop's eyes. "Hal, in Korea, I had orders to do that. My sniper partner was selling secrets, so they sent us out on a mission and gave us a target, and after he shot the target, my orders were to shoot him. I did it." Kaye leaned in close to Northrop and put his hand on the special agent's shoulder. "Now you know my secret. What's yours?"

Northrop was looking back into Kaye's eyes, trying to think fast and decide what to do, when they were interrupted by the sound of the cell door opening.

CHAPTER FORTY-NINE

The large steel door to the large heptagon-shaped cell door opened with an echo and a bang; it had clearly been opened quicker and louder this time for effect. There was a statement behind the action. When the door had slid open all the way, the intimidating figure of Briggs walked into the cell with Pike slumped over his shoulder like a bag of grain.

Pike was a large man in his own right, standing six feet and pushing a muscular two hundred pound frame, but over the shoulder of the silverback Briggs, he looked to be no more than a child.

Briggs marched to the center of the room, with his hands at his sides and Pike bent over his shoulder, displaying just how broad and massive Briggs' frame truly was. As soon as Briggs made it to the table at the center of the cell, he shrugged his shoulders, and Pike slid and landed hard on the concrete ground and bounced.

Next, Briggs looked at Northrop and then at Kaye, challenging them to move towards Pike. Neither man moved. After a few moments with an intense stare-down, Briggs turned and strolled out of the cell; the door closed behind him.

After Briggs was gone, Kaye ran to Pike and tried to help him up, displaying mock concern, but Pike pushed Kaye away.

"Keep your damned mitts off me, Blinkey." Pike struggled to roll over and push himself to his knees.

"I was just trying to help you to your feet," Kaye said.

"If you ever try to help me again, I'll kill you." Pike was deadly serious.

Pike reached out and put his hand on the table, and as he did, Paxton emerged from behind his curtain and walked over to Pike. By the time Paxton made it to Pike, Pike was on one knee and had one palm flat on the table. Paxton put his hands under Pike's arms and helped him from the floor into a chair, both men straining under the effort due to their injuries.

Once Pike was in his chair, Paxton selected the chair beside him and set himself into it. The two men looked at each other and began to smile, on the verge of laughter, like two friends sharing a private joke. Paxton's smile revealed pearly white teeth, and Pike's smile was all gums where his front teeth used to be. Paxton then hauled the cigarettes out of his shirt pocket as Pike pulled the lighter out of his pants pocket. Paxton simultaneously put a cigarette between each man's lips as Pike flicked open the lid on his lighter and sparked a flame; they leaned into the flame. Once the cigarettes were lit, Pike snapped the lighter closed and both men enjoyed a long drag.

"You should be in bed," Pike said.

"I had to see how badly you got beat. Doesn't seem that bad," Paxton said.

"No?" Pike said as reached into his pocket and pulled out what was left of his false teeth and dropped on them in the centre of the table.

"No," Paxton smiled. "They let you keep your teeth."

"I need to carry them in my pocket," Pike said.

"So they did let you keep them." Paxton winked and both men laughed.

Northrop watched and waited until the men had settled, and then he joined them at the table. Kaye followed Northrop's lead and did the same.

After Northrop and Kaye took their seats, Northrop waited until Pike and Paxton had stopped laughing and resumed smoking before he spoke.

"Anything to report, soldier?" Northrop asked Pike. Pike and Paxton traded glances.

"Only that the army's been good to me." Pike took a long slow drag.

"Bullshit," Paxton said with a laugh.

"Bullshit," Pike responded with a laugh.

CHAPTER FIFTY

Lieutenant Colonel Samantha Braun could be as petty as she was vicious, and it was the combination of these two traits that had her smiling at her own wicked reflection in the window of her office. Despite the position she planned to take on the argument that was coming, a position she knew was weak and transparent, she had actually taken great pride in giving Master Sergeant Withers the order to beat Lieutenant Kelley Pike. Braun had no idea prior to the torture what Pike knew, if anything, but she knew that Dr. Reynolds did not want her beating and torturing any more of the five, and she wanted to use her methods and prove him wrong. The Lieutenant Colonel was now convinced Pike knew nothing of value.

Braun was expecting the see the doctor fly through her door any time now in more of a rage than they day they had first met. Braun wanted to humiliate the doctor for the way he had spoken to her, and she was looking forward to doing just that. Braun felt cheated by what happened next.

There was a soft knock at the door, and the Lieutenant Colonel turned towards her door, a little surprised by the softness of the sound. Braun had not expected anyone ahead of Dr. Reynolds. "Come," Braun said, and the door opened.

When the door was opened it revealed a very calm Dr. Reynolds, with a cup of coffee and a doughnut. The doctor's doughnut was lying over the top of his coffee mug, and the steam from the coffee was rising up through the hole in the centre of the doughnut. With his free hand, Dr. Reynolds calmly closed the door; he then he picked up his doughnut off the top of his mug, and with both hands busy carrying an item apiece, the doctor walked to the front of Braun's desk, and spoke quite casually.

"Colonel, are you deliberately trying to tank this experiment, or are you just that blasted stupid?" In truth, Dr. Reynolds knew the answer: she was trying to tank Experiment FIVE, but she was also so firmly entrenched in her parading, she was incapable of strategic and tactical linear correction. Braun may have been a West Point phenom, and she might have had a decorated career, but this was the first test of her skills in a non-traditional environment, and she was failing.

"Doctor?" Lieutenant Colonel Braun responded in a confused tone, so shocked by the calm manner of the doctor that she could not properly phrase any of the competing questions flooding in to her mind.

"You had Pike beaten," Dr. Reynolds said as he sat down, uninvited. "Today."

"You had your talk with Captain Pell, Doctor," Braun offered, struggling for a way to regain footing. "It went so badly he killed himself. Your methods were failing. I stepped up."

"So the answer is 'stupid.'" Reynolds took a bite out of his doughnut.

"Doctor, I will not be spoken to in that manner in my own office..." Braun was becoming agitated by the calm manner Reynolds was projecting.

"Pell's suicide was planned. I introduced it as a catalyst to target responses from the other subject that would lead to loose lips and revelation. That is why I orchestrated it to occur over Christmas." Reynolds took a sip of coffee.

"You are living in a fantasy, Doctor. It was not even Christmas," Braun argued.

"But they thought it was, Colonel." Reynolds took another bite of his doughnut. "Christmas is a depressing time of year for many, more so for soldiers, more so for soldiers away from home, and more so still for soldiers locked in a crypt with a suicide victim. It was the catalyst to get them talking. There is a reason we have microphones and cameras in there." Reynolds took another bite of his doughnut.

"What does any of that have to do with Pike being aggressively interrogated?" Braun asked.

"Aggressively inter...which screw is the loose one? What we do is torture...aggressive yes, interrogative no." Reynolds swallowed the last bit of his doughnut.

"Say what you will, Doctor, but my methods have proven effective." Braun stepped up to her desk and took a file out of her top drawer.

"Oh?" Reynolds raised an eyebrow.

"Anything to learn about the Pike subject is in this folder. Clearly not a subject of consequence, Doctor."

"Then he told you about Colombia?" Reynolds took a nice sip of coffee and grinned.

"What happened in Colombia?" Braun asked.

"Well Colonel, I have no earthly idea, but then again, that really is the point of all this now, isn't it?" Reynolds got to his feet and took another sip from his mug, and enjoyed the moment. Lieutenant Colonel Samantha Braun was becoming desperate and unhinged, and the doctor grinned as he quietly reflected on their first meeting. *You do not get to be Benedict Cain's top guy if you can't play the long game*, Reynolds thought to himself with pride.

Chapter Fifty-One

Pike was on the cot in his sleeping area, beaten halfway to death and unsure why it was only halfway, when Kaye came to see him, just the way he had gone to see Paxton after his beating. Like Paxton, Pike saw Kaye's shoes and spoke to him.

"What do you want, Blinkey?" Pike said, and Kaye stepped in through the curtain.

Kaye looked nervous, and scared. He was worried that eventually he would be the one taken for a beating. Kaye desperately wanted to manipulate the situation first, bargain his way out of the cell. Kaye was hoping desperately to avoid a beating like Paxton's or Pike's.

"Was it bad?" Kaye asked.

"You wouldn't like it, Blinkey," Pike said dismissively.

Kaye processed that, and he did not want to be on the receiving end of Briggs. Kaye decided, should they come for him, if he knew anything that would stop his beating, he would talk before the first punch.

"What is it you know that they want to know so badly?" Kaye asked.

"Jack-all, Blinkey. I don't know a goddamned thing.

Never have," Pike said.

"Yeah. I don't know jack either," Kaye said, while trying to think if he knew anything at all. Kaye could not think of anything else to say, so he turned and began to walk away. He pulled the curtain back, and then a thought occurred to Kaye, so he turned and asked Pike another question. "Pike, why do you call Northrop 'Company'?"

"Walks like company, flaps like company, stinks like company," Pike said.

"I don't know what you mean," Kaye said.

"I mean, he knows what's going on here. Exactly what is going on."

"How do you know that?" Kaye asked.

"Company secret." Pike began laughing at his own joke and Kaye began to feel very uncomfortable.

CHAPTER FIFTY-TWO

Paxton and Pike were sitting at the table, beaten, swollen, and sore, but in the best spirits either man had experienced in some time; for better or worse, they had seen action, and that was all they really knew. The two men were both recovering from the beatings they had endured at the hands of Sergeant Briggs, and they were both claiming to have had the worse beating while insulting the other one for being so easily injured. They were having fun. Pike and Paxton had passed the whole day this way, right into the night. When the lights had dimmed to the evening cycle, and Northrop and Kaye had both long gone to bed, the two soldiers felt safe to speak candidly and Paxton changed the direction of the conversation.

"Pike, what's the history with you and Northrop?" Paxton asked Pike.

"What did he say?" Pike asked Paxton.

"Nothing, but Withers did thank him for the dart idea," Paxton said, and watched Pike as the other man sighed and rubbed the back of his neck, trying to decide how to best answer his friend's question.

"Do you know why I didn't kill Northrop the day he crawled out of that cot back there?" Pike pointed towards Northrop's sleeping area.

"No," Paxton admitted. "But ever since I overheard him talking to Withers I have been wondering about that."

"Spite," Pike said.

"That sounds like you," Paxton admitted. "So your history is what I think it is?"

"Yes," Pike said.

CHAPTER FIFTY-THREE

A dark figure lurked about in the heptagon-shaped cell, checking all the corners, listening for any noise, and making an educated guess as to how much time would pass before the lights came up. Satisfied that there was no one else awake, the figure moved to Captain Pell's sleeping area and quietly pulled the curtain that covered the body down off Pell's face. Lifting the fallen pilot's head, the figure took Pell's pillow before replacing his head and pulling the curtain back up over Pell's body.

After stealing Captain Pell's pillow, the figure crossed the cell and stretched an arm out. At the end of the arm was a hand, and in the hand was a gun: a single-action Colt revolver. The figure used the nozzle of the pistol to gingerly open the curtain and then slipped inside the sleeping area of his prey.

CHAPTER FIFTY-FOUR

Special Agent Hal Northrop emerged from his sleeping area with a lot on his mind. He was desperate to find leverage, and his calm and confident demeanor was eroding away, so he was taken aback by what he saw.

Lieutenant Kelley Pike was sitting in his usual spot at the round table in the centre of the heptagon-shaped cell, and he was staring right into Sergeant J.P. Kaye, who was standing over top of him, clearly agitated. Northrop joined the men, and as soon as he approached them, Kaye began to speak.

"Pike murdered Paxton, Northrop," Kaye stated. "He's dead."

Northrop looked from Kaye to Pike. "Pike?" Northrop asked with shock in his voice.

"He's half right, Company," Pike replied.

Northrop went to Paxton's sleeping area, pulled the curtain wide, and went inside; Kaye followed. After a moment, Pike struggled to his feet and followed.

There was an entry wound in Paxton's forehead, and what was once inside Paxton's skull was now all over his cot and pillow. Beside Paxton's cot was a second pillow that had been shot through. Northrop picked up the second pillow.

"Silencer," he said.

"Silencer?" Kaye repeated as a question.

"Yes. Whoever shot Paxton used the pillow to muffle the sound of the revolver. A silencer," Northrop explained.

"Then that makes it easy," Kaye said. "We need to check everyone's sleeping area, and then whoever no longer has a pillow is our killer."

"Fuck, you're stupid," Pike said, and then walked back to the table and sat down in his chair.

"It won't work, Kaye," Northrop said. "If the killer was smart enough to use a pillow, he was smart enough to take Pell's pillow."

"Why Pell's pillow?" Kaye asked.

"Because dead men tell no tales, Blinkey." Pike hollered from the table.

"And," Northrop added, "we don't know who came in overnight. Someone comes in with gruel and someone left the revolver. That same someone could have killed Paxton to turn us against each other."

"Little late for that, Company," Pike said.

The three men stayed where they were a few moments: Pike at the table, Kaye and Northrop right by Paxton's cot with the curtain pulled wide open. It was then that the door to the cell opened and Dr. Reynolds entered, flanked by Briggs.

"Kaye," Pike said. "Somebody's here for you."

CHAPTER FIFTY-FIVE

When Kaye heard Pike's voice, he turned and looked at the table to see Dr. Reynolds and Sergeant Briggs standing there at the opposite end of the table's diameter from where Pike was sitting. Kaye was overcome with fear. He shuffled out, away from Paxton's cot and over to the table, stopping beside Pike.

"Pike...?" Kaye asked.

"What, Blinkey?" Pike answered with a chuckle.

"Aren't you going to...you know...stand up and tell them I don't need to go?" Kaye asked.

"Nope," Pike said.

"Why not? You did it for Pell," Kaye said.

"But I don't like you, Blinkey."

Kaye looked up again at the doctor and then at the silverback in sheer terror.

"Sergeant Kaye, we are just going to talk. As long as you don't resist, Briggs will not lay a hand on you. You have my word," Dr. Reynolds said.

"But when you talked to Pell..." Kaye started.

"Sergeant, Captain Pell was a monster; you are a soldier. I think you will enjoy our chat. You will come back better than ever," Dr. Reynolds said. "And at no time did Sergeant Briggs ever lay a finger on Captain Pell; Pell's death was at Pell's own hands." Defeated, Kaye walked around the table, past Dr. Reynolds, and headed for the door. Reynolds followed him, and Briggs brought up the rear. As they were exiting the cell, Briggs turned back and looked at Pike.

"How are your teeth, tough guy?" Briggs asked, mocking Pike.

"They don't bite into my cheek anymore," Pike replied. "How do you like breathing through your mouth, ape?"

"Briggs! Leave it alone!" Reynolds hollered back into the cell, and Briggs followed the sound of Reynolds' voice out into the corridor.

After the cell door shut, Northrop looked at Pike. "You really don't like him very much, do you?"

"Nope," Pike replied as he struggle to his feet. "But don't feel too bad, Company. I don't like you either." Pike walked over to Northrop. "Are you done with your crime scene, Company?"

"Yes. Go ahead, Pike." Pike pushed passed Northrop and went to Paxton's cot. Pike then struggled down to his knees beside Paxton, just as he had done for Pell. Pike began offering a prayer over Paxton's body, doing his best to offer some sort of last rite. Northrop had taken up post behind him, hands clasped in front with his head bowed down, the way Paxton had done when Pike was praying over Pell.

After Pike had completed his prayer, he looked down at Paxton's body, and he stiffened. Northrop watched closely, and he was shocked by what he saw. Pike was crying.

CHAPTER FIFTY-SIX

The long walk down the dark, cold, grey corridor outside the cell was the longest walk in Sergeant Kaye's life. Kaye walked the length of the corridor shoulder to shoulder with Dr. Reynolds, but it was the sound of Sergeant Briggs walking behind him that made the corridor seemed to stretch on forever.

When Kaye and his escorts, Master Sergeant Withers and Sergeant Briggs, arrived at the end of the long corridor, there was a steel door. This new steel door was much smaller and less ominous than the steel door on the opposite end of the corridor that lead to the heptagon-shaped cell. The second door was a double door, large enough for maintenance and building materials to pass through, but the first door, the one leading to the cell, was larger, thicker, and somehow scarier.

Through the new door was a different kind of corridor. This new corridor was no different than any other corridor in any military base the world over. There were fluorescent lights, grey paint over steel walls, and the smells of disinfectant cleaners and stale recycled air. This new corridor was identical to the corridors Kaye had walked along his entire military career. Kaye suddenly felt at ease.

"Sergeant Kaye," Dr. Reynolds said, "I have a few matters to attend to before we have our chat, but rather than have you wait for me in the interview room, I want you to go with Sergeant Briggs. Briggs will see to it you get a much-needed hot shower." Reynolds looked at Kaye, and after a few moments, Kaye nodded, slowly and silently, in agreement. "Very good, Sergeant Kaye," Reynolds continued. "Briggs, please see to it that the Sergeant gets some fresh clothes as well."

"Yes sir, Dr. Reynolds," Briggs replied, and then he ushered Kaye onward up the corridor the way one might help a passenger on a train or a theatre-goer find their seat.

Briggs took Kaye through the military complex, not through the main level above them, but along the twists and turns of the subterranean level where they were located; had Kaye not been focusing on controlling his fear, he might have realized they were below ground by the absence of windows.

As Briggs led Kaye through the well-lit familiar labyrinth that was a generic military base, he was beginning to sense a turn in his luck. Kaye reasoned that he would not be allowed to see the whole of the facility if they had simply planned to beat him down like a dog, the way they had beaten Paxton and Pike. Kaye began to slowly allow his pride to swell within his chest. Kaye concluded that he had something they needed or wanted, and they were willing to deal.

After they snaked their way through the facility, Briggs finally brought Kaye to the locker room. It was huge. There were double-sized lockers along the walls, and long benches for dressing. In one corner there was a leisure area with a few sofa chairs and a television. There was a sauna and a steam room off one wall, and there was a door to a restroom facility, and beyond that, showers, and sinks with mirrors for shaving, but it was what came next that impressed Kaye the most.

Briggs took Kaye to a locker that had his name affixed to it with a small brass nameplate: *Srgt. Kaye, J.P.* Kaye was beginning to see the upside of his ordeal; the light at the end of the tunnel was shining through, and Kaye intended to go to the light.

When Kaye opened his locker, he found brand new battle dress fatigues and boots; all of them looked to be a perfect fit. There was also a large bath towel, some soap, shampoo, a shaving kit, and even moisturizing lotion.

"These are mine?" Kaye asked Briggs, staring into his locker in a state somewhere between disbelief and hope.

"Yes. Dr. Reynolds told me you were the guy. I don't see it though. Get cleaned up, but stay around here. I will be here to take you to the doctor when you're ready." Kaye nodded his agreement to Briggs, and Briggs retired to the back corner, the leisure area where the chairs were, and turned on the television. His orders were to not make Kaye feel watched, and to partially ignore him, so Briggs did his best to pretend to be doing that.

Kaye's first move was to go to the steam room, where he unknotted. After fifteen minutes in the steam, Kaye sat on the bench and waited for his body to stop sweating. Then Kaye moved on to the main event, a hot shower. Kaye had no idea how long it had been since he last had a hot shower, but he knew it was well overdue. Kaye showered for nearly thirty minutes.

The hot water and soap felt good on his skin, and when he emerged from the shower, Kaye's body felt renewed, and his mental state crisp and positive. Kaye had never felt better.

After his shower, Kaye wrapped himself in a towel and shaved. First, he used the scissors from the shaving kit to cut his beard down to avoid painfully pulling his facial hair with the blade. Next he shaved to the bare skin with his new razor blade. Finally, Kaye splashed on the moisturizing lotion, slicked back his hair, and looked at himself in the mirror. Kaye had never been prouder of his reflection.

Next, Kaye dressed in his new, crisp, perfectly fitting fatigues. Kaye had never realized how good new clothes could feel on a man, but now he did. They were new clothes and he was a new man. After a good long look at himself in the mirror, Kaye walked away from the mirror and over toward the area where Briggs had been pretending to ignore him.

Kaye's stride had changed after he had enjoyed his hot shower and donned his new clothes; Kaye was walking fully erect with pride and purpose. When he made it to Briggs' side,

Kaye spoke with more authority and confidence than he had displayed in his voice in a long time.

"I'm ready now. Take me see the doctor." There was even arrogance in Kaye's voice as he looked up at the monster of a man charged with delivering the sniper to the psychologist.

Chapter Fifty-Seven

Special Agent Hal Northrop was sitting at the round table in the heptagon-shaped cell, staring at the slowly ticking clock on the wall, but not focusing on the faulty timepiece. For Northrop, the clock had simply become a direction point to stare at as he waited.

Lieutenant Kelley Pike was lying flat on the concrete floor of the heptagon room, his body stretched away from the table with his feet up on a chair, smoking a cigarette. The men had sat in silence for some time before finally Pike inhaled his cigarette and spoke.

"Company, you never said what it was you did at Gitmo." Pike exhaled his smoke and it rose towards the ceiling.

"Does it matter much now?" Northrop replied, trying his best to hide his nervousness from his voice.

"Not anymore." Pike inhaled his cigarette again. "So where do you think we are?"

"I don't know," Northrop lied, while thinking, *does he know?* "Where do you think we are, Pike?"

"I don't know." Pike exhaled smoke. "For all I know, we are in a sub-basement at Guantanamo Bay."

"You think?" Northrop responded, trying sound cool and detached, while thinking, *Does he know?*

"I don't know, Company," Pike said, and the two men sat in silence for a long time. Northrop was just beginning to relax when Pike spoke again.

"Hey, Company, have you ever been to South America?"

"No," Northrop lied while still thinking, *Does he know?*

"I spent a lot of time down there before some spook pinched me." Pike inhaled the last bit of his cigarette and tossed the butt. "I don't think you would like it down there, though."

"Why is that?" Northrop asked.

"American spooks stand out down there. Big feeling guys in cheap suits. You bastards just can't ever seem to blend in." Pike exhaled smoke.

"Then I'll stay clear of the southern hemisphere," Northrop replied, but he was thinking, *Does he know?*

CHAPTER FIFTY-EIGHT

Dr. Reynolds' office was not a large office, nor was it a small one. The doctor's office consisted of a window, a desk, a small table, chairs, and several filing cabinets. In fact, Reynolds' office was identical in dimensions to Braun's, and the government-issue furniture in each office was likewise identical. The only real difference between Dr. Reynolds' office and that of Lieutenant Colonel Braun was the illusion of Reynolds' office being smaller because Braun had no filing cabinets in hers. Of course, Dr. Reynolds was not really waiting for Sergeant Kaye in his office, because much like Braun, the doctor's office was on the surface, and Kaye was to be confined to the subterranean facility.

Dr. Reynolds was sitting in the first chair at the rectangular table in the very interrogation room where he had given Captain Pell his cyanide capsule. Opposite where Dr. Reynolds was sitting was the empty chair once occupied by Captain Pell, and the cameras were once again trained at that chair. The camera located on the ceiling where the south wall met the west wall looked down at the empty chair and captured part of Dr. Reynolds on the edge of the frame. The camera on the ceiling where the north wall met the east wall had a tighter focus waiting on the new occupant of the chair to fill the frame: Sergeant Kaye.

On the rectangular table there was a metal serving tray with a metal cover over it, and beside the tray there was a glass of water and a mug of coffee, hot, with steam rising out of the mug. There was a second mug of coffee gripped tightly in Dr. Reynolds' hand.

Reynolds had been timing the meal to coincide with the expected arrival of Sergeant Kaye to the room, and the coffee was indeed still hot when there was a knock at the door.

"Come in, Briggs," Reynolds replied to the knocking sounds at the door. The door to Dr. Reynolds' office opened and Sergeant Briggs ushered in Sergeant Kaye. "Thank you, Briggs. Please give us about an hour, then come back," Reynolds ordered.

"Yes sir," Briggs replied and left the doctor's office, closing the door behind him.

"Sit, Sergeant Kaye," Reynolds said, pointing to the empty chair, and Kaye sat right down.

Once Kaye had sat down, Dr. Reynolds reached across the table and took the lid off the serving tray to reveal a hot meal of bacon, eggs, Texas toast, hash browns, and some fruit.

"Please, Sergeant, help yourself to your breakfast." Dr. Reynolds sat back and sipped his coffee.

The table between the two men was a contrast to the table back in the cell. The table in the cell was round, with no clear head and therefore no clear power dynamic; the prisoners lived in equality. The rectangular table in front of the two men was different from the round table in both shape and symbol. The rectangular table had a head position, even though neither man was sitting at it. In fact, the clear absence of a person at the head of the table suggested that both men had a higher-ranking commander to answer to, and by inference that officer was the same entity. Kaye was now subconsciously perceiving Reynolds as his teammate a little bit more with each passing moment.

Dr. Reynolds had five bases running this scenario, and in all five he had identical tables in each cell and each interrogation room. The tables became symbols; in the cell they were the center of a fragmented and disenfranchised community, and in the interrogation room, they were the structure of a more formidable community. The symbol the rectangular table represented to Kaye was structure and opportunity; for Kaye it was a chance to belong again, and a way out.

Kaye pulled the steel serving palate of hot food towards him, and he began to eat. This was the first meal of substance that Sergeant Kaye had enjoyed in a very long time. Dr. Reynolds watched the way Kaye took into the food, and through his body language he knew that Kaye was the man he needed to be talking to, so the doctor smiled and began to talk as Kaye continued to eat.

"It is good," Dr. Reynolds said, referring to the meal Kaye was eating. "One of the few luxuries we have here is the mess. Of course, by 'we,' I mean staff, and not you, obviously...not yet, anyway." Reynolds was choosing his words with purpose. "It is among the best in the military. I have eaten at a few in my time, but the food here, at the base – well, it is definitely top quality food, to say the least." As Reynolds was speaking, Kaye had kept his head down and his focus on the food in front of him.

"Soldier's instinct," Reynolds said, referring to the manner with which Kaye was eating. "Eat when you can, sleep when you can. It is amazingly similar to the behavioral patterns of incarcerated men. I have always found that fascinating."

Kaye finished his meal quickly and without speaking. After he was done, Kaye reached for the mug of coffee, picked it up, and sat back in his chair.

"I am sorry about the milk and sugar, or lack of, I should say. It seems that they were omitted." Reynolds then timed it so that he and Kaye took a sip of coffee. "Nonetheless, it is good coffee."

Dr. Reynolds continued to sip on his coffee, waiting for Sergeant Kaye to take the initiative, and the bait, and ask the question he had been fed. After a minute, Kaye did just that.

"What did you mean by 'not yet'?" Kaye asked, once he had allowed his meal a few minutes to settle in his belly.

"Direct. I like that. It is what I expected of you." At that moment, Reynolds knew he had Kaye fully committed to the sinister plan; the pawn had been moved ahead on sacrifice. "Well, we will get to that, Sergeant, but first, tell me something. Do you know why you were brought here, to this facility specifically? You and your cellmates, I mean."

"We know things you want to know. You want our secrets, our military secrets. It is the only reason that makes sense," Kaye said.

"Sergeant Kaye," Dr. Reynolds replied. "You know nothing, have nothing, and in no way have knowledge of any military secret I want. Everything there is to know about you, I already know."

"Are you sure?" Kaye responded with arrogance.

"Are you referring to the Middle East? You and your partner...Hamilton, wasn't it?" Dr. Reynolds had planned the flow of this conversation perfectly, exactly anticipating Kaye's responses to his questions.

"Yes," Kaye replied. "Hamilton was selling secrets. We were sent to eliminate a target. After he shot the target my orders were to..."

"His orders, you mean." Reynolds cut Kaye off, and Kaye became confused and anxious, shattered. "You see," Dr. Reynolds continued, "I know the truth. They were Hamilton's orders. You were the one selling secrets, not him. He was ordered to eliminate you. You reasoned it out, changed the assignment. You shot him right through the scope before he ever even shot your target." Reynolds enjoyed a long sip of his coffee.

"H-h-how?" Kaye stammered in surprise.

"I have very good clearance, and the moment you shot him I heard about it, and that was when you were selected for this experiment. Consider yourself lucky...had I passed on you, your next partner would have eliminated you." Dr. Reynolds was now becoming very stern in his address.

"So...why am I here?" Kaye asked nervously.

"Because, Kaye," Reynolds replied, "you are a survivor. All that matters to you is surviving: not living, not growing, not duty. Surviving." Dr. Reynolds took another sip of coffee and then he continued to address Kaye. "It was your attention to detail and your analytical skills, the skills that led to Hamilton's assassination, that saved your life: your will to survive at all costs and your ability to ferret out the details," Reynolds lied. "So back to your question, the first one: what I meant by '*not yet.*' The moment you asked that question, I knew you were the one to deal with."

"What do you mean?" Kaye asked.

"My name is Doctor Reynolds. I am here to develop some aggressive interrogation techniques. Your entire group, your cell, the environment: those are the elements of my research. When I run this scenario, there are always one or two out of the five soldiers selected with information I want to extract – the rest I know everything about. They are window dressing. In your group, I am concerned with Lieutenant Pike. You get me Pike's secret, and I will make you part of my team. Prove you can manipulate information out of others, and you will be on my staff. Every time we run this scenario, you will be in the room, and I will rely on you to sniff out secrets from the other four. When you're not in the holding room, you will eat like this every day and go back on Uncle Sam's payroll." Dr. Reynolds smiled because he knew that he owned Sergeant Kaye.

"What do you want me to find out, sir?" Kaye asked dutifully.

"What happened in Colombia," Reynolds said.

CHAPTER FIFTY-NINE

The heavy steel door to the heptagon-shaped cell opened and Sergeant J.P. Kaye walked in briskly. Kaye was no longer walking with the body language of a prisoner; he was walking like a man with pride and power. Northrop saw Kaye, and he knew exactly how the conversation with Reynolds had gone. Northrop had been hoping that Reynolds could not turn Kaye on the rest of them, but Kaye's strut said it all.

Kaye strolled right to the table and sat down. Pike began to force himself off the ground, one grunt and groan at a time.

"Well, you look fresh as a daisy," Northrop said to Kaye, looking across the small table at the sniper.

As Northrop was speaking, Pike made it to his feet, and stepped over to Kaye, then sniffed the air.

"They fed you," Pike barked at Kaye.

"How did you know?" Kaye asked Pike.

"Because," Northrop interjected, "you smell like coffee and bacon."

"Figures," Pike said. "They beat me, then they feed Blinkey. Northrop, you'll probably get a day at the beach." Pike set himself down in his chair and took out one of

Paxton's cigarettes, put it between his lips, and then fished out his lighter. Pike's lighter did not spark on the first strike, but on the second strike the flame appeared, and Pike drew the flame into the nail before shutting the lighter off and then slinking gingerly back into his chair.

Kaye looked to Northrop and made eye contact, and then nodded past him towards the corner with the clock. After that, Kaye got up and walked to the corner and stood below the clock. Northrop looked at Pike, who was now smoking with his eyes closed, and then he stood up and walked over to the clock.

When Northrop made it to the corner, Kaye leaned into him and began whispering in hushed tones.

"Hal, we need to work together," Kaye said.

"To do what?" Northrop asked, knowing the answer.

"We need to discover Pike's secret. We are going to be next unless we break him." Kaye paused and leaned in very close before continuing. "Hal, if we can break him, I can get us out of here."

Northrop turned his head away from Kaye and stared at Pike. *Does Pike know?* Northrop thought.

"Kaye," Northrop said, "guys like Pike, they do not break. They break others." As soon as Northrop had finished speaking the door to the cell opened and Withers strolled into the dark, grey room, once again flanked by Briggs and Patterson. Without opening his eyes, Pike called out to Northrop from the table.

"Northrop," Pike said, casually, "your ride to the beach is here." Northrop took a breath and then crossed the room and approached Withers.

"Benedict here yet?" Northrop asked Withers, with forced bravado.

"Not yet, sir," Withers replied.

"He will be here soon," Northrop said.

"Most likely, sir," Withers agreed, and then Northrop walked past Withers, through the large steel door, and out of the heptagon-shaped cell. Withers turned smartly and followed Northrop; Patterson turned smartly and followed Withers.

Briggs lingered a moment and looked at Pike. Pike had not opened his eyes. After a moment, satisfied he had made a point, Briggs turned and walked to the cell door, and just as it was about to close, Pike spoke from the table, still relaxed with his eyes closed.

"We are going to dance again, Sunshine, you and I," Pike stated in a calm challenge to Briggs. The silverback's head snapped back to look towards Pike, but the large steel door closed before Briggs had the opportunity to respond.

After the steel door closed on the heptagonal cell, the room grew silent. Kaye remained by the clock, staring at Pike, who remained at the table, slunk low in his chair with his eyes closed. "So tell me the truth, Blinkey," Pike said, "how do you really feel about me?" There was silence for several moments before Pike continued, "Yeah, I thought so." Pike inhaled his cigarette deeply, flicked the butt away, and then exhaled the smoke.

CHAPTER SIXTY

Special Agent Hal Northrop walked out of the cold grey cell briskly, as if exiting that tomb was in itself his resurrection and he was returning to his former position within the company ranks. Once he was seven or eight feet deep into the corridor, Northrop paused and listened. Northrop heard all of the soldiers fall in line, and then he heard the cell door close.

"I believe you know the way, sir," Withers stated.

"Which one are we in?" Northrop asked.

"It doesn't matter, sir. The floor plans are identical," Withers replied. "But that was a nice try," he added.

Northrop began to walk briskly, head held high with false bravado, taking crisp, sharp steps and long purposeful strides down the long corridor. Withers followed Northrop, Patterson followed Withers, and Briggs followed Patterson.

Northrop got halfway down the corridor and paused to speak, without looking back.

"Withers, are we going to the doctor's office, the interrogation centre, or the other place?" Northrop asked.

"The other place, sir," Withers replied with a sinister smile.

"Damn," Northrop said, and then resumed his purposeful stride straight towards his oncoming fears.

CHAPTER SIXTY-ONE

Lieutenant Kelley Pike was leaning his head back on his chair, smoking a cigarette with his eyes closed, but still he knew exactly what was happening in the heptagon-shaped tomb. There was only him and Sergeant J.P. Kaye in the cell now, just like it had been so very long ago when Kaye woke up in the lion's den with the alpha beast.

Kaye was now sitting on the floor, directly beneath the clock, with his legs pulled in close to his chest; all his confidence had walked out of the cell with Hal Northrop. Kaye hated Pike. Kaye hated Pike because Pike was bullying him. Kaye hated Pike because Pike was an alpha dog and Kaye had always been a beta. Kaye hated Pike because Kaye wanted to be more like Pike, intimidating and rugged, but mostly Kaye hated Pike because Kaye was afraid of Pike.

"So, tell me, Blinkey," Pike said, as he exhaled cigarette smoke. "Have you ever killed anyone without using a sniper rifle five hundred yards out, hiding in a tree or on a rooftop?" Pike took in the silence that filled the slot in the air reserved for Kaye's response, and then he continued. "Have you ever killed anyone up close? Like a man would? With a machete, or just your bare hands?" Pike paused. "Or even a Colt revolver?"

Kaye listened to Pike, and then he sat in silence for a few moments before he abruptly stood up and walked off into his sleeping area to sit on his cot, leaving Pike in the main cell area alone, laughing.

CHAPTER SIXTY-TWO

The door to the torture chamber opened, and Special Agent Northrop walked into the room briskly, like he owned it. Truthfully, that was not too terribly far from the truth, from a certain point of view. As soon as he was through the door, Northrop surveyed the room and saw it was mostly empty, but not completely. In the center of the room there was a wooden chair with a wooden spoke back and wooden arm rests; the chair was identical to the chairs in the heptagon-shaped cell. Beside the chair were steel pails filled with water, and on the chair were cable ties and a black hood. *Water-boarding,* Northrop thought. *Ironic.*

Northrop moved a few steps to one side of the door and permitted Master Sergeant Withers to enter the room, followed by Patterson and Briggs. "You like the setup, sir?" Withers asked.

"I liked it better on your end of the experiment," Northrop replied.

"This was one of your favorite techniques, was it not, sir?" Withers asked mockingly.

"I believed it to be efficient," Northrop responded evenly.

"Did it ever work?" Withers asked.

"It would have on a few," Northrop justified.

"The ones that drowned, sir?" Withers asked, rhetorically.

"You were there, Withers," Northrop reminded the Master Sergeant.

"Yes, I was," Withers smiled. "If you had let me do it, those men would have lived...at least long enough to talk." Withers paused briefly before continuing, "Shall I ask the soldiers to seat you?"

"No, no need." Northrop walked to the chair, and he stood in front of it a long time looking at the chair and the hood. Finally, Northrop picked up the hood and cable ties and sat down. Northrop was still racing through his thoughts, looking for an exit.

"You got away with it a long time, sir," Withers said, and then nodded to Briggs and Patterson, who in turn took the cable ties from Northrop's hands and began to secure his wrists and ankles to the chair.

"It was not exactly discouraged by our government," Northrop said. "But I was smart enough not to do it to Benedict Cain's subjects. Are you sure this is the route you want to go down? Benedict is very protective of this experiment."

"I have my orders, sir," Withers responded with a large smile. Withers waited until Patterson and Briggs had secured Northrop to the chair before he put his hand out, and Briggs passed him the hood, and then he continued to speak. "It's a woman, by the way, sir."

"Who, Withers?" Northrop said, but truthfully he knew what Withers was referencing, even if he did not know to whom.

"Your replacement," Withers replied. "Cain chose a woman this time. And not a company woman; he selected a soldier. A lieutenant colonel." Withers took a few steps forward and stopped just in front of Northrop. Withers held out the hood, as if he was going to place it on Northrop's head, and then he said, "We do not have to do this, sir."

"Yes, we do," Northrop replied, knowing that he knew nothing that Benedict Cain or Dr. Reynolds did not already know. His only secret, the one that put him here, must have been discovered, or he would not be strapped to the wooden chair waiting to be water-boarded.

As Withers began to put the hood on Northrop, the door to the room opened and Dr. Reynolds walked into the torture chamber.

"No, we don't need to do this," Reynolds said. "Withers, cut him loose." Withers nodded to Briggs, who unsheathed a knife and cut the cable ties around Northrop's ankles and wrists. "Withers, you and your men can wait outside."

"Very good, sir." Withers nodded to Patterson and Briggs and they exited, followed by Master Sergeant Withers, who closed the door behind him.

"Bill," Northrop said to William Reynolds by way of greeting.

"Hal, why did you do it?" Reynolds asked.

"Ambition, I guess," Northrop answered.

"You didn't think he would know?" Reynolds asked.

"I didn't think he was omnipotent," Northrop replied

"I always assumed he was," Reynolds said gravely.

"So where are we?" Northrop asked Reynolds.

"You know better, Hal," Reynolds replied.

"At least tell me if we are still at Gitmo." Reynolds ignored the question and instead went to the door and knocked, and Withers opened it. "Master Sergeant, send down to the mess and get me two cups of coffee."

"Yes, sir." Withers closed the door and Reynolds went over to one of the buckets and dumped the water out, then he turned it over and sat on it like a stool.

"You know, we have these facilities on certain bases, and not even the soldiers on the bases know we are there." Reynolds thought for a moment. "Hal, I can't tell you which base we are on, but you're a bright guy, so you probably have that figured out already anyhow. I am not putting my neck out. I will not cross Benedict Cain."

"Can you tell me why I am here?" Northrop asked.

"You know why, Hal. You crossed him." Reynolds paused. "No one gets to do that."

"How do we fix this, Bill?" Northrop asked. "There has to be a way." As Northrop finished speaking, there was a knock at the door.

"Come," Reynolds said to the door, and it opened to reveal Sergeant Patterson with two cups of coffee. Patterson walked over and gave a coffee to each man. "Dismissed, Patterson." And with that, Patterson exited.

Reynolds and Northrop both enjoyed a few sips of coffee before Reynolds spoke again.

"Lucky for you I showed up, or they would have water-boarded you to death, because you really do not have any information that I don't know, and they would never believe that."

"I had it pegged as a stress test," Northrop said.

"Yes, well, with this new C.O., you got lucky I claimed you first." Reynolds took a deep breath. "I had nothing to do with your cellmates being beaten."

"I didn't think so," Northrop said. "You know I never touched any of your subjects."

"I know," Reynolds agreed. "You did put a lot of tough guys through the gears though," Reynolds stated.

"Yeah, and I really believed I was right," Northrop said.

"Believed?" Reynolds asked. "Past tense?"

"The cell has me rethinking it."

"Why?" Reynolds pushed.

"I have never seen eyes as dead as Pike's." Northrop took a sip of coffee. "I finally believe you. Guys like him….you just can't break a man that is already that broken."

"Well, Hal, Pike is the answer to your question. The one about a way back," Reynolds said.

"What do you mean?" Northrop asked, afraid he knew the answer and that Reynolds was about to propose a no-win situation.

"Usually, I have two guys in there with secrets I need, but you got one of those spots, and I know exactly what your secret is, so this time there is just one guy, Pike. I have more pull with Benedict Cain than anyone, you know that. If you can get it out of him, I can save your life." Reynolds took a sip of coffee.

"What about my facility? Will I get that back?" Northrop asked.

"No. But I can get your life spared. I can get you on my team, and over time maybe some privileges. I can give you the position we always promise someone. It's a start, Hal. Benedict is not a forgiving man; this is a once in a lifetime opportunity. It is the only shot you will ever have, and the clock is ticking. You know no one has lived through this yet. Hal, let's make you the first."

Northrop gave his coffee cup a hard long look, and he thought, *damned pride*. "All right, Bill. Let's do it. What can you tell me about the secret?"

"Well, it should be easy for you. Find out what happened to Pike in Colombia," Reynolds replied. "Benedict sent you personally to Colombia to get him, so you should have some clues."

"Damn," Northrop said. "He is going to be hard to crack."

"What do you mean by that?" Reynolds asked.

"He already lied about it to me once," Northrop replied.

"How?" Reynolds asked.

"He said it was a five man operation," Northrop explained.

"That's what Benedict said in the briefing, but that is about all he said. He just told me it was part of a five man operation in Colombia, and that Pike was the biggest asshole in JTF2."

Northrop raised his coffee cup to his lips and took a sip.

"He went into the jungle alone. It was a one-man mission," Northrop revealed to Reynolds, with his eyes cast down at his coffee and desperation in his voice.

CHAPTER SIXTY-THREE

Special Agent Hal Northrop was wearing a black power suit and unnecessarily expensive dark sunglasses; his suit was not a very good selection for a trip into the jungle, and his elaborate glasses were not a very good selection to win the respect of the front line soldiers. The look was all about image, and rising to the top of the company was more about the image than it was about the sensible choices that earn respect from the men beneath you. Northrop was an excellent image builder.

Northrop was riding shotgun in a military Jeep travelling north to a base camp at an undisclosed location from a secret landing strip at another undisclosed location; officially, Northrop's mission did not exist, and this journey through the jungles of South America was not happening.

The unofficial drive on the nonexistent mission was about two hours, and required secretly crossing over the border from Peru to Colombia. As the Jeep neared the base camp, Colonel Hauser, United States Army Ranger, stepped out of his tent to watch the approach.

When Colonel Hauser saw how Northrop was dressed, he thought, *Typical company man.* The Jeep pulled to a stop a few feet from where the colonel was standing, and he waited for the typical show to be done.

Northrop pulled up on the roll bars and then slung his legs out from the Jeep, as if he wanted to ensure all eyes were on him. He threw himself out of the Jeep, and then he put his palms on his lower back and arched backwards before standing up slowly, deliberately, and just for display. Northrop scanned the area right to left and up and down, and then finally he walked over to the colonel and stretched out his hand. "Special Agent Hal Northrop," Northrop said.

"I know," Colonel Hauser responded gruffly. *Typical company man,* he thought again, *arrogant.* Hauser had long ago given up offering a handshake to men like Northrop, but since Northrop did offer one, Hauser shook hands; to Hauser, this handshake was a political maneuver to protect his career, nothing more.

"Let's go into my command tent." Hauser pointed to his tent and Northrop walked in first.

The tent was as spacious as a small cabin, and it had a desk and chairs. Hauser passed Northrop, went to his desk, and selected the chair behind it and waited. Hauser had given up offering seats to men like Northrop; instead, he just waited for the show, and the show began.

Northrop took his sunglasses off slowly, moving them partway down his nose and then scanning the room, and pretending he was satisfied with an inspection he was not really conducting, Northrop then fully removed his glasses.

Northrop thought his techniques for establishing himself as an authority worked very well; Hauser thought he was pain in the ass.

"When will Lieutenant Pike be back?" Northrop asked as he sat down in a chair opposite Hauser.

"If he is on schedule, at oh-fourteen hundred hours. So I am going to say noon." Hauser responded.

"Really?" Northrop asked.

"Do you know what we soldiers call Pike?" Hauser asked the special agent. "He has a bit of a reputation."

"No," Northrop admitted.

"Effective but expendable," Hauser stated. "You see, he is very, very good at what he does, and damned near impossible to kill."

"Then as an asset, why is he expendable?" Northrop asked.

"His personality," Hauser said flatly. "That is why we were able to get him on loan from JTF2; none of us like to loan out our best." Hauser waited a beat and then continued, "How do you plan to abduct him?"

"I am going to slip something in his dinner at the mess. It is what I always do. It works," Northrop said with arrogance.

Hauser reached into his desk and produced a dart and a gun, and then he slid it to Northrop. "This will work better."

"Colonel, I know my job and I am very good at it," Northrop stated.

"And I know Pike," Hauser said coolly. "And if you try it that way, he'll kill you, and probably the rest of us. It won't work. Pike sees a company man and he kills him on sight, no questions asked and no concerns about the consequences. You would not be the first one."

"I doubt that," Northrop said.

With respect, Special Agent Northrop, Kelley Pike is a killer." Hauser's voice became very grave. "And I don't mean he has killed in the line of duty, like a soldier. And I don't mean he left a dozen bodies in a dumpster or alley like a psychopath or serial killer. I mean, in the coldest sense, Pike is a killer. No thought, no compunction, no remorse. And no one is better at killing than him."

"And with all due respect, Colonel Hauser," Northrop replied in a condescending tone, "no one just kills company men. No one would be that foolish."

"Oh?" Hauser raised an eyebrow. "You realize you guys are the reason he went to a Russian Gulag? You guys screwed him over. Don't test your theory, Northrop. It will just get us both dead."

Northrop looked at Hauser, and then he reached out and picked up the gun and the dart.

"It is getting pretty close to noon, Mr. Northrop."

"Special Agent," Northrop interrupted and corrected Hauser.

"You are no one special to me, son," Hauser responded. "You may want to be scarce. When Pike gets here you don't want to be seen, and I sure as the devil do not want to be seen with you."

Northrop stood up and tucked the gun and dart away. "Do you have any men out there watching for them? So we can get a proper E.T.A?" Northrop asked.

"Them?" Hauser said.

"There were five men deployed into that jungle. I have copies of the orders," Northrop said.

"I just sent Pike," Hauser said.

"What?" Northrop was not often shocked, but he was now. "Just one, for a five man mission?"

"Mr. Northrop, Pike *is* five men. Four more would have slowed him down," Hauser said.

"Colonel…" Northrop started, but Hauser cut him off.

"Do you know what this mission is, what Pike was sent to do?" Hauser asked.

"No," Northrop admitted.

"Well I do, and I don't know of any other man in the military with stomach enough to do this, let alone keep it secret," Hauser said. "No, Mr. Northrop, Pike was perfect for this because he is effective and expendable, and so I kept the other four men here. They have no clue what Pike's mission is, and I don't want them to ever know. That alone would be hard to live with. I haven't been able to sleep since Benedict Cain told me about this sick…"

"What is the mission?" Northrop asked with genuine, morbid, ambitious curiosity.

"Mr. Cain didn't tell you?" Hauser asked.

"No. But I can handle it," Northrop replied.

"Then ask Benedict Cain to tell you, because I will not be telling anyone."

"You realize how high my clearance goes, right?" Northrop said, making a veiled threat. "With my influence working against you, your career could be over."

"You could be the Pope himself taking my deathbed confession. I will not cross Benedict Cain."

"Colonel, you don't need to worry about Benedict Cain very much longer. I am his successor; he just doesn't know it yet. Don't fear the puppet, fear the puppet master."

"You want to be careful talking that way, Northrop." *Pride goeth before the fall*, Hauser thought. *Arrogant.*

"Colonel, I have been two steps ahead of Benedict Cain my entire career. I manipulate him to my ends, not the other way around," Northrop said, adding, "As I said, he is the puppet and I am the puppet master." With that, Northrop walked out of Hauser's command tent, and then Hauser took a glass and bottle of gin out of his desk and had a drink, and he waited.

About thirty minutes after Northrop left the command tent, Lieutenant Kelley Pike walked into the command tent unannounced, as if he owned the place. Pike was covered in blood, head to toe, and in his left hand he was holding a machete; the blade was also coated in dried blood. Over Pike's right shoulder was a bloody duffel bag, likewise caked in dried blood. Pike dropped his machete, and then he un-slung the duffel bag from his shoulder and tossed it to the floor in front of Hauser's desk.

Pike walked over to the desk and sat down in a chair opposite Hauser. Hauser stood up and passed his bottle of gin to Pike, who took a pull right out of the bottle and then passed it back. As Hauser sat, he poured himself a drink into a glass. Pike threw his feet up on the desk and pulled out a plastic tube, opened it, and produced a cigar. Next, Pike fished out his lighter. Pike bit the tip off his cigar, flicked open his lighter, sparked a flame, and began to draw the flame into the cigar. Once the end of Pike's cigar was burning red, he slapped his lighter closed and put it in his pocket.

"Your report, Lieutenant," Hauser commanded.

Pike took a long puff off his cigar, and then he took it out of his mouth and held it between his thumb and forefinger, and watched it burn as he spoke. "We are all going to burn in hell for what we did here." As Pike began to put his cigar back to his lips, Northrop stepped into the tent with the dart gun drawn and he fired; the dart landed in the side of Pike's neck, where the neck met the shoulder. Pike's head pitched forward and his eyes popped out wide. Pike got to his feet and turned to see Northrop.

The two men locked eyes and Pike began to walk towards Northrop, but he fell to one knee, and then two knees. Finally,

Pike looked Northrop deep in his eyes and began to smile, then Pike pitched forward and passed out on the ground with a cruel smile on his face.

Colonel Hauser shut his eyes for a moment when he heard Pike's body hit the ground. "God help us both, Mr. Northrop," Hauser said. The colonel slowly stood up out of his chair, and then reached for his glass of gin and shot it down in a single swig. Next, the colonel made his way out from around his desk and walked over to where Pike lay motionless on the floor. Hauser took a long look at Pike and then said to Northrop, "Take your prize and get the hell away from my base camp. If you are still here in ten minutes, I will have you shot and killed."

"Colonel, there is no need to panic. He will be out for a long, long time," Northrop said. "Are you that afraid of this man?"

"Yes," admitted Colonel Hauser. "Pike is the second most dangerous man I have ever met, and he terrifies me."

"And who is the first, Colonel?" Northrop asked.

"Benedict Cain," Hauser said.

Chapter Sixty-Four

Special Agent Hal Northrop's return trip from South America to Guantanamo Bay, Cuba, was uneventful. He had accompanied the Pike subject a portion of the way, but they were destined for different bases, and Northrop had detoured to Langley for three months. Northrop also knew the recruitment drill: none of the facility leaders were ever sent to harvest the subjects for their own base. It was one of Dr. Reynolds' rules, and Northrop never questioned it; he enjoyed the harvesting trips.

Northrop's facility was so secret, even the soldiers stationed at Gitmo were unaware of its existence, with the notable exception of the men that were directly assigned to the facility. The facility looked like a small building in a quiet part of the larger base, and inside it there were only two offices: one for Northrop, one for Dr. Reynolds. There was also a small reception area with two desks and some cabinets. One of those desks was unassigned, and the second was assigned to Master Sergeant Withers. The reception desks were dead center in the reception area, and the offices were in opposite rear corners of the facility. Along one wall, the wall that ran between Dr. Reynolds' office and the front of the facility, there was an elevator.

The elevator went down to a larger facility, one with long maze-like corridors, mock training facilities, a locker room, an interrogation room, and a room reserved for torture. Most significantly, there was a long corridor that led to a very large, very thick, very ominous, steel door that served as the barrier to a very large, very grey, very scary, heptagon-shaped cell; the steel door was the only point of entry, or exit, to the tomb.

Walking into the facility, on the right, the next three corners were small sleeping areas consisting of nothing more than a cot and a pillow, and were separated from the rest of the room, and each other, by long black curtains. In the next corner there was a large wall clock, and beyond that the next two corners were sleeping areas like the first three, identical in every way. Beyond the last two sleeping areas was once again the large steel door, the sole point of entry to the cell. There were four more such facilities hidden on four other American military bases. Special Agent Hal Northrop had been on the team that designed the facilities.

When Northrop finally returned to Guantanamo Bay and his plane had landed, he went directly from the plane to his office; not to his quarters, not to the mess. Northrop had prepared a file on the plane, and he wanted to put it in his personal files right away. The file was titled "Pike," and he had written a report to show how he had managed to abduct Pike; however, in his file, Northrop took credit for the dart gun idea.

Eventually Northrop planned to lecture on his espionage techniques.

Northrop entered the facility, and paid no real attention to the fact that Withers was not at his desk. Northrop had assumed that Withers was below ground, which was quite common. Northrop went past the desks and to the left; in the rear left corner was the door to Northrop's office. Northrop arrived at his door, opened it, and went inside to discover Master Sergeant Withers.

Withers stood silently beside Northrop's desk, hands clasped in front of him, waiting and smiling. Behind Northrop's desk, his large, high backed chair was turned around, facing away from him.

"Withers?" Northrop asked, looking for an explanation.

"Sir," Withers answered with a sadistic smile, offering no explanation.

"I am very surprised Lieutenant Pike didn't kill you," a voice said from Northrop's chair as it swiveled around to reveal Benedict Cain.

"Come on, Benedict," Northrop said, trying to hide his confusion. "If you didn't think I would get him, why would you send me?"

"Because I wanted him to kill you, Hal," Benedict said coldly, and Northrop's chin dropped involuntarily with shock. "Don't get me wrong, Pike is an excellent choice for Experiment FIVE, but there are many other uses for him. I would have been fine with either result, but I fully expected he would have killed you." Benedict Cain leaned forward. "Now, Withers here, though, he said you were way too lucky for that."

"Better to be lucky than good, sir," Withers agreed.

"Now hold on here, Benedict. We go back a long way. What has he told you?" Northrop asked Cain while pointing at Withers.

"Withers?" Cain said. "Nothing, except that you had a horseshoe up your ass. He is not why I'm here, Hal," Cain said. "You and you alone are the reason we are at this point."

"I am not sure I understand, Benedict," Northrop said. "What exactly is this all about?"

"You forgot who was who, Hal," Cain responded.

"What?" Northrop asked, confused.

"Hal, I am the puppet master, and you are the puppet, and you seem to have forgotten that," Benedict Cain said viciously. "And that, Hal, is a sin I cannot forgive."

CHAPTER SIXTY-FIVE

Dr. William Reynolds was sitting on the upside-down pail looking at Special Agent Hal Northrop; Special Agent Hal Northrop was sitting in the chair looking at Dr. Reynolds. Their coffee cups were empty now, and the room felt heavy and thick.

"Dammit, Hal," Reynolds said, "I always knew you were ambitious and arrogant, but why would you ever plan to usurp Benedict? You should have known this is how it would end for you."

"I was always two steps ahead of him, Bill. I wish I knew how he found out," Northrop said.

"Hal," Reynolds answered him, "you were never two steps ahead of Benedict. No one ever is. If you thought you were, it is because he wanted you to think that." Reynolds and Northrop were quiet for a long time. "There is only one way back, Hal."

"I know," Northrop agreed.

"You need to find out what happened in Colombia," Reynolds said, stating the obvious.

"Will that be enough?" Northrop asked.

"I hope so. I will go to bat for you, Hal, but you need to get that out of him," Reynolds said with urgency. "And you need to do it before he comes."

"Pike already is lying to me about Colombia. He said it was a five-man mission. It was just him," Northrop said, strategizing out loud.

"It was meant to be five, Hal," Reynolds said. "You know how to do interviews. Use that skill. Make sure he sees you and him as being on even footing. Find a way to make Pike your ally. Read between the lines. Deductive reasoning."

Northrop's mind was in overdrive as he looked around the room, then finally he said to Reynolds, "You thinking what I am thinking?"

"I think so," Reynolds responded.

Northrop stood up for a moment and removed his suit coat, and then he ripped his shirt open, popping all the buttons off. Next he laid down on the floor and nodded to Reynolds. Reynolds picked up a full pail of water and poured it out all over Northrop.

Once Northrop was drenched, Reynolds helped him to his feet. Northrop grabbed his suit coat and threw it across his forearm.

"How was the water?" Reynolds asked sarcastically.

"Cold." Northrop shivered.

CHAPTER SIXTY-SIX

Kelley Pike was sitting at the round table in the center of the heptagon-shaped cell, alone. He had slunk down into his chair with head his laying against the back, eyes closed, a foot up on the table, and a cigarette burning between his lips. Pike had long ago accepted the tomb and the way of life inside the prison, and very little seemed to get a reaction from him anymore, so when he heard the cell door open, he didn't even open his eyes. When Pike heard the slouching sounds of wet clothes walking, and the wet slapping noise of soaked shoes on the concrete, he didn't open his eyes. When Pike heard the steel cell door close, he didn't open his eyes, and when Pike heard the noise of a chair being pulled out from the table and Northrop's wet body slump into it, he didn't open his eyes.

"How do you feel?" Pike asked, with his eyes still closed.

"Waterlogged," Northrop replied.

"Waterlogged, eh?" Pike still had not opened his eyes.

"Yeah. They water-boarded me." Northrop was studying Pike's reaction, but there was none. Northrop scanned the room, and he didn't see Kaye anywhere. "Where's Kaye?"

"In on his cot," Pike said, still keeping his eyes closed. "He went in there shortly after you walked out of here and he stayed in there the whole time. I am beginning to take it personal." Pike's eyes were still closed.

"Well, Kaye is an odd duck," Northrop said. Then after a long, awkward pause, he continued. "Pike, can I get one of those nails?"

Pike reached into his pocket, pulled out the cigarettes, and tossed the pack to Northrop; Pike had still not opened his eyes. Northrop put a cigarette between his lips.

"How about a light?" Northrop asked.

"Sure thing, buddy," Pike said, and then he reached into his pocket and fished out his lighter. Pike flipped the lid open and sparked the flame, still keeping his eyes closed. Then, unexpectedly, Pike pulled his leg off the table and straightened his posture, sat up in the chair, and leaned into the table, reaching out with the lit lighter. Northrop gingerly leaned in to the flame and began to draw it into his cigarette, and that is when Pike opened his eyes and looked right into Northrop's eyes. As Northrop sucked on the cigarette and turned the end of it red, Pike said, "I remember everything."

Northrop turned white and his mouth opened, almost causing him to lose his cigarette. "Remember what?"

"You, Company. I remember you." Pike snapped his lighter shut, put it back in his pocket, closed his eyes and slunk back deep into his chair. He rested his head on the back of the chair and threw his leg back up on to the table. "Interesting development, eh?"

CHAPTER SIXTY-SEVEN

It was very late at night, and Special Agent Hal Northrop was sitting at the table in the center of the cell, alone, soaked to the bone, and shivering cold. Northrop's gambit had not paid off; even if Pike did believe Northrop had been water-boarded, he didn't care. Pike had no sympathy for Northrop because Pike remembered.

He knew, Northrop thought to himself. *The son of a bitch knew this whole time.* Northrop was becoming anxious because he knew his life was worse than forfeit if he did not find out what Pike actually did in Colombia before the Secretary of State arrived.

Northrop kept looking at the door with the same intensity that Kaye had always done, though with less focus. When Kaye stared at the door he was examining it, studying the seams and rivets, looking for a weakness in what was a very strong barrier; for Northrop, the door was a place to stare as he tried desperately to create a point of leverage, to generate a strong position out of a weak one. That was when a strange, new thought occurred to Northrop: *If Pike knew the whole time, why didn't he kill me?*

CHAPTER SIXTY-EIGHT

Lieutenant Colonel Braun walked into her office that morning to discover Dr. William Reynolds sitting in a chair with his morning coffee.

"Doctor, why are you in my office?" Braun said as she briskly walked past the psychologist, circled behind her desk, and set down her valise.

"Well, technically, this office belongs to the government, not you." Reynolds took a sip of coffee.

"Doctor, I do not have time for riddles or games," Braun said.

"You are a manipulative bitch, Colonel. I just wanted you to know that I know that about you." Reynolds took another sip of coffee.

"Manipulation is your department, doctor. I am more of a schoolyard bully." Braun sat down opposite Dr. Reynolds and then continued. "Just the same, Great Manipulator, you have not produced any results. We will be going back to my methods."

"Colonel, the second you began beating my subjects I knew it was just a matter of time before Benedict Cain would be coming here. I could have called him, but I knew I didn't have to." Reynolds reached into the inside pocket of his suit coat, produced a sheet of paper, and passed it to Braun. "You should see this. I got it last night, and I was too giddy to sleep. That's why I beat you in this morning. It's better than Christmas Eve; just like Santa, Benedict Cain is coming to town." With a very large smile on his face, Reynolds continued to enjoy his coffee as Braun read the note.

"How did he know I changed the parameters?" Braun asked, growing anxious.

"He knew because he is Benedict Cain," Reynolds stated matter-of-factly.

"He is really upset." Braun was speaking more rhetorically, but Reynolds answered her anyway.

"Benedict does not like it when anyone deviates from his plan. He considers it to be disloyal. It never ends well."

"Will I lose my command? My rank?" Braun asked.

"If you fix things, maybe that will be all." Reynolds was enjoying this, and it showed.

"What do you mean?" Braun asked.

"Disloyalty is as near an unredeemable sin as anything to Benedict Cain." Reynolds straightened himself in his chair, leaned into the desk, and locked eyes with Braun. "Do you know who the last occupant of this office happened to be? He was disloyal to Benedict Cain as well."

"No, Doctor," Braun admitted. "Who was he?"

"Hal Northrop." Reynolds leaned back into his chair and enjoyed the moment. It took Braun a few moments to process what Reynolds had just told her, and even longer to begin to articulate a question.

"Doctor," she asked, "are you telling me the Northrop subject in the cell is the man I replaced here?"

"Yes," Reynolds replied in a flat tone. "And he had been one of Benedict's guys longer than me. Long before ever there was an Experiment FIVE." Reynolds watched Braun's body language as she changed from defiant to fearful. After Reynolds had enjoyed his moment, he got up out of his chair and to his feet, and then added, "Only one thing can save you now, Colonel." And Reynolds then walked to the door, leaving Braun on the hook.

"Wait. Doctor!" Braun exclaimed. "What is it? What can save me?" There was desperation in Braun's voice.

"You need to find out what happened in Colombia," Reynolds said. "You need to break Pike." And with that, Reynolds walked out of Braun's office, leaving her in a panic as she tried frantically to compose herself.

Braun was beginning to come apart, due in no small part to the manipulations of her emotions at the hands of Dr. Reynolds. Reynolds had been waiting for his revenge since the day they first met and he discovered the lieutenant colonel had had Paxton beaten. Reynolds was very territorial about Experiment FIVE.

After Braun had composed herself, she briskly walked out of her office and straight to Master Sergeant Withers' desk, where she addressed him.

"Master Sergeant, I have just received word that the Secretary of State is coming to our facility," Braun announced.

"Benedict Cain is coming here, sir?" Withers asked, though he had been expecting it for some time.

"Yes, Master Sergeant, he is," Braun confirmed. "He will be here in a little less than twenty-four hours."

"That is highly irregular, sir." Withers knew in that moment that Braun was almost certainly going to die. The question was whether it would be quick, or long and slow in the cell.

"Withers," Braun said, interrupting his musings, "before Mr. Cain arrives, I need you to break the Pike subject."

"Break Pike?" Withers asked, knowing it was indeed a tall order, but a challenge he would enjoy.

"Yes, Master Sergeant," Braun confirmed, and then added, "and Withers, use any means necessary."

"Understood," Withers replied.

Chapter Sixty-Nine

Sergeant J.P. Kaye knew that Hal Northrop was back in the heptagon-shaped cell, so when he pulled back his curtain and stepped into the main area of the cell, it was with a renewed arrogance in his stride. He approached the table and looked it over.

On one end of the table Pike was slunk down in his chair, with his head leaning against the chair back, a lit cigarette in his lips, and his left leg up on the table, the same way he had always sat.

At the table, seated in the chair opposite Pike, was the lifeless corpse of Special Agent Hal Northrop. Northrop's head was on the table with a bullet wound through his head, and blood and brain matter on the table.

"Good morning, Blinkey," Pike said.

The two men stayed were they were for a few moments: Pike smoking with his eyes closed and Kaye staring at Pike, studying him. As the silence was cresting, the men heard the steel cell door open; Kaye turned to look at the door, while Pike kept smoking with his eyes closed.

Master Sergeant Withers entered the room, flanked on either side: Patterson on his right and Briggs on his left. Withers marched up to the table and looked at the lifeless remains of Northrop. Withers squatted beside Northrop and leaned in to look at his head. Withers lifted Northrop's skull, and the stringy blood pasted between the table and Northrop pulled and then released. The exit wound had left only half a face on the dead man, but the dead man was undeniably Northrop. Withers smiled and dropped Northrop's skull back onto the table, and then stood up and looked at Kaye first, then at Pike.

"Round two, Pike," Withers announced.

Pike hauled his leg off the table, and then pushed himself out of his chair and opened his eyes, arched his back and stretched. Pike began walking around the table, and he stepped right up to Briggs, looking up into his eyes.

"I've been waiting for another crack at you, asshole," Briggs said.

"You hurt my friend. I will kill you," Pike replied. Pike pushed past Briggs and walked out of the cell with a stride of confidence.

"Interesting," Withers said as he watched Pike walk away. As Pike exited the cell, Withers began to walk after him, followed by Patterson and Briggs.

Once Pike, Withers, Patterson, and Briggs were all out of the cell, the steel door closed and Sergeant J.P. Kaye stood alone.

CHAPTER SEVENTY

Sergeant Briggs was very bloody. Briggs' torso was crimson, his hair was caked to his skull, and his knuckles, more than any other part of his body, were saturated with blood: Pike's blood.

The blood Briggs was wearing over his skin and hair had come out from inside the body of Lieutenant Kelley Pike one long, painful second at a time. Pike was fastened to a wooden chair with a spoke back and wooden armrests by cable ties. The cable ties were wrapped around Pike's wrists and ankles, and his head was slumped forward with his chin resting on his chest. Slowly, and with great effort, Pike raised his head and looked up at the giant silverback that had been beating him. Pike could tell that Briggs' body was nearing exhaustion just from the sheer effort of beating him, hour after hour after hour.

Pike opened his mouth, and blood poured out over his lips and into his blood-soaked tank top-style undershirt. Once his mouth was clear of blood, Pike began to whisper: "You hurt my friend." Unsure of what Pike was saying, Briggs leaned in, huffing and puffing from the exertion of beating the lieutenant. "I am going to kill you." Pike forced himself to smile, and Briggs broke Pike's nose.

Briggs stepped back and slumped over, putting his hands on his knees as he tried to catch his breath. It was at that moment that door opened and Master Sergeant Withers walked into the room with a folding chair in one hand and a bottle of water in the other.

After Withers entered the room, he paused and took a look around the chamber. Both Briggs and Pike were covered in Pike's blood, as was the wall behind Pike and floor surrounding him. Next, he tossed the bottle of water to Briggs, who opened it and drank it down in an instant.

Withers entered the room all the way, and Patterson came in behind him carrying a bucket of salt water. Patterson set the bucket down in front of Pike, and then Withers passed Patterson the folding chair, and Patterson set the chair up facing Pike.

As Patterson was setting up the chair, Withers approached to Briggs. "Did he spill anything?" Withers asked.

"Just blood," Briggs replied.

"You all right?" Withers asked, somewhat concerned about the level of fatigue Briggs was showing.

"I'm fine. Beating this loser is a hell of a workout, though."

"You fine to keep going? We need to break the bastard fast," Withers stated.

Briggs straightened his posture. "I'm going to fuck him up, Master Sergeant."

"Good." Withers said, "But on my lead, soldier." Withers walked over to the chair opposite Pike and sat down. Withers looked at Pike; Pike was half dead, half alive. Pike's head was slumped and his chin was resting in his chest. Whatever real teeth might have been left in Pike's mouth at one point were likely gone. Pike's nose was pointing more towards his ear than his chin. The cable ties had cut deep into his wrists. Despite all this, Pike was still awake. "Remarkable," Withers commented aloud. "A remarkable specimen. I do wish I had more time with this one." Withers nodded to Patterson, and Patterson lifted Pike's head so that he was forced to look at Withers.

Withers stared into Pike's eyes for a moment, and he was convinced Pike was coherent, so he spoke.

"This," Withers said, indicating the bucket that Patterson had carried into the chamber, "is a bucket of salt water."

"Not thirsty," Pike responded.

"Funny," Withers said. "Briggs, the right one," Withers ordered.

Briggs stepped up to Pike and grabbed his shirt, then ripped it down the center, exposing Pike's chest and abdomen. Briggs then unsheathed his knife and stepped in between Withers and Pike, reached out with his thumb and forefinger, and pulled Pike's nipple out from his body and cut it off. Pike screamed violently and blood poured out of his fresh wound.

As Pike screamed, Withers smiled. Withers reached into the bucket and pulled out a sponge. Withers played with the sponge, dropping it into the bucket and then picking it up, again and again, as he waited for Pike to stop screaming. Even after Pike's screams ceased, Withers played with the sponge until Pike's breathing became regular, and then he pushed the sponge full of salt water into the cavity on Pike's chest that used to be his right nipple. Pike screamed.

When Pike's screaming stopped and his breathing again became regular, Withers spoke to him. "You're holding out on us, Pike. All we need to know is what happened in Colombia."

"Is that what this is about?" Pike asked.

"Yes, Lieutenant Pike, that is exactly what this is about," Withers replied.

"I discovered something," Pike said, fading, and whispering as blood poured from his mouth.

"Discovered something?" Withers asked. "What did you discover in Colombia, Pike?"

"The world's richest coffee beans," Pike said, and began to laugh.

Withers backhanded Pike and screamed, "Colombia!"

"University," Pike replied, and Withers hit him again. Pike's head snapped sideways and blood sprayed out of his mouth as his head rotated.

After a few moments Withers regained his composure and looked to Briggs. "Cut the other one."

Briggs stepped in between Withers and Pike, and using his thumb and forefinger, he stretched Pike's left nipple out form his chest and cut it off with his knife. Pike screamed in pain.

As soon as Pike stopped screaming, Withers pushed the salt-water sponge into Pike's nipple wounds, and Pike screamed again.

Withers sat back and waited for Pike to stop screaming; as he did, Pike looked Withers in the eyes and said, "Water's cold." Withers soaked the sponge in the salt water and applied it to Pike's wounds again.

"Colombia!" Withers demanded, as he squeezed the sponge into Pike's wounds.

"Go spit!" Pike screamed back as the sponge released salt water into Pike's open flesh.

CHAPTER SEVENTY-ONE

Lieutenant Kelley Pike was a bloody mess, fastened to a bloody chair. His head slumped forward as he sat half alive in the torture chamber. The bucket that had previously held salt water was empty and laying sideways in the floor, and in his semi-lucid state Pike almost sounded as though he were laughing softly. Pike was dying, and he had never felt better. Pike had been in less physical pain before, but emotionally the lieutenant had never felt better. Pike felt free.

When the door opened to the chamber, Pike turned his head, and he saw Master Sergeant Withers return to the room followed by Sergeant Briggs. Briggs was wheeling in a battery charger.

"I missed you guys," Pike said, and then spit out some blood.

Withers smiled and then he nodded to Briggs. Briggs rolled the device up to the chairs. Next, Briggs took a long cord from the back of the device and found an outlet. Briggs turned on the device and it made a small hum. Finally, Briggs took out the large alligator clip ends, held them at the ready, and waited.

Withers reclaimed his chair and sat down opposite Pike again. Withers smiled at the lieutenant, and nodded towards the charger.

"This, Lieutenant Pike, is a large battery charger. It will hurt, Lieutenant. Are you sure you wouldn't rather just tell me what happened in Colombia?" Withers asked with a sadistic smile.

"Spark me up," Pike responded.

Withers nodded to Briggs, and Briggs clamped the alligator clips where Pike's nipples used to be and shocked him. Pike screamed as the electricity passed through him, and then when he was released from the device, his body slumped and his breathing became labored.

"This all ends as soon as you tell me about Colombia," Withers told Pike.

"And the band played on," Pike whispered defiantly, and Briggs put the battery charger into Pike's wounds.

As soon as Briggs pulled the alligator clips away from Pike, Withers punched Pike in the face.

"Tell me about Colombia!" Withers ordered, and Pike spat in Withers' face defiantly. Withers spat back at Pike and then struck him, and nodded to Briggs, who again blasted Pike with the battery charger. Pike screamed.

When Pike ceased screaming, Withers leaned forward, reached out with his left hand and grabbed Pike's right ear, and pulled his face in close. "I want you to tell me what you did in Colombia," Withers ordered again.

"Ain't never been there," Pike answered defiantly and smiled at the Master Sergeant.

Withers grabbed both sides of Pike's face and stood up, driving him and his chair into the concrete wall. Withers continued to hold onto Pike's head, and as Pike bounced back out form the wall, Withers twisted to his right, using momentum to throw Pike, still lashed to his chair, onto the hard, cold, floor; Pike landed with such force that the chair broke apart. The arms of the chair became free, as did the back, leaving Pike's hands free; however, as Pike crashed onto the floor, his left shoulder took the full force of the fall, dislocating his shoulder and fracturing his collar bone.

Withers walked over to Pike and kicked him a few times, and yelled "Colombia!"

"Is that all you got?" Pike said in quiet, defiant, raspy voice, with his face against the hard concrete.

Withers turned to Briggs. "Take his eye," Withers ordered.

Briggs unsheathed his knife and held it in his left hand, and then walked over to Pike, and grabbing Pike by his hair, Briggs lifted the beaten man to his feet and then shoved him against the wall. Briggs pressed his left forearm against Pike's throat to hold him there, and he moved his knife towards Pike's right eye.

Just as the tip of Briggs' knife was about to make contact with Pike's eye, Briggs heard a voice command, "Stand down, Briggs." Briggs froze in place and turned his head to face the door, and standing there was Dr. Reynolds, accompanied by Patterson.

"We have our orders, Doctor," Withers protested.

"Einstein defined insanity as doing the same thing over and over again expecting a different result," Reynolds countered as he moved further in to the chamber. "Briggs, lower your weapon."

Briggs relaxed his left arm, the one leaning into Pike's neck, slightly, but still held him to the wall; he lowered his right arm, the one holding his knife, to his side. Briggs turned his head so he could watch Dr. Reynolds.

"Your point, Doctor?" Withers responded.

"You have been at this nearly twenty-four hours. Beating this man will not work. He is waiting for you to kill him, and right about now he is probably wondering what is taking you so long," Reynolds said as a statement of fact.

Pike looked up, and his eyes were surprisingly clear of blood at that moment. He saw that Withers and Briggs were both fixated on Reynolds. Pike's left arm was beyond useless, but his right arm was still functional. Pike mustered all his remaining strength, pushed out from the wall with his foot, and grabbed Briggs' knife with his right hand. In a fluid motion, Pike twisted the knife free of the gorilla's hands and shoved it deep into his rib cage into the big man's lung, then twisted and pulled the handle downward.

Briggs' mouth was open and his lung was punctured, so there was no sound emitting from the silverback's mouth. He turned his head around to face Pike, and Briggs had a look of confusion on his face. Pike looked into Briggs' eyes and said, "I killed you."

Briggs' body slumped down and he died as he hit the floor. Pike steadied himself by leaning his back into the wall. Pike looked out at Withers, Patterson, and Dr. Reynolds. Pike noticed the looks of shock on the other men's faces. "He hurt my friend," Pike said, and then he slid down the wall and sat on the floor slumped against the bloodstained wall.

"Remarkable," Withers observed.

"Remarkable," Reynolds agreed. Reynolds walked over to Pike and squatted down in front of him. Pike fished at his pocket and hauled out Paxton's last pack of cigarettes using only his right arm, unable to move his left. Pike shook the cigarette package until one of the nails protruded the top of the package, and then Pike bit the nail and pulled it out. Next Pike used his right hand to fish into his left pocket and find his lighter. Pike flicked the lighter and the lid opened, then he moved the lighter up to his face and flicked his thumb on the wheel. Nothing happened. Pike tried it again, and this time the lighter sparked a flame. Pike drew the flame into the cigarette and lit it; as Pike snapped the lid of his lighter shut, he inhaled. After a moment, Pike exhaled a cloud of smoke.

"Those things will kill you," Dr. Reynolds said with a smile.

"Fuck it," Pike said. "I'm ready to go."

Reynolds picked up the package of cigarettes from where they lay on the ground beside Pike's broken body; Reynolds took out another cigarette and set it between Pike's lips. Pike began to shake his head, smile, and laugh as he raised his lighter and sparked the nail for Reynolds.

After his cigarette was lit, Reynolds moved from his position, squatting in front of Pike, to take up one sitting against the wall beside him and on the left; the two men smoked in silence as Withers and Patterson watched quietly. As they were smoking, Reynolds took another cigarette out of the pack and slid it behind Pike's left ear.

Pike and Reynolds sat in silence until they were done their cigarettes, then Dr. Reynolds forced himself to his feet. Reynolds looked at his watch and then he looked at Withers. "Master Sergeant, wait about an hour, and then take Pike back to the cell."

"Sir?" Withers asked, with a raised eyebrow.

"After the last twenty-four hours, I think the lieutenant earned a little break before dying."

"Yes sir," Withers said. "And where will you be?"

"I will be meeting a plane out on the tarmac," Reynolds said.

CHAPTER SEVENTY-TWO

A private plane landed at the airfield at Guantanamo Bay. The plane was carrying a very important and very sinister man.

On the tarmac, the door to the plane opened and the stairs were powered out. Two men in dark suits and dark sunglasses climbed down the stairs. Each man had a small bud in his ear with a spiraling white cord running out from the ear-bud and down into the collars of their shirts.

When the first man reached the bottom of the steps, he took a step sideways to the right. When the second man reached the bottom of the stairs, he took a step sideways to the left. The men looked at each other and the first man nodded to the second man, and the second man then spoke into his wrist.

Next, the very dangerous man stepped through the door and looked around. The man was in a navy power suit, and standing at the top of the small set of airplane steps; the man put on a pair of dark sunglasses and a fedora, and then walked down the stairs and paused briefly at the bottom as he stood between the two men in the dark suits.

After his pause was complete, the man began to walk towards the facility, and the two men in dark suits followed him, one step behind, one of them on either side of the man. The man was walking toward the edge of the tarmac where Dr. Reynolds was standing, waiting.

The man's name was Benedict Cain.

CHAPTER SEVENTY-THREE

Lieutenant Colonel Braun was no longer self-assured and arrogant; she had degenerated into a very insecure and anxious woman. Braun felt her command slipping away, and even worse, she felt her life was slipping away. Braun was scared.

Braun was pacing from one end of her office to the other. She had begun chewing her nails, and she was growing more nervous each moment. Braun knew that the plane carrying Benedict Cain, the Secretary of State, had landed and that he was on his way from the landing strip to her office.

Braun was pacing towards her desk with her back to her office door when the door opened. Braun spun around and watched in silence as two men in dark suits entered; the first man to step through the door moved sideways to his right, and the second man to walk through the door moved sideways to his left. Next, Benedict Cain walked through the door and walked directly to the center of the room. Dr. Reynolds entered the room next and took his place beside Benedict Cain.

Braun was taken aback as the men entered the room, which was not typical of her, but receiving Benedict Cain and the fear of possibly having failed him was the most stressful situation that the lieutenant colonel had ever endured. Braun marched to the center of the room with her hand outstretched and tried to introduce herself to Benedict Cain.

"Mr. Secretary, it is an honor, sir," Braun said, with her hand out in the air; Benedict Cain did not accept Braun's handshake.

"Colonel," Dr. Reynolds explained. "Benedict Cain is not interested in small talk with you. He is only ever interested in positive results."

"Colonel," Benedict Cain said coldly, "show me your results."

It took Braun several seconds to compose herself. Braun retracted her hand from the air and responded, "Of course, Mr. Secretary. If you will all follow me, we have a place to observe the subjects. Your timing is quite fortunate. I expect the Pike subject to break any moment."

Braun walked out of her office briskly, followed by Benedict Cain, then Dr. Reynolds, then the second man in a dark suit, and finally the first man in a dark suit.

CHAPTER SEVENTY-FOUR

Lieutenant Colonel Samantha Braun led Secretary of State Benedict Cain to the elevator; Dr. William Reynolds followed Benedict Cain, and the two men in dark suits followed Dr. Reynolds. Once they arrived at the elevator, Braun pushed the call button and the doors slid open. Braun stood aside and Cain entered, then Reynolds, and finally Braun. The two men in dark suits did not enter the elevator; the first man stepped to the right of the elevator and turned to face outward, and the second man moved the left of the elevator and turned to face outward.

The two men in dark suits took up their guard positions and stood silently while all three of the elevator occupants looked straight ahead. Benedict Cain and Dr. Reynolds stood with their backs only inches from the rear wall, and Lieutenant Colonel Braun stood front and center. Braun pushed the down button. The elevator doors closed and the car began its dark descent.

The atmosphere in the elevator was tense, thick, heavy and clinical. Benedict Cain's presence alone filled the car, making the space seem far more cramped than it was, and a feeling of claustrophobia overwhelmed Braun, though she tried hard to conceal that weakness.

Lieutenant Colonel Braun had not travelled into the basement of the facility since her first tour of it. Braun saw no reason to lower herself to the basement level; that was for her clerk, Master Sergeant Withers. The basement was beneath her in every respect. This was therefore only Braun's second ride in the elevator, travelling down to the subterranean laboratory of Experiment FIVE, but the ride seemed much slower than she remembered or thought it would.

Dr. Reynolds felt the presence of Benedict Cain in the elevator car, but despite the fact that Cain had a larger-than-life presence, Reynolds was not feeling suffocated by it at all. Reynolds was enjoying the descent, waiting for what he knew was coming. Reynolds knew exactly how dangerous and temperamental Benedict could be; Benedict Cain was driven by ambition at all costs. There was a much larger plan behind Experiment FIVE for Cain, and it was a plan built solely for the purpose of satisfying Cain's own personal, power-seeking agenda. When the elevator car stopped and the doors slid open, Dr. Reynolds smiled.

When the elevator doors opened, Braun was the first to exit, followed by Benedict Cain, and then Dr. Reynolds. Braun led the men through the labyrinth of corridors even though both men knew the way through the facility much better than the lieutenant colonel.

The trio snaked through the corridors and eventually found the long, straight one that led to the large steel door guarding the heptagon-shaped cell. The steel door was a sinister and intimidating on the outside as it was inside. As Lieutenant Colonel Braun, Dr. Reynolds, and Benedict Cain approached the door, they discovered Master Sergeant Withers and Sergeant Patterson were in the process of closing it, sealing the cell.

As Braun approached the Master Sergeant, she was surprised, but Dr. Reynolds was not. Things were progressing exactly the way that Reynolds had planned, and his smile widened.

"Withers!" Braun exclaimed. "What's going on here?"

"We just re-introduced Pike to the cell, sir," Withers said.

"Now?" Braun asked.

"Yes, sir." Withers continued, "We worked on him for twenty-four hours."

"So he broke?" Braun began to smile, sensing victory. No one could endure twenty-four hours of sheer torture.

"No, sir," Withers said. "Pike did not break, but he did kill Briggs." Braun's face turned white and her jaw dropped; she was in a state of shock.

"Master Sergeant," Reynolds spoke up to break the silence, "would you turn on the monitor for Mr. Cain?"

"Yes, sir," Withers replied, and then turned on the wall monitor. They could see Pike's husk of a body on the floor just inside the door, just beginning to stir.

CHAPTER SEVENTY-FIVE

Sergeant J.P. Kaye was pacing nervously in the large heptagonal cell, as if he knew his time was growing short. He could feel his opportunity slipping through his fist, like grains of sand squeezing out between this fingers, and the more he squeezed, the less he held. Kaye was sweating and mumbling, and growing increasingly uneasy when he heard the now-familiar sound of the large steel cell door opening.

To Kaye, it felt as though the steel door was opening slower than ever before, which was without a doubt the impact of the nervousness he was experiencing, knowing his time was running out. Kaye turned to the door and waited, staring intently as the steel slid along the concrete floor, and then, once the door was about halfway open, Kaye saw two men: Master Sergeant Withers and Lieutenant Kelley Pike.

Withers stood tall, proud, and ominous. He looked demonic, calm and impatient, and most of all, sadistic. In front of Withers, slouched, unsteady, and teetering, was Pike. Pike looked smaller than he had before, far from intimidating, and far from alpha status. Pike looked done.

Withers looked at Kaye and smiled widely, then grabbed Pike by his shoulders and pushed him forward and down, hard, onto the concrete floor just inside the steel door. Pike landed in a heap, bloodied and battered. Next, the door began to slide closed, and again, Kaye listened to the sound of the steel sliding along the concrete. When the large door finally sealed the tomb shut, it became the backdrop for the husk that was Pike.

Kaye stared at Pike. Pike was unrecognizable to Kaye, not just as Pike, but also as a human. Pike was covered in dried-up blood, his shirt was little more than tattered rags, and one of his eyes was swelling shut. Pike's nose was over on his right cheekbone, and there seemed to be few, if any, teeth left in his mouth, real or fake. Pike's left shoulder was grotesquely descended from his shoulder girdle. To Kaye, Pike no longer looked macho, he looked pathetic.

The husk that was Pike began to move. Pike crawled from the door, inch by inch, leaving a blood stained trail in his wake, until he arrived at the round table in the center of the heptagonal cell. Pike lifted his right arm up beyond the tabletop, placed his right palm on the table, and used his hand to pull himself upward. Pike swayed on his buckling legs and leaned his hip against the table, then moaned as he lowered and dumped his body into the chair. Once he was in his chair, Pike took a few minutes to get his breathing under control.

"You look like death," Kaye said, still standing a few yards away from the round table and Kelley Pike.

"Don't worry Kaye, it feels a lot worse than it looks." Pike reached behind his left ear with his right hand and pulled his last cigarette down and put it in between his lips. Next Pike struggled to fish his lighter out of his left pocket with his right hand. After he retrieved his lighter, Pike took a moment to again catch his breath and it became clear to Kaye that Pike's ribs were also broken.

"I can fix this, Pike," Kaye offered.

"No you can't, Blinkey." Pike struggled to flip the lid open on his lighter, and once he had, he tried three times to spark a flame by flicking his thumb down the wheel; three times he failed. "Figures," Pike said.

"Why can't I fix this?" Kaye asked.

"'Cuz there ain't nothing broken, Blinkey," Pike said. "This is exactly what they planned."

"No Pike, there is always a back way out." Kaye refused to accept that he was little more than a bait and switch.

"We're loose ends, Blinkey," Pike replied. "We don't walk out."

"I can fix this for us, Pike," Kaye pleaded emphatically, desperate to sacrifice Pike and save himself. "I can manipulate the situation. I can talk us out of here. I have a plan." Kaye paused. "Trust me, I'm a survivor."

"So what do you need from me, Blinkey?" Pike asked, as he flipped the lid of his lighter open again to try and spark it once more. This time, when Pike snapped his thumb down over the wheel, the flame sparked, and as it did, Kaye spoke.

"Pike, for my plan to work, for me to get us out of this prison, I need to know what happened in Colombia," Kaye answered.

Pike paused just a fraction of a second and then he moved the flame from his lighter closer to his cigarette and drew the flame in to light the end of the nail. As soon as his cigarette ignited, Pike moved his lighter out in front of his gaze and stared into the flame, and as he did, it died with the lid of the lighter still open.

After a moment, Pike snapped the lid of his empty lighter shut and tossed it to the center of the table, then inhaled a long drag of smoke.

"You know why I don't like you, Blinkey?" Pike asked. "Because you're a sniper, and I hate snipers." Pike exhaled smoke and turned his eyes away from Kaye, opting instead to look at his cigarette as it burned in his hand. "Snipers are cowards. Social rejects. Outcast misfits that never had the strength of character to man up." Pike moved the cigarette back to his lips and inhaled a long drag, then exhaled the smoke into the air around him.

Pike was enjoying his last cigarette, and he continued to watch it burn in his hand. "Real men don't hide in a tree, a thousand yards away, in the dark, clutching their scopes. Cowards do that, Blinkey, not men." Pike paused and took another drag. "Then again, Kaye sounds like a woman's name anyway." Pike began to laugh slightly as he continued, "I bet you were the queen of basic." Pike took another drag; he was speaking calmly and deliberately, but smoking fast, with long, deep lungful after lungful of smoke, making sure he could enjoy the whole cigarette; timing his speech and his nail, burning them out together. "JTF has a sniper unit too, you know, but no ladies allowed. Hell, even the women in JTF2 are more man than you, Kaye." Pike paused, and looked at the cigarette in his hand, nearly burned all the way down to his forefinger and thumb.

"Snipers," Pike continued with derision. "Sneaking around in the dark, not man enough to approach someone in the light of day. Snipers are just half-witted half-soldiers of half-men." Pike took his last drag from his last cigarette and then threw it away as he calmly and dismissively said, "I should have snapped your neck the moment you showed up here."

Pike had not looked at Kaye throughout his entire speech, choosing instead to focus on his burning cigarette. This was a deliberate choice Pike was making to enrage Kaye. Pike's speech was a success; it had made Kaye very angry. Pike's plan had been to push Kaye to a point where he would lose his self-control, and it worked. When Pike finally looked up at Kaye, the lieutenant found he was now staring right into the barrel of the single-action Colt revolver.

Kaye had been pointing the gun at Pike, waiting. Kaye could have shot Pike dead at any second, but he had waited; Kaye wanted Pike to know who was killing him. Kaye wanted to end Pike's life on his terms, but just as Kaye was beginning to squeeze the trigger of the Colt, Pike spoke.

"Was it something I said?" Pike smiled as he finished his statement, knowing it was too late for Kaye to stop squeezing the trigger. As Pike's words registered in Kaye's ears and his brain recognized the smile on Pike's face, the bullet flew out of the muzzle of the pistol and flew through the air. Only after it was too late by a fraction of a second for Kaye not to have understood what Pike had said and done, the bullet went through Pike's forehead, sending his body flying out of the chair, causing it to crash onto the concrete floor. Kaye registered what Pike had done; Pike had gone out on his terms, not Kaye's. In death, Pike was still tormenting Kaye.

CHAPTER SEVENTY-SIX

Benedict Cain was standing front and center of the monitor outside of the large steel door that guarded access to the large heptagon-shaped cell. Behind Cain and to his right was Dr. William Reynolds, and behind Cain and to his left was Lieutenant Colonel Samantha Braun.

When the monitor transmitted the image of Sergeant Kaye shooting Lieutenant Pike through the forehead, Benedict Cain did not react. Dr. Reynolds turned slightly towards Lieutenant Colonel Braun and smiled. Braun turned pale.

After a few moments of silence that Reynolds enjoyed and Braun did not, Benedict Cain turned to his left and looked at Braun. Braun was unable to bear the intense power of Benedict's stare, and turned to Withers.

"Master Sergeant, open the cell door," Braun ordered the clerk.

"Yes, sir," Withers replied, and then walked to the control panel and keyed in the command to open the door.

As the large steel door slid open along the concrete floor, Braun walked quickly towards it. Once the door was fully open, Braun entered, followed by Benedict Cain, Dr. Reynolds, and finally Master Sergeant Withers.

CHAPTER SEVENTY-SEVEN

J.P. Kaye did not speak when he decided to kill Kelley Pike. He just raised the revolver, aimed, and waited for Pike to look at him, then when Pike turned and made definitive eye contact with Kaye, the sniper began to squeeze the trigger. The muzzle flashed, the sound cracked, and Pike flew to the ground, dead. Kaye had wanted to kill Pike for quite some time; he had wanted to kill Pike more than he had wanted to kill Paxton or Northrop. Kaye hated Pike, and this should have been a great moment of triumph for Kaye, but Pike had ruined it for him.

Kaye had wanted to kill Pike as he groveled for his life and said he was sorry for being a bully. Kaye had wanted to kill Pike after he found out what had happened in Colombia. Kaye had wanted to kill Pike after he had given Pike the hope that he might live; it was the thought of giving hope to Pike and then taking it away that Kaye had been most looking forward to, but Pike had ruined it all.

At the moment when Pike was supposed to be groveling for his life at Kaye's feet, the JTF2 soldier elected instead to bully Kaye again, to mock him, and to enrage him. Pike had said some things to Kaye that Kaye deemed unforgivable, so Kaye decided to kill Pike right then and there, to forego giving him hope and to forget about making Pike reveal the truth about Colombia. Kaye had thought, *at least Pike will die on my terms, knowing that I am the one that killed him.* Kaye took the revolver out from under his shirt, raised the gun, and aimed it right at the center of Pike's head; Kaye had excellent aim. And then Kaye waited. Kaye was anticipating victory, but Pike ruined it for him.

Kaye was very good at waiting; it was second nature to a sniper. Kaye waited because Pike was just looking at his damned cigarette while he was berating and ignoring Kaye. This was making Kaye angrier and angrier. Kaye was ready though. He would wait for Pike to turn his head and look him right in the eyes, and lock eyes just long enough for Pike to be able to register that Kaye was the one killing him. He would show Pike who was the alpha in the cell; Kaye was going to kill Pike up close and personal. And then it happened.

Pike looked up at Kaye. As they were making eye contact, after Kaye's brain gave his fingers the command to squeeze but before Kaye's fingers had registered the command, Pike had spoken. *Was it something I said?*, Pike had asked him, and then Pike smiled. There was still just enough time for Pike to see Kaye's face change as he registered the Canadian's words and smile, and there was not enough time left for Kaye's brain to belay the order it had given his finger to squeeze. Pike had stolen Kaye's victory.

Kaye had not been able to make Pike suffer. In fact, Kaye realized as Pike was smiling and his forefinger was in the process of squeezing the trigger of the Colt, that Pike had wanted Kaye to shoot him all along, that Pike had been waiting for it to happen. Kaye had played into Pike's hand, and Pike had taken Kaye's victory and Kaye's last chance to ever get even. Pike had won and Kaye had lost.

The gun was still in Sergeant Kaye's hand and still smoking as the steel door to the heptagonal tomb opened, and Lieutenant Colonel Braun entered the cell for the first time. She was followed closely by Benedict Cain, Dr. Reynolds, and Master Sergeant Withers.

Braun walked briskly towards Kaye. The motion and noise brought the sniper back to his surroundings and out of his thoughts. Kaye turned square on to Braun and saluted her. Braun returned the salute out of reflex, not respect, and put her hand out towards the revolver; Kaye handed her the Colt.

"Sergeant, tell me you got it," Braun said. "Before you killed him, tell me you figured it all out. I know you asked him, but please tell me that was just a verification, that you have the answer."

"Sir?" Kaye asked.

"Colombia, Sergeant. Did you find out what happened in Colombia?" There was fear in Braun's voice.

"No, sir," Kaye said.

"Why not, Sergeant?" Braun asked, now with a mixture of anger and fear.

"Because he, Pike," Kaye said, pointing at Pike's corpse, "had to die first." To Kaye the answer seemed perfectly logical.

"If you didn't get my secret, what good are you to me?" Braun asked, exasperated.

"I learned other secrets, about the other men. We can use that information," Kaye reported.

"Sergeant," Braun replied, "I do not care about those secrets." Braun raised the Colt revolver and aimed it at Kaye's forehead.

"But, sir," Kaye said with surprise, "I'm a survivor."

"You used to be, Sergeant," Braun replied, and then she shot Kaye through the forehead, killing him instantly with the fourth and final bullet. Braun tossed the Colt onto Kaye's corpse and then turned smartly and approached Benedict Cain. Her mind had already imagined a scenario that would vindicate her and put Dr. Reynolds under the bus. This is what she had learned at West Point.

"Mr. Cain," she said, "my results speak for themselves. Experiment FIVE failed; the doctor's research methods have failed. My results have disproven his hypothesis. Dr. Reynolds is a drain on our research. Give the project to me." Braun spoke with bravado.

Cain looked at Braun, and he removed his fedora. Next, Benedict Cain removed his sunglasses and put them in his fedora, and then Cain handed his fedora to Dr. Reynolds.

"You want Experiment FIVE, Colonel?" Benedict Cain asked.

"The doctor cannot handle the task," Braun replied. "My results speak for themselves."

Benedict Cain reached into his coat and produced a Walther P5 Compact pistol. Cain raised the pistol and aimed it at Lieutenant Colonel Braun.

"Colonel, I do not accept your results." Cain squeezed the trigger of his Walther P5, the muzzle flashed, and Braun fell to the floor, dead.

Benedict Cain put his pistol back inside his concealed shoulder holster, and then he stretched out his hand towards Dr. Reynolds, who in turn placed Cain's fedora and sunglasses in his hand. Cain took his sunglasses out of his fedora and slid them into his pocket, and then he placed his fedora on his head, looked at Reynolds and gave him an order.

"Doctor, find me five more," Benedict Cain said, and then he turned to walk toward the cell's door. Once at the door, Cain paused and added, "Doctor, I trust your report will again indicate suicide?"

"Yes, Benedict, again," Reynolds replied.

Benedict Cain walked out of the heptagon-shaped cell and made his way through the facility to the elevator. Once at the elevator, Benedict Cain went back to the surface, and then he and the two men in dark suits went to the airstrip, boarded the private jet, and left Cuba.

Reynolds remained in the cell for some time, standing alone in a tomb full of bodies and lies. The cell had become a tomb for Lieutenant Colonel Braun, as well as the five: Sergeant J.P. Kaye, Captain Bradley Pell, Special Agent Northrop, Sergeant Michael Paxton, and Lieutenant Kelley Pike. They were not the first five to die here, and they would not be the last, but as Reynolds stood there among their bodies, bodies that were rotting and decaying, he realized that in a very real sense, this place was his tomb as well.

CHAPTER SEVENTY-EIGHT

As the old man finished his story and painted that haunting picture of Dr. Reynolds standing alone in the empty prison room, with the decaying bodies of Braun, Northrop, Kaye, Pell, Paxton, and Pike, I felt a chill go deep into my spine; a chill that has never left me, a chill that has followed me the rest of my life. I reached for the glass of brandy the old man had put in front of me, and I had the first drink of my life, and I drank it in one swoop – I have continued to drink every day since my meeting with the old man.

I stood from my chair and walked towards the door silently; the old man followed me. I opened the door. The rain had stopped and dawn was upon us; the sky was turning red and the air was still damp.

I walked to my car and I looked back to the house. As I stood by my car, I looked back at the door, at the way the old man was standing there in the door, alone, mournful. With the perspective and distance, it had an eerie resemblance to the picture the old man had painted in my mind.

As I looked at him with an expression that was a quizzical mixture of surprise and contempt, he answered my silent question. "Yes Mr. Washington, I am Dr. Reynolds, and this story, these actions…they are my legacy to science and my contribution to humanity. Now that I am old, and I am dying, I have told you this story to try and clean my slate, to look for God's mercy on my soul, though I doubt I shall have it."

Dr. Reynolds turned and walked back into his house and closed his door on me. I stood there a moment before driving away and locking this story in my vault until I was old and dying, and now, like Reynolds, I am telling this story. By hiding it, I was complicit in these events, and now, praying for mercy, I am trying to wipe my own slate clean.

. . . .

After Charles Washington had concluded recording his story, he turned off his recording devices, and he sent the video files out to his contacts in the world news media. Then Charles Washington went upstairs to his kitchen and sat at the round kitchen table in his modest home and reflected on his life. It was a life where he had amassed no real possessions, which was not in and of itself a bad thing, but he had never married, never fathered any children, and never settled into his life, and those were bad things, wasted opportunities. Charles Washington had spent his life chasing news and reporting news, while keeping the most important news story of his life silent.

Charles Washington had been trapped all his life by the sins of Benedict Cain, just like the five men in the dark cell, and just like Dr. Reynolds. And even though Washington had finally told the world about the dark shadows of the world's leaders, he realized he had missed his entire life because he was desperate to carry this knowledge deep inside himself, either unwilling or unable to share his burden of knowledge until he was at a point where his life was at its very end. In turn, that meant that Charles Washington had built walls around himself, and now that he had finally broken out of his metaphoric tomb, he knew he would die old, alone, and full of regrets, and nothing could change that now.

As Charles Washington had nothing left in his home to drink, he made his way to his bedroom, prepared himself to retire for the night, crawled into bed, and died in his sleep.

ACKNOWLEDGEMNTS

Images used in the cover art are stills frames from the feature film *FIVE,* and appear courtesy of Groove Hill Studio and Jeffrey Kelley

Cover Images feature (Left to Right On Front Cover): Ian Estey, Jeffrey Kelley, Scott Brownlee, Jon Blizzard, Josh Gaudet

Photo Credit: Joseph "Jpoq" Comeau

Novel Edited by: Scott Brownlee

Cover Design: Jeffrey Kelley

Made in the USA
Middletown, DE
23 June 2021

42963285R00196